FLOWERS ON THE WALL

♥♥♥ ♫ ♥♥♥

HART of ROCK and ROLL BOOK ONE

MARY J. WILLIAMS

© 2016

ABOUT THE AUTHOR

Writing isn't easy. But I love every second. A blank screen isn't the enemy. It is the opportunity to create new friends and take them on amazing adventures and life-changing journeys. I feel blessed to spend my days weaving tales that are unique—because I made them.

Billionaires. Songwriters. Artists. Actors. Directors. Stuntmen. Football players. They fill the pages and become dear friends I hope you will want to revisit again and again.

Thank you for jumping into my books and coming along for the journey.

HOW TO GET IN TOUCH

Please visit me at these sites, sign up for my newsletter or leave a message.

http://www.maryjwilliams.net/home.html

https://www.facebook.com/maryjwilliamsauthor

https://twitter.com/maryjwilliams05

https://www.pinterest.com/maryj0675/

https://instagram.com/2015romance/

https://www.goodreads.com/author/show/5648619.Mary_J_Williams

TABLE OF CONTENTS

PROLOGUE

COUNTING FLOWERS ON the wall. That don't bother me at all. Playing solitaire 'til dawn. With a deck of fifty-one.

He hated the song. It was the music that nightmares were set to. When the first familiar note pounded through the broken-down trailer, he knew what it meant. Their fragile peace was at an end.

Smokin' cigarettes and watching Captain Kangaroo. Now, don't tell me. I've nothin' to do.

When he was younger—still innocent enough to believe that this time would be different—he would cover his head with his pillow and pretend the music hadn't started. He didn't have to worry about his sister. At least he knew she would be fine. She was practically a baby and blessedly, the monster left her alone.

He was the one it sought out. *He* was the one who felt its wrath.

Was it a joke that the walls of his tiny room were covered in daisies? The faded wallpaper made his skin crawl. Taking it down wasn't an option. He had tried. The scars in his hand had been his punishment. Or—as the monster put it—his reward for being such a clever little boy.

Counting flowers on the wall. That don't bother me at all.

"I need my little boy." The voice was sing-songy, and though the words were slurred, they were unmistakable.

The bedroom door slammed open.

"There he is." The monster grabbed his arm, jerking him out of bed. His breath was foul. Sour from cheap whiskey and stale cigarettes. "Come keep Daddy company."

"I have school tomorrow."

He knew the slap was coming. Not across the face. Teachers noticed when he showed up for class with a swollen lip. The monster knew better. He aimed low where a mark would be covered by long-sleeved shirts or blue jeans.

"What good is school? Don't I teach you everything you need to know? How to pour a drink. How to light my stogie?" The monster took his cigar from his mouth, blowing on the end until it glowed red. "How to put it out?"

The hot tip hovered near his face. Closing his eyes, he waited for the pain.

"Nope. I'm not done with it yet." The monster threw him through the door, his teeth holding the cigar as he unbuckled his belt. Eyes narrowing, he slowly slid the leather from the loops around his waist, then slapped it against his hand.

"Why?" Asking never helped. The answer didn't hurt as much as the belt. But it was close.

"Why?" the monster jeered, slowly advancing. "Because I can."

CHAPTER ONE

THE KNOCK ON the dressing room door was firm and decisive. Whoever it was seemed to know what they wanted. He sighed. Pushy or tentative—it seemed someone always wanted something. All *he* wanted was a hot shower and a few blissfully uninterrupted hours of sleep. He should have gone straight to the hotel instead of collapsing on the sofa. After all these years, he knew better.

He didn't answer when the pounding got louder. With a sigh, he slung an arm over his eyes and hoped against hope that whoever it was would take the hint and go away.

"Mr. Hart?"

Shit. Hadn't he locked the door? He heard the doorknob turn. *Nope. He definitely hadn't locked the door.*

"Mr. Hart? Ryder? Do you mind if I come in?"

Ryder didn't bother to look. She had a nice voice. A little husky. But his interest was zero. Neither his brain nor his dick was in the mood.

"Sorry, sweetheart. I don't fuck groupies. Try two doors down. I hear the opening act isn't picky."

"They might not be, but I am. Don't worry, Mr. Hart, your virtue is safe. I'm not looking for bragging rights. My name is Quinn Abernathy. We have an appointment."

"I don't think so, honey."

"It's Quinn. Not sweetheart. Not honey. If you can't remember my name, I occasionally answer to *hey, you*. But keep the sugary platitudes for your adoring fans."

Interesting. In spite of himself, Ryder raised his arm enough to get a look at the lady with the acid tongue. *Well, shit.* He had hoped she would look like somebody's aunt. Instead, Quinn Abernathy was a knock-out. He felt a stir of interest. But not enough to do more than roll over so his back was to her. It was meant to end the conversation.

"I spoke with your manager, Mr. Hart. He—"

"Jesus H. Christ." Ryder whipped around. "I don't give a fuck. My head is pounding. My knee has swollen up to twice its normal size, and I need something to eat besides the crap they put out in my dressing room. Whatever you want, can it wait until morning?"

"Sure." Concerned, Quinn's blue eyes lowered. "What happened to your knee?"

"Old war injury."

It wasn't far from the truth. Ryder's entire childhood had been lived in a war zone. He survived because he learned how to avoid the ever-present landmines. One time, when he was ten, he wasn't fast enough. The result had been a baseball bat to his knee. It had healed. But now and then—like tonight—it flared up.

Ryder didn't know what the lovely Quinn thought of his explanation. She had a mighty fine poker face.

"I won't keep you. Get some ice on that knee. And I would recommend a steak. The hotel where you're staying serves a mean ribeye."

"How do you know?"

"I had one for dinner."

"Wait." All of sudden, Ryder wasn't as anxious for her to leave. "Are you staying at the St. Regis?"

Quinn nodded.

"What floor?"

Shaking her head, her lips curved. Nice lips tinged with a touch of red gloss. Ryder wondered about the flavor.

"Not yours." Halfway out the door, Quinn paused. "I'm a photographer, Mr. Hart." She patted the bag that hung over her shoulder. "Not a groupie."

"I don't have sex with groupies."

"I remember." Quinn laughed. "I'm not immune, Mr. Hart. And maybe—somewhere down the line—we'll see what we see. But for the time being, let's keep this professional."

"I didn't proposition you." Ryder wasn't used to women setting boundaries. That was his prerogative.

"You were going to." With that closing shot, Quinn shut the door.

Refusing to let her have the last word, Ryder hurriedly limped across the room.

"Hey, you," he called out. Quinn was already at the end of the hallway, but she heard him. To his delight, she stopped. Slowly, she turned toward him. In the glow of the harsh fluorescent lighting, Ryder could see that she tried not to smile.

"You bellowed?"

"Why do I need a photographer?"

"Because I'm the best."

Ryder loved a woman with confidence. "That doesn't answer my question."

"I guess you'll have to wait and find out."

"Lunch? One o'clock? My room?" When Quinn hesitated, Ryder laughed. "I promise… your virtue is safe. For now."

"I don't know your room number."

There were at least a dozen women roaming the hall. Ryder already had their attention. When his room number was mentioned, they practically began to salivate.

"Call my manager. He'll give it to you."

Ryder watched until Quinn was out of sight, then closed his dressing room door. This time, he made certain it was locked. He hadn't noticed the other women. At this point in his life, he rarely did. Before he became famous, when he and his band played one-nighters for peanuts, the women were always around.

It was the music. Rock and roll. Country. Jazz. Classical. If a guy could play an instrument, he could get laid. It was a truth as old as time. Ryder imagined back in prehistoric days, the first caveman who figured out how to carry a beat with a stick and rock found himself beating the women off with his club.

However, everyone had their saturation point. Ryder liked sex. Hell, it was one of life's great pleasures. But after over a decade of countless anonymous women, he no longer went for quantity over quality.

Nobody would call Ryder Hart a monk. He simply liked to know a woman's name before he stuck his tongue down her throat. Or any other place on her body.

Quinn Abernathy. It was a nice name.

"I DON'T KNOW, Dad. I just started a new project. However, I will try to get there for Cora's birthday."

"How often does someone turn thirty?"

Quinn wondered if that was a trick question. Cora, her father's third wife, had celebrated her thirtieth birthday last year and the year before. At this rate, it wouldn't be long until her stepmother magically became younger than Quinn.

"How are *you* doing?" There were times when a change of subject was the only solution. "Are you sticking to your diet?"

"No caffeine and one small whiskey a day? Don't get me started on the steamed vegetables. Have you ever tried to live on broccoli and kale?"

Quinn could almost see her father shudder. Michael Abernathy was a man who had always lived life on his own terms. He made his own rules and lived with the consequences. That attitude had made him one of the most successful corporate lawyers in the country. Which meant he was reviled as much as he was admired. Just ask his ex-wives. One hated him—with good reason. The other loved him— despite the extramarital affairs and the divorce.

"The doctor and Cora are trying to keep you alive. Those chest pains you suffered last year were a warning sign, Dad. I would like you to stick around for another thirty years or so."

"Your mother would have snuck me a little hollandaise."

"My mother would dance on your grave."

Michael laughed. "Belinda had passion. Still does. I miss her, Quinn."

Then you should have treated her better when you had her. Her father had a habit of rewriting history. In his mind, he hadn't destroyed his first marriage with lies and betrayals. It had simply been a series of unfortunate misunderstandings. The fact that her mother hadn't spoken to him in twenty years was a minor matter he chose to overlook.

"Mom is happily remarried, and you have Cora." Whether her father was happy was up for debate. "Be glad you have someone who cares enough to make sure you eat properly."

"Cora is sweet. But she doesn't challenge me the way your mother did." Michael sighed. "Speaking of which. How's the job?"

That was her father's less than subtle way of saying, like his wife, her job was fluff, and she never should have dropped out of law school. He was wrong on both counts. However, Quinn knew it was a pointless argument. There were only so many times that she could knock her head against that brick wall. It resulted in nothing but harsh words and headaches.

Not today.

"I was on my way out the door when you called. Give Cora my best. I love you."

Her father didn't make it easy, but Quinn did love him. It helped that they didn't speak often and saw each other even less. There had been a time when pleasing him was all she cared about. She had been a year from getting her law degree when she had come to her senses. She didn't want to be a lawyer. Working at her father's firm would have ended in disaster—Quinn had no doubt.

Convincing her father was another matter. He was convinced that photography was a frivolous whim. When she was ready to return to the real world, he promised not to say I told you so—more than every other day for the rest of her life.

Photography was her passion. Her joy. The reason she spent long hours in her studio only to drop exhausted into bed. Quinn had a reputation as a perfectionist—something her father would appreciate in anyone else. She never settled for a shot that was *almost* right. She pushed herself to be the best. Nothing was going to stand in her way. Not her father. And not a rock star with an inflated idea of his own appeal.

I don't fuck groupies. Ryder Hart had said it with such disdain. As though the women who threw themselves at him were beneath contempt. He might not fuck them now, but Quinn would bet he had at one time. And hadn't blinked at doing so. How had he spoken about them then? Not much better, she imagined. Arrogant prick.

She had hinted that she would sleep with him because it would feel so good when she turned him down. *After* he gave her what she wanted.

Quinn checked the clock. Quarter to one. She slid her feet into her boots before checking her reflection. The heels brought her to just under six feet tall. Her long legs were encased in her favorite pair of jeans. They were soft from frequent wear and washings. Her leather jacket was a pale gray and underneath, she sported a bright yellow t-shirt. Her look was casual but trendy. She loved when comfort and fashion meshed.

Quinn had kept her makeup to a minimum. A little mascara. Some blush and a touch of color for her lips. She left her shoulder-length auburn hair loose. A pair of silver hoops in her ears and she was ready to go.

This assignment was going to lift her career to the next level. A full spread in Rolling Stone. It was a coup for any photographer. Covering the final weeks of Ryder Hart's wildly successful world tour was the chance of a lifetime. He and his band were notoriously publicity shy. Access to the inner circle was harder to come by than a ticket to one of their concerts.

Grabbing her camera bag, Quinn took a deep breath. Whatever it took, short of using sex as an inducement, she was determined to win over Ryder Hart.

CHAPTER TWO

"SHE'S A GODDAMNED photographer, Ryder."

"I'm aware."

"Why are you going to so much trouble? She's here to do a job. *If* she impresses you. Not the other way around."

"Room service went to the trouble, not me." Ryder shifted the salt shaker, aligning it with the pepper. "I picked up the phone and placed the order. And what is wrong with adding a little class? Would you prefer I had a pizza delivered and popped the top on a couple of beers?"

"Rather than lobster and a five-hundred-dollar bottle of wine? Yes."

As managers went, Ryder supposed that Alden Christopher wasn't any more protective than the next guy. But how would he know? Alden was his first and only.

Ryder had hustled his first paying gig when he was sixteen years old. A few bucks under the table and a couple of hot meals had meant the world to a kid struggling to get by. Things got better. But it had been a slow, hard fight. Alden had been the first person who believed in Ryder's talent. For that reason alone, he would have put up with a lot.

"Relax. Aren't you the one who convinced me to meet with her? I don't like anyone hanging around the band. And for two weeks? I want to get a feel for Quinn Abernathy. A nice, relaxed lunch will be a good start."

"Why didn't you invite the rest of the band?" Alden frowned as Ryder fussed over the place setting. "Vote like you always do. Either she's in or out."

"Nothing will be decided until everyone has a say." Satisfied that everything looked the way he wanted, he gave the chilling wine a turn around the ice bucket.

"Ashe won't care one way or the other. Dalton will say no. And Zoe will be a wild card. Nothing changes. We always end up on the same page eventually. Otherwise, it's a no. Simple as that."

"You want to sleep with her."

"All discussion of my sex life is off limits, Alden. Always was, always will be."

It was a sore subject with Alden. It rankled because he knew that Ryder never thought about what had happened all those years ago. And Alden thought about it all the time.

"If she's as professional as Rolling Stone claims, it won't be an issue. Quinn Abernathy doesn't sleep with anyone she photographs. It's practically written on her résumé."

"Ever?"

"No! Goddamn it, Ryder. I wasn't issuing a challenge."

Ryder grinned, the green in his hazel eyes seemed to gleam brighter than usual. "Isn't that a gauntlet I see on the floor?" With a flourish, he made a production of picking up the imaginary item. "Challenge accepted."

"I thought you didn't treat women as trophies." Alden's only hope was to appeal to Ryder's sense of chivalry.

"I won't sleep with the lovely Quinn unless she knows the rules." Ryder patted Alden on the back. "Relax. I've been celibate too long. A little fun under the sheets might be just what I need."

"But—"

"It's been a long tour, Alden. And I've been a very good boy." There was a knock at the door. "Don't I deserve a treat?"

This was not a discussion Ryder wanted to have with Alden. Or anyone. Except Quinn. And wasn't he going to enjoy that conversation? When the time came. But he planned on enjoying the dance. Let Alden think what he wanted.

"Ms. Abernathy. Right on time." Ryder stood back so Quinn could enter the room. "This is my manager, Alden Christopher. I believe you've spoken."

"Mr. Christopher." Quinn nodded as Ryder took her bag. "Careful. You have my livelihood in your hands."

"I will treat it as if it were one of my guitars."

Quinn relaxed. She had read that Ryder's guitars were his babies. She knew how he felt.

"I suppose I should leave you to get acquainted."

"Yes, you should." Ryder carefully set Quinn's bag on the sitting room table. "Make sure Paul is here to pick us up by five. The sound check was iffy last night, and I don't want to leave it to the last minute."

Alden nodded, sending Ryder one last look before he exited.

"Doesn't the show start at eight?" Quinn asked.

"That's right."

"Do you always get there three hours early?"

"Wine?" Ryder picked up the bottle.

"Please."

"I like to think of myself as a perfectionist. My bandmates aren't as complimentary." He handed her a filled glass. "But we agree on one thing. We want to put on the best show possible. Every night. The fans who shelled out their hard-earned money don't care that we've been touring for a year. This could be the only time they see us live. It has to be perfect."

"That's admirable. Do all entertainers feel the same?"

"I can only speak for myself. But I hope so."

Quinn knew the answer. It was a big fat no. She had been at performances where it was obvious the artist phoned it in. Last night had been her first Ryder Hart concert. It was a dazzling experience. She looked forward to seeing them again tonight. And hopefully every night for the next two weeks.

"How is your knee?"

"It's kind of you to ask." Ryder was surprised by the genuine concern in her voice.

"Better. A couple of Advil and some ice fixed it right up." There was a time he would have chased that with a snort of cocaine, but thankfully those days were over. "Are you hungry?"

"Famished." Quinn wasn't a breakfast person. That meant she usually ate lunch around noon. One o'clock meant her stomach was past ready to be filled.

"Lobster? I ordered the chicken in case you had an allergy to shellfish."

"Lobster is fine. Great. Thank you."

This was not what she had expected. Ryder held her chair, sitting her at a table with a spectacular view of the New York skyline. White linen. Expensive plates and silverware. Quinn would have been fine with pizza, beer, and paper plates. Though she had to admit, she preferred lobster and cold white wine.

"You smell amazing."

"Excuse me?"

Quinn had been so busy taking in the view and the table service, she had almost forgotten Ryder. Almost. He wasn't a man one could ignore for long.

"What is that fragrance?"

Ryder didn't sniff at her like an overly friendly dog. He simply breathed in without touching her. It was a strangely erotic moment.

"It doesn't have a name. Just a mixture of soap, shampoo, and body lotion. Unscented."

"Then it's you."

"I guess so."

Without further comment, Ryder took the seat opposite her and began serving lunch. Quinn quickly forgot about the city view. Her attention was focused on him.

Ryder Hart photographed like a dream. She knew because she had closely studied everything that was available. Poses or candid, the man didn't have a bad angle. But as she discovered last night as she watched him perform, pictures didn't do him justice.

A photo could capture his rugged good looks. It could show off his dark wavy hair that just brushed the collar of his shirt and his long, lean body with arms that looked like sculpted bronze. Ryder was a staggeringly good-looking man. Sexy as hell. Those qualities were easy for a photographer to capture. It was the animal magnetism they missed.

On television and in videos, he reached out and grabbed you. Pulling you in. Forcing you to listen as his voice completed the seduction. But in person, it was even more intense. Ryder Hart bombarded you non-stop with his charisma. Was it any wonder his concerts sold out in seconds?

Quinn's hands itched to pick up her camera. She knew she could do what nobody else had been able to accomplish. She was determined to capture Ryder's sexual energy.

"I recognize that look on your face," Ryder said with an easy smile.

"You do?" He caught her staring. How embarrassing. And unprofessional. Quinn hoped the floor would open up and suck her in.

"It's a spectacular view, isn't it?" Ryder turned his head toward the window. "The first time I saw New York from here, it blew me away. It's a lot different than at street level in the Bronx."

"That's where you grew up?"

"Until I was twelve."

Something flashed across Ryder's eyes, but it happened so quickly, Quinn couldn't be certain what it was. Pain? Anger? She knew his story. Or part of it. His childhood hadn't been an easy one.

"I try not to take it for granted." He looked Quinn directly in the eyes, his lips curving slightly. "It's easy to forget that all of this isn't the norm. Most people will never see that view. Not in person. Now and then, I have to remind myself of that."

"I grew up staying at the best hotels. Eating in the best restaurants." Quinn sipped the cold wine, sighing with pleasure.

"Now that I have to watch my pennies, I finally appreciate what I used to take for granted."

"Did your family lose their money?"

"No. My father pulled his support when I chose photography over the law."

"I'm sorry."

"It was the best thing that could have happened to me. This poor little rich girl had to learn to stand on her own two feet." Quinn raised her foot, showing off the black leather boot. "It's amazing what you can get on eBay."

"You and my sister will have a lot to talk about. All through high school, she dressed like a trust fund princess while making minimum wage at Dairy Queen."

"I'll look forward to trading stories." She didn't push her luck. Just because Ryder mentioned his sister didn't mean Quinn had the job.

"You mentioned that you gave up the law for photography? Why?"

"Why do you write songs? Or perform?"

Ryder nodded. "It's in your blood. So this job isn't about the paycheck?"

"Not entirely," Quinn laughed. "Don't get me wrong. I like to eat. And having a roof over my head is a must. But I would swallow my pride and move in with my mother before I gave up taking pictures. It's who I am."

"Do you always eat like that? Or is it the excitement of a free meal?"

Quinn looked at her plate. She had practically eaten off the pattern. Rather than feel embarrassed, she took another helping. "This is me. I was blessed with good genes and a fast metabolism. I can eat most men under the table."

"If you like, I can get you a doggy bag for later."

"You think that's funny, but I won't say no. When midnight rolls around, a roll piled with lobster will hit the spot."

14

"I won't caution you to save room for dessert."

Ryder lifted a silver cloche to reveal two pieces of chocolate cake.

"Oh, heaven help me. I think I'm in love."

"THE DECISION IS up to you—as always."

Ryder looked from face to face. These people were his friends. His family. He would trust them with his life. And there wasn't a thing in the world he would hesitate to do for them. He wanted Quinn to photograph the waning tour. But if they said no, he would respect their choice.

"*You* want to say yes."

"That's my vote," Ryder nodded.

Reading Zoe wasn't as easy as when they were kids. She used to have an open expression. Now, he had to look hard to figure out what she was thinking. Right now, it could have been anything from what she had for lunch to who she was backing in the next presidential election.

"Are you hot for the photographer?" Dalton asked. Reading him was easy. He believed in letting people know how he felt. It was a trait that Ryder appreciated in a bandmate. But in the past, it had gotten his friend into a lot of trouble.

"Fuck, son. Why didn't you say so in the first place? You've been flying solo for too long. A duet is exactly what you need."

"Jesus, Ashe." Zoe slung a magazine at his head. She had a good arm, but Ashe knew her moves. He ducked just in time. Dalton wasn't as fortunate.

"Hey." Dalton rubbed the side of his face. He picked up the magazine ready to throw it back, then changed his mind. "At least you tossed me the latest *Sports Illustrated*. I haven't read this one yet."

"Are we done, children?"

"Is Dalton right?" Zoe's dark brown eyes narrowed on Ryder. "Is this about sex?"

"Not everyone is happy living like a monk, Zoe. Or in your case a nun."

"It's better than screwing everything that moves."

Unconcerned by the accusation, Dalton shrugged. "I'm making up for lost time."

"That was an excuse two years ago." Zoe pinned him with her gaze. "Now? It doesn't fly. You screw around because you can. Not because you went without."

"She's right." Always happy to egg on any argument, Ashe nodded.

"Enough! All I wanted was a vote. Our various sex lives—"

"Those of us that have them." Dalton was unable to resist one more jab at Zoe.

Rather than explode, Ryder calmly picked up his guitar. "You know what? Figure it out yourselves."

He walked out of the room without a backward glance. Sometimes he wondered why he put up with their shit. Sitting on an equipment case, he slowly picked out some random chords. Liking what he heard, he added a few more.

"I'm sorry, Ryder." Zoe rushed out of the dressing room. She ignored the guitar, throwing her arms around him. It was a spontaneous gesture that she only showed to him. "I acted like a child. Why do you bother?"

"Because I love you."

"You have to. I'm your sister."

On the outside, Zoe looked about as tough as spun sugar. Her long blond hair, delicate features, and slender build suggested an easy mark—a woman who would cave at the slightest push. However, looks could be deceiving—and dangerous.

More than one man had made the mistake of thinking he could take what he wanted from her. His sister was no shrinking violet. If her sharp tongue didn't do the trick, he had better watch out for her right cross. It was a dandy. Ryder knew. He taught it to her.

Zoe's tough exterior seldom showed a crack. Dalton and Ashe rarely saw her softer side. Only Ryder understood that under her armor, lurked the remnants of a scared, vulnerable little girl. He had tried his best to shield her, but it was impossible to deflect that much ugliness.

"Love has nothing to do with the blood that runs through our veins. Or shared DNA. We know that as well as anyone."

A shadow zipped across Zoe's dark eyes. Ryder recognized it. He had seen it enough when looking in the mirror. To their credit, they had gotten pretty good at shaking it off—as Zoe demonstrated when she smiled. She didn't do it often enough, but when she did, it lit up her entire face, turning her from beautiful to stunning.

"It isn't fair that you have to play peacekeeper."

"More like zookeeper."

"I wish I could argue, but we do behave like wild animals."

"On occasion. Then again, on occasion, so do I."

Zoe chuckled. It was a good sound. One Ryder wished he heard more often. "I guess we do belong together."

Ryder gave Zoe a reassuring squeeze before letting her go. "None of us had it easy growing up."

Zoe raised her eyebrows. It was Ryder's turn to laugh.

"All right. Ashe had an unblemished childhood. But he's been knocked down a time or two. The point is, we came together and made a family. Right?"

"At the moment, I would like to disown Dalton. But I agree." Zoe sighed. "And as a family, we have decided to let your girlfriend play shadow for the next two weeks."

"Not my girlfriend. Her name is Quinn Abernathy."

"Dalton wasn't far off, was he?" Zoe gave him a speculative look. "She must be gorgeous. I've never known you to let your dick do your thinking for you."

"My dick has nothing to do with it." When Zoe shot him another unconvinced look, Ryder sighed. "I like her. She's smart. And ambitious."

"And attractive."

"Yes," he conceded. "And attractive."

"Gorgeous?"

"In the right light." Or the wrong one. From what he had been able to ascertain during their two meetings, Quinn was gorgeous— period. But he didn't want to add any more fuel to Zoe's speculation. "You'll like her."

"I'll make up my own mind," Zoe bristled. "But I will try to keep an open mind."

"She shops eBay."

Ryder could tell he had piqued his sister's interest.

"Don't try to sweeten the pot, Ryder." Zoe tapped her temple. "Open mind. That's all I can promise."

"Sounds fair." Ryder stood. "Tell Dalton and Ashe to get their asses in gear. We have a sound check in fifteen minutes."

Knowing he could count on Zoe to put a flame under their bandmates' feet, Ryder headed toward the stage. He wouldn't admit it to anyone—not even his friends, but he was relieved. He wanted Quinn around. Maybe he would charm her into bed, maybe he wouldn't. However, it had been a long time since he had gotten excited about *any* woman. Perhaps it was because Quinn wasn't a sure thing. Or maybe it was the fact that he enjoyed her company.

Ryder smiled to himself. Why couldn't it be both? Two weeks. Just enough time to have some fun. But not long enough for her to get any ideas. He was in the mood to play. Light and easy. No expectations. No strings. That was how Ryder Hart rolled. Quinn might be the perfect playmate. As long as she understood the rules.

CHAPTER THREE

THE EXCITEMENT GREW with each passing minute. The opening act had done a nice job of warming up the crowd, but they hadn't paid their hard-earned cash to watch an up-and-coming band from Kentucky. They were here to see the headliner. The rock god with a voice like spiced Tupelo Honey. They were here to see Ryder Hart.

The spiced Tupelo Honey reference was one that Quinn heard while standing in line. A group of heavily made-up female college students had gushed non-stop as they inched their way toward the entrance.

Ryder this. Ryder that. Occasionally, one would throw in a sigh over the drummer or the hunk on the keyboard. Dalton Shaw and Ashe Mathison had their followers. But far and away, the women were here to see Ryder Hart.

Quinn still had a bit of a buzz herself. Lunch had been a revelation. Okay. Maybe that was a bit of an overstatement. But she hadn't expected Ryder to be such a laid-back, down-to-earth man. And funny. It wasn't as if he were *on* all the time. He was witty. And smart.

And, oh, boy. She was in trouble. It was one thing to find Ryder attractive. The world was with her on that score. But a sense of humor to go with his killer smile? It wasn't fair. The man had been blessed with *too* many irresistible qualities. Quinn wasn't an undisciplined fool. She wasn't ruled by her hormones or the twinkle in a man's eyes. Even eyes like Ryder's. *No* was a prominent word in her vocabulary.

If Ryder asked—and she was almost positive he would—she was capable of turning him down. She was a professional. And she was determined to remain friendly but not *too* friendly. Flirting was fine. After last night, and this afternoon, she would say it was mandatory. Why did it have to progress beyond that?

Because deep down you want more? Quinn groaned. *That kind of thinking won't help. Stop. Stop now.*

"Did you say something?" The woman in the seat next to hers sent Quinn a questioning look. She was in her mid-twenties with bright red hair and lipstick to match.

"Nothing important," Quinn smiled. One of the reasons she had chosen to watch the concert down here instead of backstage was so she could get a feel for the crowd and the fans. This woman with her *I love Ryder* t-shirt was a great place to start. "Is this your first time?"

"At a *Ryder Hart* concert?" the woman scoffed. Though to give her credit, she managed not to sound insulting. "I follow the band. At least, as much as I can. I try to get to twenty or thirty concerts a year. When they're touring."

"That's amazing. Just here in the U.S.?"

"I've followed them to Japan and Australia. And Canada, of course. That was a breeze. I would have loved to see them in Paris last week, but my international budget was tapped for the year. I can get around the U.S. on the cheap." She pointed down the row. "The eight of us travel together. We share expenses."

"I bow to the über fans." When the woman laughed, Quinn held out her hand. "I'm Quinn, by the way."

"Ren."

"Like the bird?" Names fascinated Quinn. Hers had been a mistake. It was supposed to be Queen. Thank God there was a miscommunication between her parents. Her father loved the regal moniker. Her mother swore she misunderstood what he had said. Whatever the truth, Quinn was grateful. *Queen.* She shuddered at the thought.

"Ren as in *Footloose*. My mother's favorite movie."

"It's different."

"I like it now. And Kevin Bacon *is* hot." Ren laughed. "But nobody spells it correctly. And kids are brutal when they think your name is funny."

"Kids are brutal. Period."

"True. Sugar and spice, my ass. There were girls in my school who came out of the womb playing mean."

They commiserated for several more minutes. Now and then, Quinn took a few candid shots of Ren and her friends.

"Do you mind?" Quinn lowered her camera.

"Not at all." Ren posed, hands on hips, her lips pursed in a flirty pucker. "Are you a reporter?"

"No. I tell my stories with pictures. And a few captions. But I leave the writing to someone else." Quinn pulled out her iPad. She carried around a digital release form wherever she went. Passing it down the row, she made certain she had permission to publish the photos. "Last night was my first time seeing them live. They put on quite a show."

That got Ren and the other women talking. They raved about the production values. The lighting. The acoustics. But mostly they spoke of the performances.

"We don't have to tell you about Ryder's voice." Ren sighed. So did her friends. "It kills me when he rocks out. But when he does a ballad? The man is a walking advertisement for sex. We've all used his music to get in the mood."

"Works every time. I'm Milly, by the way." The woman next to Ren held out her hand. "I love my husband; Ryder in the background adds a certain something."

"I like Dalton," another of Ren's friends called out. "Those drummer's arms make me drool."

"Give me Ashe any day."

"Ladies." Ren held up a hand when the discussion turned heated. "We could go on like this all night. The band is hot. Scorching." Ren lowered her voice so only Quinn could hear. "Brenda? The one on the end? She has a thing for Zoe. But she's married with three children so we don't make a big deal about it."

"The band's sex appeal can't be your only reason for following them. This is a pricey hobby."

"We all have our reasons. For me, this is my passion. I don't go to the movies. Or knit. Or collect do-dads. Or spend much on my wardrobe. This is it. Besides," Ren grinned. "My husband likes to go to Vegas. I think our marriage is stronger because of my love for Ryder Hart and his for blackjack."

"May I quote you on that?"

"Are you kidding?" Ren bounced with excitement. "Quote away. Any chance I'll see it in print."

"Rolling Stone." Quinn gave Ren the publication date.

"No kidding?" Ren shook her head. "Wow. You're like the big time."

Quinn took another shot of Ren's beaming face. "Not yet. But I'm getting there."

RYDER NEVER TIRED of the energy the audience gave him. It was the best drug going. Better than cocaine. Alcohol had nothing on the buzz that rushed through him from the moment he stepped on stage. In all of his twenty-eight years, he hadn't found anything that came close.

The first set rocked the house. He and his band—his family—began with their latest hit. It released a month ago at number one and was still riding that lofty perch on the charts. *Steel and Lace* was a collaboration between him and Ashe.

From the very beginning, Ryder insisted they write their own material. Dalton, for all his tough words and troubled past, was a poet. Ballads and love songs came easiest to him. Zoe—surprise, surprise—changed like the wind. He never knew what kind of song she would produce.

However, it was Ashe who had metal in his veins. A headbanger before he knew what that was, Ashe could make the rafters shake with his melodies. Ryder added the words. And between them, a multi-platinum hit was born.

One reviewer called the first thirty minutes of the show a non-stop cardio explosion. Nobody, not the band—or the audience—was allowed to take a breather. Ryder knew what he was doing. He wanted the crowd involved from the first note. And they were. By the time he picked up his acoustic guitar and strummed the open chords to *Out of My Heart*, every single person in the stadium was mesmerized.

"You might recognize this one," Ryder's voice crooned to the crowd.

Of course, they did. The ballad was the band's first number one song. In fact, five years ago Billboard named it the song of the year. It wasn't the last time they achieved that distinction. The awards had started rolling in as soon as they became the latest industry darling. An overnight sensation—ten years in the making.

The trick with that kind of success was to keep it going. To grow. Artistically all the time increasing their commercial success. It hadn't been easy. There were bumps. Hell, there were fucking mountains that they had to overcome. But they had a secret weapon. They were not four individuals looking for fame and fortune. They were a unit. Solid. Unbreakable.

Ryder sang the first line. He knew his gifts. Not the least of which was his ability to reach out to his audience. Not as a whole. One by one. The person in the front row, the back row, and every row in between would leave the concert convinced that Ryder had sung every song just to them.

The music coursed through him. Ryder felt every note. Every beat. And the words. Oh, the words. It was his specialty. It always had been. The music was his muse. The words his salvation. They carried him through some grim times. To right here. Right now. In front of forty thousand screaming fans. Who would have predicted that when he was seventeen and trying to find someone—anyone— to give him a shot.

It didn't take Ryder long to stop thinking and simply feel. The hell with his nightmare childhood. Fuck the doubters and the haters. This was where he was free. Where he could fly. And for two and a half hours a night, he soared.

When the song ended, Ryder was in the center of the darkened stage. One light illuminated only him. Eyes closed, his head fell back. His arms dropped to his sides. And the stage went black. A split second passed. Then, as always, the audience erupted. It was crazy. Bedlam. And Ryder reveled in it.

"Show off." Dalton chuckled as Ryder grabbed a towel from behind the drum set.

There was a small table filled with bottles of water. During the concert, nobody went near it except Linc, the band's longtime roadie. For two and a half hours, Linc had one job. Watch the table. Nobody except the band was allowed near it. They learned their lesson on that score the hard way. They were in Atlanta, about three years ago. Ashe drank from a bottle that had been doctored with roofies. He had passed out halfway through the concert and was rushed to the hospital. Ryder, Dalton, and Zoe had some bad moments until they found out Ashe would be all right.

Linc took his job seriously. He was devoted to the band. And he guarded the table with the ferocity of a Doberman pinscher.

Ryder nodded toward Linc. He was a wall of a man. Thick and sturdy with muscles on his muscles. If he liked you, he was a pussy cat. If he didn't? You didn't want to find out.

"I'm not a show-off, asshole." Ryder chugged down the water, pouring the last bit over his head. "I'm an artist."

"Fuck you."

"Not in this lifetime."

On the run, Ryder detoured around the back so he would enter the stage from the side. As Zoe played the introduction of the next song on her classic Gibson. She made the guitar sing. And Eric Clapton bow at her feet. Literally. Ryder had seen it happen. His little sister played like an angel. Or the devil. It depended on the song. And her mood.

The stage manager tossed Ryder his guitar, and as he did every night, Ryder caught it without breaking stride.

"Are you ready for something hot?"

24

The audience went wild.

"I said, are you ready for something hot?"

Somehow, the volume of the crowd increased.

Ryder looked over his shoulder. First at Zoe. Then Ashe. And finally, Dalton. As one, they nodded. In perfect four-part harmony, they began the chorus of *Hot Summer*. It was the last song of the night. Not counting an encore. Or two.

He wasn't tired. It was one of those nights when Ryder felt he could have played for hours. And by the look of his bandmates, they felt the same.

Back to back, Ryder and Zoe played the song they knew by heart. But they made it sound as if it were the first time. Fresh. Alive.

He used to tell her that nothing could bring them down. Not as long as they stuck together. The world could be a cold, merciless place. But here—on stage—it was always perfect.

CHAPTER FOUR

THE BACKSTAGE ATMOSPHERE differed greatly after a concert compared to before. Instead of the frantic rush to get everything set up, there was a determined rush to tear it all down and make sure it was loaded on the trucks. The next stop was Philadelphia—day after tomorrow.

The crew chief, his assistant, and the roadies who worked under them had the vital task of making sure that all the equipment arrived and that it was in perfect condition. Not an easy job considering the size and scope of *The Ryder Hart Band—Hartbeat Tour*.

"Careful." Alden Christopher pointed toward the large stack of boxes. "The easiest way to get hurt is to not be aware. You never know when something might fall on you. If you don't keep your eyes peeled."

Why did that sound more like a threat than a warning? Suddenly wary, Quinn followed behind Ryder's manager. For a man who arranged with Rolling Stone for her to be here, he wasn't the friendliest person she had ever encountered.

"Is there a problem, Mr. Christopher?" Quinn skirted a roll of cable. "Ryder informed me that the band was on board with me taking pictures."

"It was a close vote."

Close? Ryder had told her that unless everyone was on board, she was out. That meant the vote had to have been unanimous. How was that close?

"I appreciate their faith in me. I know this is the first time they've given anyone this kind of access."

"Remember. As quickly as you were let in, you can be let out again."

Okay. Alden Christopher was not a fan. Perhaps he had expected someone else to get the assignment. Someone with more experience. Quinn understood. To a point. She was used to proving herself. But she hadn't expected Ryder's manager to be her first obstacle on this job.

"I'm very good."

Alden paused outside Ryder's dressing room.

"That may be." Looking her up and down, his expression was skeptical. "But keep this in mind. Ryder never plays with one toy for very long. You have two weeks. Make the most of it."

Before Alden could knock, Quinn grabbed his arm. "Hey. I'm a photographer. Period. Not a toy. Or a plaything. My lack of a dick doesn't mean I will automatically flop on my back with my legs spread."

"There is no need to be crude, Ms. Abernathy."

This time, it was Quinn who looked at him. Long and hard. "I agree."

Quinn's meaning wasn't lost on him. She was saying, *you started it. I have no problem finishing it. When it comes to my job? Back off. Or else.* Quinn had dealt with one or two schoolyard bullies in her day, making it easy for her to recognize one when she saw him.

"As long as we understand each other." Alden stood his ground. Though the animosity in his eyes had been joined by a touch of caution. He wasn't dealing with a pushover. And now he knew it.

"You are clear as crystal, Mr. Christopher. Ryder is lucky to have such a fierce protector."

"He doesn't think so," Alden mumbled.

"No. But you and I know the truth."

Quinn didn't expect Alden to become her bosom buddy. But if he believed she wasn't interested in Ryder, he might back off just a bit. Of course, it wasn't true. Quinn was more than interested. But there was no reason Alden needed to know.

Besides, she *had* been telling him the truth when she said she wasn't here for Ryder's pleasure. *His toy? Really?* Even if it weren't about her career, Quinn did not fly that way. She was not any man's plaything. Ever. For her, sex had to be about mutual respect as well as attraction. She had thought Ryder felt the same. Had she read him wrong? Maybe. Ryder Hart was a rock star. The world—and its women—were his at the snap of his fingers. She had spent a few hours with him. Assuming that she understood him—or his proclivities—would be a huge mistake. If for no other reason, she owed Alden a thank you for reminding her of that.

"Ready?" Alden asked as he knocked.

"Have camera, will travel."

Alden gave her a blank look. She didn't know if he hadn't gotten the reference or he had no sense of humor. When his upper lip curled into a slight sneer, Quinn voted for the latter. The dressing room door opened, making it a moot point. The chances of her spending much time alone with Alden in the next two weeks was slim to none. His lack of humor was his cross to bear—not hers. Thank goodness.

"There you are." Ryder moved aside so they could enter. "I was beginning to wonder if you were swallowed up by the crowd."

Ryder had showered. Still damp, his dark hair curled slightly. Quinn was only human. She wanted to touch it to see if it were as soft as it looked.

"No. Considering the frenzy you worked them into, I found your audience surprisingly well behaved."

"Good." Ryder took her hand. He didn't take it any further. Not so much as a hug or a kiss on the cheek. However, when Quinn tried to pull away, he held on. "Thanks for escorting Quinn to my door, Alden."

Ryder had dismissed his manager. Not in his words. In his tone. Quinn heard it clear as day. So did Alden.

"Where are the others?"

Alden seemed reluctant to leave Quinn and Ryder alone. She rolled her eyes. For Pete's sake. What did he think would happen? Oh. Right. How could she forget so quickly? Alden Christopher had sex on the brain. At least when it came to Ryder.

"Zoe is in the middle of her post-concert meditation. Dalton poked his head in a minute ago. A young woman wanted some advice. He'll be in his dressing room—with her—for a while."

"What kind of advice?"

Ryder sent her a *are you kidding me* look.

"Oh."

"Oh, indeed." Alden sighed. "Can't he keep his pants zipped for one night?"

"Dalton has a fear of celibacy."

"For Christ's sake. He's been out longer than he was in. Tell him to get over it."

Eyes narrowing, Ryder released Quinn's hand, then turned to face Alden.

"You tell him, Alden. I dare you."

Alden turned white. Literally. Quinn had heard of such a thing happening, but she had thought it was a myth. Not anymore. Alden's healthy olive complexion lost every ounce of color. To add to the phenomenon, he repeatedly swallowed as though he was trying not to vomit. It seemed the threat of pissing off Dalton was enough to make Alden lose his cool demeanor.

"Dalton is an adult."

Ryder nodded. "Given a little time, I thought you would see it that way." Ryder crossed his arms over his chest and waited.

"Was there something else?" Alden's color returned, but he still looked a little nauseous.

"You didn't ask about Ashe."

"Ashe is the last of your group to cause me any worry."

Ryder laughed. Quinn didn't know why—she had no idea what kind of sub-text floated around the room—but she had to smile. The gleam in his eyes. The exasperated way he looked at Alden. It was funny. Though from the expression on Alden's face, he didn't agree.

"You don't know us at all, do you?"

Alden stiffened, his nose twitching as he raised it slightly. "I take umbrage at that."

"Umbrage." Ryder turned his head, his hazel eyes locking with hers. "Do you know what that means?"

"I do." So did Ryder. Quinn was certain of it.

"College girl." He winked before addressing Alden. "Give us an hour. We'll meet you on the bus."

"But—" One glance at Ryder had Alden wisely dropping his argument before it started. "We should be on the road by midnight."

"We will be."

With a nod, Alden left. But it seemed he couldn't resist another look at Ryder. Then at Quinn. It didn't take a mind reader to figure out what he was thinking.

"Does he carry the key to your chastity belt?" Quinn was a lousy locksmith. Ryder's virtue was safe with her.

"No."

"But he would like to." Dalton Shaw had slipped into the room without Quinn noticing. He was a big man. His dark hair was cut short, emphasizing the chiseled lines of his face. If Ryder were drop-dead gorgeous, Dalton had a more rugged look—but not less charismatic. The blue eyes didn't hurt. "Alden is petrified that some wily woman is going to get Ryder in trouble."

Quinn hid her smile. "In trouble. As in pregnant? Is there something you haven't told me, Ryder?"

"Yes. Dalton is a jackass." Ryder leaned closer until his breath caressed her ear. "As for me? I'm all man."

"No hidden lady parts?"

Dalton barked out a laugh. Taking a beer from the mini-fridge, he sprawled out on the black leather sofa.

"I like her, Ryder." He patted the cushion next to him. "Come and tell me all about Quinn Abernathy."

"Down, boy." Ryder kicked Dalton's foot as he walked by. "Would you like something to drink, Quinn?"

"Water would be great." She shook her head when Dalton quietly patted the seat again. "I admire your stamina. Weren't you *occupied* a little while ago?" Quinn put air quotes around occupied.

"Who said?"

She dipped her head toward Ryder as he handed her the water.

"Tattletale." Ryder tapped his beer against her bottle. "Cheers. I told Alden about Maggie."

"Did you now?" Dalton said it slowly. He appeared calm, but his teasing had been replaced by an underlying tension.

"I may have forgotten to mention her name."

Dalton relaxed. "I had Linc take her to the airport. She'll be in Buffalo before we get to Philadelphia."

"Did I miss something?" Quinn asked.

"That depends. Are you asking as a reporter or an acquaintance?"

"I'm not a reporter." Quinn had the feeling she would be saying that a lot in the next two weeks. Dalton simply looked at her. *Damn*, she thought. *These men had the steady stare down pat.*

"Acquaintance. Maybe, if you don't get sick of having me around, future friend."

"Fair enough. You heard that, Ryder. This is off the record." Dalton invited her to join him, but this time, he didn't leer. "I doubt any of us will get tired of you, sweetheart."

Before she could correct him, Ryder did it for her.

"The name is Quinn. Not sweetheart. Not honey. But on occasion, she answers to *hey, you.*"

"Now I'm the one who missed something." Interested, Dalton looked between them.

"You had to be there."

"When were *you* there?" he demanded of Ryder. "You met twenty-four hours ago, and you already have in-jokes?"

"I'm a fast mover," Ryder shrugged.

"Ashe is a fast mover. You, my friend, are a glacier." After another speculative look, Dalton turned to Quinn. "Maggie is my sister. We don't get to see each other very often. She could only get away for the day."

"If that husband of hers weren't such an S.O.B., Maggie wouldn't have to sneak around to see her own brother."

"Norris believes he's protecting his wife." Dalton's expression was unreadable. "He's a good husband."

"Are you certain?" Ryder didn't sound convinced.

"Yes."

The one word, spoken with conviction, seemed to be enough for Ryder.

"Did you catch a glimpse of Ashe on your way in?"

Sipping his beer, Dalton nodded. "He was chatting up a leggy redhead."

"The one he met our first night in town?"

"Mmm," Dalton sighed. "Since he hasn't sealed the deal, he's sweet talking her into coming to Philadelphia."

"That sounds like Ashe. When he lays on the Southern charm, women fall from the trees."

Quinn listened as the men carried on their conversation as though she wasn't there. Her boss had told her over and over again how insular the band was. They didn't welcome outsiders. Especially reporters. To which Quinn threw in that she wasn't a reporter. Her boss didn't see the distinction. He wasn't alone.

Now and then she would snap a shot. These were the pictures she loved the most. Casual and relaxed. Two friends shooting the breeze. For such a private group, they were awfully at ease around her. Quinn didn't know why, but she wasn't complaining.

"Where the hell are they?" Ryder checked his watch. "I need to put a fire under Zoe and Ashe. The whole point of meeting before we got on the bus was to introduce you all to Quinn."

"I'll get them. Stay and keep the lovely Quinn company." Dalton jumped to his feet. For a big man, he was surprisingly quick. He was across the room and out the door, giving Quinn only enough time for one picture.

"Why did you make your manager think Dalton was…"

"Fooling around with a groupie?" When Quinn nodded, Ryder sighed. "Alden keeps the band running like a well-oiled machine. But at times he's judgmental. Which is odd for a man who makes his living in this business."

"Sex, drugs, and rock and roll?"

Ryder tapped his finger on the table as though the random beat helped him think.

"There has been plenty of each of those. Especially in the early days. We were a wild bunch of kids. Feeling our oats—so to speak. Alden kept us out of trouble whenever possible."

"And when it wasn't possible?" Quinn wasn't unfamiliar with how the world of a celebrity worked. But only from the fringes. She was fascinated to hear about it firsthand.

"Alden has connections, and he isn't afraid to use them." Ryder ran a hand through his hair. In Quinn's opinion, the messy look only made him sexier. "For the most part, my friends and I have calmed down. We gave up drugs. Sex is no longer a full-out competitive sport. All that's left is rock and roll. That—to coin a phrase—will never die."

"Your fans thank you."

Ryder smiled. "As for Alden? When he gets his knickers in a twist, I refuse to placate him. He jumped to a conclusion. One I didn't appreciate."

"So you let him twist in the wind." Quinn was an outsider. She didn't understand the history or the dynamic of the group. But she knew what it was like to have someone judge her actions. It would have been nice to have someone like Ryder—someone who had her back the way he had Dalton's.

"I prefer he was hoisted on his own petard."

Impressive reference, Quinn thought. "Now who's the smarty pants?"

"But I didn't learn it at a fancy college."

Which made it all the more impressive. Quinn had done her research on Ryder Hart. Not that there was much available beyond ubiquitous press releases and gossip rag crap. But she had found out that Ryder was a self-made man. Beyond a high school education, what he knew he had taught himself. It hadn't taken long to figure out his knowledge was extensive. And eclectic.

"Dalton was right. You *are* lovely."

The change of topic threw Quinn. But just for a second. Realizing where he was headed, she quickly put on the brakes.

"Keep the sweet talk to yourself." When Ryder joined her on the couch, she wisely moved to a chair.

"You were serious about keeping this professional?"

"As a heart attack. No pun intended, Mr. Hart."

"I want you, Quinn."

Her eyes widened in surprise. "This is glacial? Maybe Dalton was talking about a different Ryder Hart."

Ryder grinned. "There's only one."

"Dim the charm, fella."

"Does that mean you aren't immune?"

He looked hopeful. Quinn tried to shoot him down.

"It means it doesn't matter. Only a fool plays willy-nilly with a chance like this. I won't risk my future by sleeping with you, Ryder."

"I appreciate your professionalism. And your ambition. I know all about wanting more." Ryder set his beer on the table. "I won't push."

"It wouldn't matter," Quinn said with more conviction than she felt.

Ryder's lips curved. His smile made her sigh. Did he know the effect he had on her? Of course, he did. Quinn had spent the better part of two hours with a group of women who followed him around the world. He knew why. The smile. The voice. The body. The man was the whole package. Damn him.

"Two weeks."

"Is that code for something?"

34

"It's a fact." He circled her. Not touching. Not coming within three feet. But Quinn felt a bit like his prey. "I want you. You want me."

"Did I say that?" Quinn searched her memory. *When had she said that?"*

"I can tell. There's a lovely flush to your skin. Your breathing is uneven. And the pulse at the base of your throat is pounding like crazy."

Quinn almost checked. But she managed to keep her hands in her lap—unclenched. She was proud of that. However, it wasn't necessary to touch her throat. She could feel everything Ryder mentioned. Her cheeks *were* unusually warm. Her heartbeat raced. And that spot at the base of her throat. Yes, she could feel that too. Damn, *damn* him.

"What is your point, Ryder?"

"Thank you for not denying the attraction." Ryder took a seat across the room.

"Thank you for sitting down."

His smile widened. "Did I make you nervous?"

"I felt as though you were about to pounce."

Ryder's expression grew serious. "Not unless you ask. I don't force myself on anyone. Ever."

"I believe you."

"Thank you."

Quinn wondered if there was a story behind his vehement reaction. If there were, it wasn't one she was likely to hear. He had made it clear that he didn't share private information. Nobody in the band did. Dalton's revelation about his sister was as much as she could expect to find out.

She told herself she was glad. The less she knew, the less involved she would become. And the easier it would be to keep saying no. No matter the temptation. And Ryder Hart was turning out to be a huge temptation. And yet Quinn couldn't resist asking.

"Here they are." Dalton entered. Zoe was right behind, followed by Ashe. "Spiderman persuaded the fly to enter his web. And the yoga queen has found her Zen—or whatever it's called."

"My center, jerk." As she passed, Zoe punched Dalton in the arm. "With you around, I need all the meditation I can get. Unfortunately, the benefits don't last long."

"And I did not lure Felicia into my web." For good measure, Ashe hit Dalton in the same spot. With much more force than Zoe. "She isn't an innocent victim. She knew the score and is willing to play by my rules."

"Please. Enough with the rules," Zoe groaned. "You're worse than Dalton. Stop obsessing over laying down the ground rules. Lay her. Enjoy. Then move on. I'm certain she will."

"But—"

Zoe cut Ashe off.

"In spite of what the press claims, you and Dalton *and* Ryder are every woman's holy grail. Felicia had a life before she met you. She'll have one after you ride off into the sunset."

"Ouch." Ashe stabbed an imaginary knife into the region of his heart.

"Amen," Dalton echoed.

"The truth can be brutal." Zoe took the scrunchie from her hair, shaking out the long blond tresses. "I feel it's my duty as a friend to finally tell it like it is."

Zoe had changed from her stage clothes into yoga pants and a snug t-shirt that proclaimed her love for leafy greens. Or marijuana. Quinn thought the sprig was kale, but it might have been cannabis. But one thing was certain. Ryder's sister was a long, lean drink of water. And in fantastic shape. Quinn liked to think she took care of herself, but the beautiful Zoe Hart made her feel like a slug.

"Save the inevitable banter for the bus," Ryder intervened. "I wanted to take a minute before we hit the road to introduce Quinn Abernathy. Quinn, this is Zoe. And the hunk of southern hospitality by the fridge is Ashe Mathison."

"We've met." Holding her gaze, Dalton took her hand, raising it to his lips.

"In every bar and dance club I've ever visited."

"Are you implying my line is not original?" Dalton winked, letting Quinn know he wasn't offended.

"Rockers don't need to be original," Quinn pointed out with a twitch of her lips. "All you need to do is walk into a room."

"Oh, she has you there." For the first time, Quinn saw Ryder in Zoe. It was in the smile. "I think I might like you, Quinn."

"When will you know?"

Zoe shrugged. "There is no timetable. A day? A week?"

"Never?" Quinn asked.

"Are you out to make a name for yourself by screwing us over?"

"Zoe!" Ryder sent his sister a warning look.

"It's a fair question." Quinn preferred when things were out in the open instead of stewing under the surface. "The answer is no. However, you don't know me. I don't blame you for your caution."

"There," she said to her brother. Her tone was almost triumphant. "Quinn doesn't need you to champion her. She can take care of herself. One more point in her favor."

"Zoe hates wimpy women."

"I hate *fake* wimps," Zoe corrected Ashe. "The steel magnolia who pretends to be a shrinking violet is the most dangerous kind of woman. Watch your back when *that* one enters the room."

"Well, shit," Ryder grumbled as he checked his phone.

Dalton looked over his shoulder to check the screen. "What's wrong? Ah. Alden is getting antsy all alone on the bus. Tell him to fuck himself. On second thought, give me the pleasure."

"Not with my phone." Ryder moved it out of Dalton's reach. "What the hell is Alden's problem lately?"

Dalton and Ashe exchanged glances. Ryder missed it. Quinn didn't. The list of mysteries was piling up. As much as she loved a good Agatha Christie, Quinn wasn't fond of a story that left her hanging. Ryder and his friends held their secrets close to the vest. That meant she would leave in two weeks with plenty of pictures, but few answers.

"Ready to hit the road?"

Without asking permission, Ryder divested Quinn of her camera bag. He slung it over his shoulder before picking up his guitar case.

Quinn nodded. She followed Zoe from the dressing room. Besides unsolved mysteries, there was something else she would take with her when the job was done. A big, heaping case of sexual frustration. Did the man have to be sexy, charming, smart, and a gentleman?

Damn, Ryder Hart.

CHAPTER FIVE

RYDER HATED TOUR buses. Always had. Always would. It didn't matter that their current transportation was head and shoulders above the bucket of bolts that had taken them from gig to gig in the early days.

Ryder had been the designated driver. Back then, he couldn't count on Dalton or Ashe to board the bus sober. Zoe was willing to spell him. But the truth was, Ryder didn't like giving up control. Not in his private life. Not on stage. And not behind the wheel.

It was crazy, but Ryder missed that cramped old bus. Not that he missed the broken heater or bald tires. It was the freedom. When they wanted, he, Zoe, Dalton, and Ashe would take off for sights unknown. They would hustle gigs to make enough money for food and gas—often sleeping in the uncomfortable worn leather seats because a motel was too expensive.

Then came the first blush of success. And a newer bus. It hadn't been a lot bigger, but it was reliable. As their fame grew, so did the size of their transportation. Three years ago, they purchased their own plane. But for short trips, they drove. Or rather, the man behind the wheel drove. Not Ryder. Instead, it was Boris—originally from the Ukraine. He was a nice guy. And a capable driver. More than capable. Most of the time, Ryder was resigned to letting someone else drive. However, it had started to rain as they were leaving the New York City limits. It made it harder than usual for him to relax.

"Stop obsessing. Boris hasn't killed us yet."

Ryder's eyes narrowed at Ashe. "I know you think that's funny."

"I do." Concentrating on the game of solitaire he had laid out on the table, Ashe didn't look up. Millions of people downloaded the game onto their phone, but not Ashe. He liked to feel the cards in his hands.

"Am I laughing?"

"Your sense of humor is an ephemeral thing, my friend. One second you're as sober as a judge. The next you're rolling on the floor. I figure if you think about it long enough, you'll get the joke."

Ryder sneered. Ephemeral. Not long ago, it was a word he would have stored in his memory to look up when he was alone. Ashe seemingly came out of the womb with a huge vocabulary. For Ryder, it came later in life. He was still learning. He hoped that never changed. But thanks to a mind thirsty for knowledge, and friends like Ashe, he already had a grasp on ephemeral.

"I get the joke, dickwad. Understanding it does not mean it's funny."

"Ryder is right." Zoe took a seat next to Ashe. "Death is nothing to joke about when the rain is coming down in biblical proportions."

"A bit of an exaggeration."

"Look out the window," Zoe prodded Ashe. "The animals are lining the road two by two."

Ryder threw his head back. He could count on Zoe. "Take note, Ashe. *That* is how you do funny."

"As usual, the Harts stick together."

Ashe said it without rancor. He had known Ryder for over ten years and Zoe almost as long. Blood was thicker than water. But in the case of Ashe and Dalton, not by much.

"Where's our little shutterbug?" Dalton asked as he returned from the bathroom.

He took the seat next to Ryder then leaned over Ashe's game so he would be able to kibitz when the mood struck. It wasn't that he liked solitaire, but he knew that unsolicited help pissed Ashe off. On a long bus ride, needling his friend was Dalton's favorite way to pass the time.

"We were talking fashion—shoes to be exact—when she conked out." Zoe shook her head with a sigh. "Lightweight."

Ryder knew that Zoe wouldn't have changed her life for anything. But she spent most of the time surrounded by men. The band. The crew. The only women were usually trying to get laid by a man in the band. Or, if that didn't work, a member of the crew.

Having Quinn around for a while would be good for his sister. Though Ryder would never say it within earshot of Zoe. She objected to anyone telling her what was good for her. Especially her big brother.

"Quinn isn't a child of the night. When she wakes up to greet the sun, we'll finally be ready for bed."

"Are you calling us vampires?" Dalton queried.

Ryder grinned. "You know how Ashe likes his steak."

Zoe and Dalton answered together. "Blood rare."

"And what is wrong with that?" Ashe demanded.

Leaving them to their inevitable sibling-like banter, Ryder drifted toward the back. Zoe hadn't exaggerated. Quinn was out like a light. Her head rested on the back of the bench seat near the window. Rain splashed against the window, the only light coming from the front of the bus where Alden, still in a snit, rested in his usual spot in a chair behind Boris.

"I promised not to push," Ryder said to a sleeping Quinn. "But what is the harm of me saving you from a stiff neck?"

Carefully, Ryder slid next to her. With impressive ease, he urged Quinn to move her head to his shoulder. She obliged, rubbing her cheek against the soft brushed cotton of his shirt, her lips curving upward in a small, sweet smile. When she sighed, Ryder rethought the wisdom of his move. Keeping his hands to himself was the honorable thing to do. When she snuggled closer, grazing his arm, Ryder gave a silent groan. Hell, he wasn't made of stone. He was tempted to gather her close so he would know what it felt like to have her body pressed against his. Without a doubt, he was certain it would be worth breaking his self-imposed code of honor. Two things kept him from caving.

First? Calvin Hart had considered all women fair game—no matter their state of consciousness. Ryder's father was an example that helped him keep a multitude of bad behavior at bay. All it took to stop him was the thought, *is this something Calvin would have done*? It stopped Ryder in his tracks every time.

Second? The look he imagined he would see in Quinn's eyes when she woke to find that Ryder had broken his word. It was a fine line, and it would be up to Quinn to interpret whether he had crossed it. But Ryder refused to make it an issue—one way or the other.

Taking on the mantle of a saint, Ryder closed his eyes and settled in—content to play pillow for Quinn. The bus contained every luxury available, yet he wasn't able to relax enough to rest. Not while it was moving. Until now. Slowly, his body relaxed. His mind unwound. His spirit calmed. Before he knew it, Ryder closed his eyes and slept.

ALDEN CHRISTOPHER STARED at the sleeping couple. No. They *weren't* a couple, and he refused to begin thinking of them that way. Quinn Abernathy was transitory—like every other woman in Ryder's life. The itch would be scratched, and she would disappear. Her name forgotten. Her face fading to nothingness.

Alden had witnessed the process for almost ten years. There was no reason to think this time would be different. Except… What? A feeling in his bones? The fact that Ryder looked at this one differently? Whatever it was, it made Alden uneasy.

Eyes narrowing, he watched as Ryder shifted toward Quinn. It was a mere inch or two, but irrationally, Alden felt it was significant. In sleep, Ryder's body sought out Quinn's. That couldn't be good.

"You have to stop, Alden." Ashe took the seat across the aisle.

"Stop?" Alden gave Ashe a cool look. "What do you mean?"

"You want to play it that way?" Ashe shook his head. "Fine. I will give it to you straight—no pun intended."

"I don't take everything personally."

"Yes, you do."

Ashe patted his knee. Alden knew it was meant to be comforting. Instead, he found it, and Ashe's tone, condescending.

"Don't get me wrong," Ashe continued. "As our manager, it is one of your best qualities. As Ryder likes to say, the devil is in the details. You care so much that you never miss a detail. It makes our lives easier knowing you will never drop the ball."

"I did this time," Alden mumbled, his gaze returning to the back of the bus. "That woman is trouble. And I'm the one who brought her here."

"Which brings me back to you, my friend. Ryder is never going to give you what you want. He can't."

Alden stiffened. This was not something he wanted to discuss. "I'm aware."

"Are you? Your attitude says differently. Ryder commented on it."

That made Alden sit up. "What did he say?"

"Relax. Ryder made an off-hand comment that you seemed out of sorts. But if you keep glaring at Quinn, it won't be long until he figures it out."

"She's inexperienced. That's all. I expected Rolling Stone to send a name photographer."

"You expected a man. Or an older woman. Quinn must have come as a shock. She's very beautiful."

"I suppose she is." Alden hated to admit the truth. "If you like that type."

"She may not be your cup of tea, but speaking as a heterosexual man, Quinn Abernathy is a head turner. Ryder's human, Alden. And straight." Ashe's gaze pinned him to his seat. "As an arrow."

"That isn't exactly breaking news."

"And yet you keep the hope alive that Ryder will what? Realize he's played for the wrong team all these years?"

"Of course not." Alden knew the chances were slim to none. But his heart wouldn't let go. Hope—slim as it was—wouldn't die.

"He's out of your league."

"I—" Alden tried to grasp what Ashe had said. "Pardon me?"

"The brutal truth is this. If Ryder were gay, you wouldn't stand a chance. He's a rock god, Alden. He would have his pick of the world's hottest homosexuals."

"And I don't qualify?" Alden knew it wasn't Ashe's intention to insult him. Yet that was exactly how it felt. Like a slap in the face. No. More like a punch.

"You're attractive."

"But?"

"You want me to make a list of your shortcomings? Hell no." Ashe stood, his expression somber. "You are a smart man, Alden. You know what I've said is true. Take my advice. Find a nice man. Settle down. And forget your Ryder fantasies. It's getting old."

Alden didn't comment. However, sitting alone as the bus traveled through the rain-drenched night, his brain began to analyze the conversation. Everything Ashe had said was true. Not that it made the pill any easier to swallow.

The first time he heard Ryder sing, Alden had known he was looking at a star. Though still a teenager, Ryder had the stage presence of a seasoned performer. Raw and powerful, he commanded the small stage. The crowd was rowdy, which was to be expected. It was Saturday night in a popular honky-tonk. However, Ryder made them pay attention with sheer talent and magnetism.

It was not the kind of place Alden normally frequented. But he had heard murmurings of a young man and his band. Alden's sources told him that with the right management, they had the potential to be something special.

It hadn't taken Alden long to decide he was what they needed to take the next step. Then the one after that. He hadn't expected to fall in love. To compound the first unfortunate mistake, he made a second that could have spelled disaster. He told Ryder how he felt.

It was why Alden didn't drink. It never ended well. Never. He could count on one hand the times he had over-imbibed. One had gotten him a chipped tooth. Another time he woke up in a pool of his own vomit. And the last time? Alden found the memory bittersweet. It was the first—and last—time he kissed Ryder.

They had only known each other for six months, but the band was already getting noticed by the right people. To celebrate, Alden popped the cork on a bottle of champagne—then proceeded to drink most of it himself. Ryder, Ashe, and Dalton preferred beer. Zoe rarely drank at all.

Naturally, Alden got sloppy. When he found himself alone with Ryder, he gave into his feelings. The kiss had been raw and passionate. On Alden's side. To his credit, Ryder didn't overreact. He easily shoved Alden away, wiped his mouth—that was a memory Alden could have done without—then calmly stated that he was flattered but not interested.

The incident was never mentioned again. Ryder treated him the same as always. As his friend as well as his manager. It had left Alden with two choices. Quit. Or hide his feelings. The answer had been obvious. Ryder Hart was on his way to superstardom—and Alden was going to be there every step of the way.

It turned out to be bad luck that Alden's feeling hadn't changed. Instead, they had grown stronger. Unrequited. God, he hated that word. It sounded strangely romantic. Romance had no place in his relationship with Ryder.

However, Alden was content to love from a distance. Women came and went without a hint of permanence. There was no reason to think Quinn Abernathy would be different. And yet...

Alden snuck another look. There was something that bothered him. He had made a study of Ryder Hart. Perhaps he read more into it than there was. Perhaps it would fizzle before it began. It was day two of what could turn out to be a very long two weeks.

Keep your eye on them, Alden told himself. It was all he could do. Alden knew Ashe was right. Ryder was out of his league on every level. But in his heart, Ryder belonged to him. And he wasn't ready to let go.

QUINN HAD AN odd feeling that someone was watching her. Like a fleeting dream, it didn't stay with her long after she opened her eyes. She frowned, trying to remember where she was and why she was sleeping sitting up. Then it clicked. She was on Ryder Hart's tour bus. With her head on Ryder Hart's shoulder.

"This is disconcerting." She mumbled the words but didn't move away. Disconcerting wasn't necessarily bad.

"Is it? I like waking up with you in my arms."

"No arms involved." Quinn sat up, surreptitiously checking to see if she had drooled on Ryder's shirt. To her relief, the answer was no. "How did this happen?"

"Don't worry. Your virtue is intact. You used my shoulder as a pillow. That's as innocent as an ice cream social."

"How many ice cream socials have you attended?"

"None. But I have a terrific imagination."

Quinn couldn't fault Ryder's words. But the way he said them made her want to squirm. In a good way. It went to prove that she shouldn't spend this much time with him in such close proximity.

"I need to brush my teeth." Quinn skirted around the seated Ryder.

"Everyone is asleep, so the bathroom is empty," Ryder smiled as though enjoying a private joke. "We'll be in Philadelphia within the hour. There's a diner where we go first thing, no matter the time. I hope you're hungry."

Quinn's stomach felt hollow. When was the last time she had eaten? Between the excitement of starting the job and meeting the band, the impossible had happened. Quinn hadn't thought of food since yesterday at lunch. "How are their pancakes?"

"The best I've ever tasted."

Quinn rummaged around in her suitcase, trying to find her toiletries bag. "That is a lofty claim. I'm a bit of a pancake aficionado."

"Me too."

"There you are." Triumphantly, Quinn waved the bag over her head. "Why is it the one thing you need is always at the bottom of the pile?"

"A question for the ages." Ryder took her suitcase, replacing it on the rack. "You look pretty."

"I've been downgraded from beautiful?" Quinn laughed. She doubted Ryder's eyesight. Her hair hadn't seen a comb since before the concert. Who knew what kind of morning gunk lurked in the corner of her eyes. But it was nice of him to say. Even if, technically, it violated the no-flirting agreement. Or had they agreed to that?

"Did you promise me you wouldn't flirt?"

Ryder's hazel eyes took on a thoughtful expression. "I don't remember. I said you had a two-week no-seduction window. Flirting is innocent enough. Isn't it?"

Depends on the perpetrator.

"Like an ice cream social?"

"There you go." Ryder reached out. For a second, Quinn thought he was going to touch her hair. He seemed to hover, then dropped his hand to his side. "Better grab the bathroom while you can. I see Linc stirring in his bunk. If he gets there first, it will be uninhabitable without fumigation."

"Lovely."

"That is the last thing I would call it."

Quinn didn't stand around quibbling. Linc's bare feet hung over the edge of his bunk.

"And Quinn?" Ryder called out before she closed the door.

"Yes?"

"I don't know what I was thinking. Pretty doesn't begin to describe you. Beautiful is better. I'll give it some thought and get back to you."

Exasperated, Quinn shut the door. The man was incorrigible. And fun. Her mother liked to tell the story of when Quinn was eight, and she declared that if she ever met a man who loved pancakes as much as she did, she would marry him. That was going a bit far.

However, she had met a few men who turned their noses up. Carbs and empty calories. Jeez. Get over yourself.

Turning, Quinn froze. This was a *tour bus* bathroom? It was nicer than the one in her father's remodeled guest suite—and Cora had gone all-out fancy. This one boasted marble countertops and a shower with multiple jets. The black-and-white tile floor gleamed. As did the antique brass fixtures. And the towels. They were wonderfully thick and soft.

"Ryder and his band certainly like to do it up right."

Quinn stood before the mirror, slowly brushing her teeth. First class all the way. It was how she had grown up. Never wanting for anything. Never worrying about paying her bills or budgeting for food. Not that Quinn was living in poverty. Hardly that. She made enough to live comfortably. But not luxuriously. It would be nice to live in this world again—for a little while.

There was a small but comfortable apartment waiting for her in San Francisco. When she moved to something bigger and better, it would be paid for with her money. Earned by her talent. Quinn dreamed of that day. However, she was content at her slow and steady pace. She would make it. Eventually. And it would be all the sweeter because she made it without her father's help.

Rinsing her mouth out with water, Quinn wiped the moisture from her lips, sighing with pleasure at the feel of the ultra-soft towel on her face. There was something to be said for luxury.

Carefully, Quinn hung up the towel. Someday, she promised herself. Someday soon.

CHAPTER SIX

AFTER STOPPING TO eat—where Quinn ate a stack of the best pancakes ever—they had checked into the hotel. Everyone dragged themselves to their rooms—presumably to sleep. Quinn felt surprisingly wired, but she tried to rest. Her internal clock wasn't used to rock band hours. The way she figured it, she should have adjusted right around the time the tour ended.

To her surprise, she fell asleep the second her head hit the pillow. Four hours later, her eyes popped open when her phone rang.

"Hello?"

"Want to hit the mall?"

"Zoe?" Quinn sat up, rubbing her eyes. "Is there time?"

"Shopping relaxes me. We'll take the limo, do our part for the local economy, then the driver can drop us at the stadium. Are you game?"

"Sure." Quinn wasn't as big of a buyer as she used to be, but she loved to look. "Should I meet you in the lobby?"

"Come up to my room. We'll take the service elevator to the parking garage."

Quinn rolled out of bed, stretching her arms over her head. Checking her appearance, Quinn was satisfied that all she needed was to fluff her hair and splash some water on her face. Okay, a little blush wouldn't hurt.

It was hard to complain about her hotel room. It had all the amenities. A comfortable bed. Hot and cold running water. A toilet that didn't flush on its own every ten minutes—try sleeping through that nightmare.

She shuddered when she thought of some of the holes where she had stayed. The life of an itinerant photographer was not as glamorous as some people might think. By comparison, her room at the Philadelphia Regent was a suite at the Ritz.

Then she stepped into Zoe's room and had to laugh.

"Want to share the joke?" the blonde asked as she slipped on her jacket.

"I think I have a case of luxury envy. First the bathroom on the bus. Now this?" Quinn motioned to the huge room with a floor-to-ceiling bank of windows. The view wasn't New York, but it would do. "I thought I was used to generic peanut butter and bargain basement sheets. Now I wonder."

"Ryder said that you grew up rich." Zoe's were a different color, but in a blink, her eyes took on the same intense look that Quinn had seen in Ryder's.

"I grew up with a rich father. I found out quickly that it wasn't my money. It was his to dole out at his discretion." Quinn shrugged. "It was a shock when he cut me off. Luckily, I'm smart and surprisingly adaptable."

"And still standing."

"Stronger than ever."

Quinn waited while Zoe applied a pale-colored lipstick. The other woman was a natural beauty and was wise not to cover it up with heavy makeup.

"How was the sound check?"

"I gave you the perfect opening to ask me about my childhood. Why didn't you take it?"

They left the suite. Instead of retracing Quinn's steps, they walked in the opposite direction.

"Did you want me to?" Quinn shot Zoe a speculative look. "Or was that a test to see if I would dig for information?"

Zoe didn't deny it. "I've never hung out with a reporter. I don't know what to expect."

"I'm a photographer, not a reporter." Quinn wondered if she should have it printed on a card. It would be easier than saying it over and over again. Besides, if she had it embossed, it would look official.

The service elevator made a creaking noise as it came to a stop. The doors opened. And though Quinn didn't hesitate to step inside, she noticed it looked as though it had been lifted from *The Shining*. Not the most encouraging image she could have summoned as the doors slid shut.

"That's what Ryder said."

"Did he?" It was good to know someone listened.

"What's the difference?"

"In my case? Quite a lot. I am not here to gather information, Zoe. Unless it's visual." Quinn tapped the camera bag she had slung over her shoulder. "This will be a photo essay. A story in pictures."

"There is a lot of money to be made from celebrity exposés."

It was understandable for Zoe to be cautious. She didn't know Quinn—none of them did. But she was human. The questions rankled—enough that Quinn felt she had to bite back.

"Did you invite me so you could suss out my intentions or insult my integrity?" When the elevator stopped at the garage level, Quinn did not get out. "I think I'll skip the girl time. If I want an afternoon of passive/aggressive bullshit, I'll call my father."

Zoe hit the hold button on the elevator panel, making certain the doors stayed open. Deliberately, she turned to face Quinn.

"Let me make myself clear. I don't have a passive bone in my body. Aggressive? Hell, yes."

"Then say what you mean."

Quinn preferred it when all the cards were on the table. That said, she wasn't a naturally confrontational person. If possible, she liked to settle things calmly and rationally. Not knowing what was coming, she braced herself.

"We make music. And we are damn good at our jobs."

"I agree."

Zoe's dark eyes narrowed. "What happened before Ryder formed the band is nobody's business. However, there is something you need to know. Ryder has watched out for me from the moment I was born. I can't tell you all the times he sheltered me; most of the time, I didn't know. He made *certain* that I didn't know. Now it's my turn. I will not let you hurt him."

Shadows crossed Zoe's expression, making Quinn want to offer a comforting hug. Something told her Zoe would not appreciate the gesture.

"I think you overestimate Ryder's need for your protection, Zoe. Whatever happened in the past doesn't seem to haunt him. He's a well-adjusted, happy man." When Zoe didn't answer, Quinn frowned. "Isn't he?"

"Most of the time." Zoe stepped from the elevator. "Ryder is the best man I have ever known. Happy? Yes. And loving. And kind. But he has demons nipping at his heels, Quinn."

Quinn found that to be a bit dramatic. Zoe must have read her expression.

"I can see why you would be skeptical. It isn't that Ryder hides his foibles. What you see is pretty much what you get. But now and then, he…"

Quinn leaned closer. "Don't leave me hanging. Now and then, he what?"

"I've said more than I should have." Ten feet away, a long, black limousine pulled to a stop. The driver rushed around to open the passenger door. As she started to get in, Zoe gave Quinn one more piece to the puzzle. "Listen to Ryder's music."

"I have," Quinn frowned. How was that supposed to help?

Tucking her long frame into the car, Zoe told her, "Not the commercial songs that fly to the top of the charts. If you want to know where to start, play *Tangled Vines*."

BACKSTAGE WASN'T CHAOS. It was worse. From the moment *The Ryder Hart Band* took the stage, there was never-ending movement. To the untrained eye, the crew seemed to go in hundreds of directions with no planned path.

But in truth, they were a well-oiled machine. This was not the crew's first rodeo. Ryder insisted on the best—from lighting to sound. From the first night of the tour, nothing had been left to chance. If something went wrong, it was fixed before the next performance. Or the person responsible was replaced—quickly.

The band had a hard-fought reputation for putting on a flawless show, and it was well earned. Ryder meant to keep it.

Quinn had learned fast to keep out of the way. Though to the crew's credit, as soon as they learned that she would be there every night, they looked at her as a mobile piece of the scenery. *Quinn is in the house,* rang out as soon as she arrived. She smiled every time; it made her feel a part of the gang.

A week had passed since her conversation with Zoe. Since then, few words had passed between them. Zoe had put Quinn on alert. *I'm watching you.* Quinn had no idea what Zoe would do if she decided to act on her vague threat. And she didn't want to find out.

Quinn had an easier time with the rest of the band. Dalton flirted—though he wasn't serious. Ashe teased. And Ryder? She had no idea what was going on with him. He was friendly. And cooperative. But the easygoing man she met in New York had morphed into something else. Ryder seemed preoccupied. Something was definitely on his mind.

There was another explanation. It could be that Quinn was looking for something that wasn't there. Ryder's schedule was brutal. He was the face of the band that carried his name. He drew the line at interviews. However, Ryder managed at least one personal appearance in every city they visited. An orphanage in Philadelphia. A hospital in Miami. A nursing home in New Orleans. What little free time Ryder had, he gave freely—and without publicity. Quinn found out by accident when Dalton let it slip. Ryder wasn't pleased. He kept his charity work hush, hush for a very good reason. If it were widely known, the requests would be overwhelming.

Quinn suspected that was only part of it. Ryder was a private man. Giving of his time was easy—and important. He didn't want accolades. Those came on stage from his screaming, adoring fans.

It was funny. Quinn felt she knew less about Ryder today than when they met. It seemed Zoe was right. There were hidden layers.

Deep—and dark. *Tangled Vines* was a perfect example. The song was from the band's second studio album. Like most people, Quinn listened to the singles the most. Radio friendly was the term. *Tangled Vines* did not fit that description.

Yet, it caught the listener from the opening chords. There was something heartbreaking in Ryder's voice as he told the story of loss and the search for redemption. The final note faded without a resolution. Hope or despair? It was left to the listener to decide. Quinn chose to come down on the side of hope. But as she found from her online search, critics and fans were split down the middle. The arguments were numerous and passionate. And the only man who had the answer refused to talk.

Great art—as one writer noted—was best when the artist allowed others to enjoy it without preconceived ideas. Would the *Mona Lisa* be as powerful if we knew why she smiled?

Quinn doubted that Ryder would put his music on the same level as da Vinci's painting, but the point was valid. Ryder Hart was a genius. His words. His music. His voice. They could lift the spirits or haunt the soul. And for his fans, that was enough.

However, it was frustrating as hell for Quinn. She had been looking for a few answers and came away with more questions than when she started. Had that been Zoe's goal? To send Quinn on a quest that had no end? Quinn wouldn't be at all surprised.

"Ten minutes. Crank the backlights. And Richie, turn on the fans. Another minute and the stage smoke will obliterate Dalton."

The last slow song of the evening calmed the overheated crowd. Quinn closed her eyes and floated on Ryder's words. Beautiful. And seductive. She might have said no, but the audience was filled with women who would kill to share Ryder's bed. The irony of her situation was not lost on Quinn.

"We hit Chicago tomorrow."

With nothing to do until the set ended, two members of the crew stood off to Quinn's right, enjoying the break before the madhouse erupted again.

"Well, shit. Why do I always forget about Chicago?"

The first man gave a long-suffering sigh. "You know why. It's the one gig where Dr. Jekyll turns into Mr. Hyde."

"We hit Chicago on the first leg of the tour." The second man shuddered. "Why not skip it this time?"

"I suggested St. Louis instead."

"And?"

"The look Ryder gave me shriveled my balls. That was twelve months ago. I'm still waiting for them to thaw out."

"Get your asses in gear, ladies," the crew chief growled at his men. "I want you breaking that stage down the second the last encore is finished."

Quinn tuned out the rest of the conversation. Dr. Jekyll and Mr. Hyde? Obviously, they were talking about Ryder. And it tied into the band playing Chicago. Ryder and Zoe's hometown. And the source of Ryder's demons?

It was another piece of evidence that the sweet, funny man that Quinn had met in New York wasn't as easygoing as she first thought.

CHAPTER SEVEN

RYDER NEVER DRANK to excess. It was an unbreakable rule forged in the memories of the evil alcohol could bring out in a normally placid individual. He had flirted with drugs. At sixteen, it had seemed like an easy way to get through his nights on the street. But he learned fast that when he was jacked up on cocaine, he lost his edge. And without an edge, the street could eat him up hard and fast.

Music became the answer. It gave Ryder a high better than any drug. And it helped him mask his demons until he no longer had to pretend that everything was okay. Happiness became a reality—not a concept. Ryder no longer began his day with dread or ended it in fear. Life was good. Damn good.

Until he remembered Chicago. The home of his nightmares. The city where he was born and wished to die. Then—miraculously—was reborn. The demons still lurked in the darkened alleys. Waiting for Ryder to join them. So rather than wait for them to come knocking, he sought them out. That meant including Chicago on their tour schedule. Every time. Sometimes—like this year—they landed here twice.

His bandmates argued. His manager cajoled. Even the tour crew put up a token protest. But Ryder would not be swayed from his path. He had a theory. To enjoy heaven's delights, now and then he had to remind himself what it was like in hell.

"I get why you won't top off the beer with a shot of Kentucky's finest." Ashe took a swig from the bottle of bourbon. "I even admire your restraint. But you need to take the edge off. For the love of God, and my sanity, find a willing woman and get yourself laid."

"We go on in less than an hour," Ryder pointed out.

"What's your point?" Looking confused, Ashe raised the bottle to his lips.

"You shouldn't be swigging bourbon, and I don't have time to get laid."

Heeding Ryder's words, Ashe lowered the bottle. "Blowjob?"

"Are you offering?"

"Over half the people in this arena are women. Give Linc the word and he will have a veritable smorgasbord of choices waiting outside your door before you can break the seal on a box of condoms."

"Sounds tempting." The lack of enthusiasm in Ryder's voice said otherwise. He reached for his old, beat-up guitar case. "I think I'll pass."

"I get it. I've lost my taste for the random screw. It was exciting at nineteen. Now?"

"Not so much." Ryder nodded. He couldn't remember his last *random* screw. If he weren't careful, *any* kind of sex would become a distant memory.

"There is always the beautiful Quinn. Unless I'm mistaken— and I never am—the interest goes both ways."

"No."

Ryder didn't want to talk about Quinn. She was light. Her smiles lit up a room, making him feel that hope still existed. Right now, he welcomed the darkness. He took his guitar from the case and plucked seven chords. Ryder took a deep, resigned breath. Instead of running from the acrid fog that always dogged his steps, he stopped to let it swirl around him.

"Not that song." Ashe screwed the lid on the bottle of bourbon. When Ryder casually began to tune the instrument, Ashe slammed the bottle onto the table. "Don't do it, Ryder."

Ryder didn't pay attention. Content that the guitar sounded right, he plucked the first few familiar notes again. Closing his eyes, he began to hum along.

"You promised that number had been retired."

"I promised I would never play it in public." As his fingers warmed up, Ryder increased the tempo. In spite of the words—and the memories they invoked—it was a peppy tune. "We are in goddamned, fucking Chicago, my friend. This song is a given. To quote the legendary Sammy Cahn, *you can't have one without the other*."

Flowers on the Wall. Some perverse part of Ryder's psyche insisted that he keep it in his personal repertoire. The old Statler Brothers' song never failed to lower his spirits—and make him want to vomit.

"Am I supposed to sit and watch your version of self-flagellation?"

"You can leave anytime. Or lend me some harmony. Take your pick."

"You are one sick son of a bitch."

But Ashe didn't leave. Ryder knew he wouldn't. Friends don't leave friends to fall into the abyss alone. If he were a sick son of a bitch, Ashe was right behind him, watching his back—as always.

Ryder took the lead and Ashe's voice blended in as smooth as Kentucky bourbon.

"SON OF A bitch."

Dalton stopped outside of Ryder's dressing room. He exchanged worried looks with Zoe—looks that Quinn didn't understand.

"Do you hear that?" Dalton asked.

"Am I deaf? Of course I hear it. Get out of my way."

Zoe calmly walked through the door. She looked at what was happening—Ryder playing, Ashe harmonizing. Without a word, she took a seat next to her brother and joined in.

"Really?" Dalton stood with his hands on his hips, watching the spectacle. "Fuck. This is some messed up shit."

With a resigned sigh, he sat and picked up his part of the harmony.

Quinn watched. She had no idea what was going on or the significance of the song they sang. More than ever, she felt like the outsider. Because she was exactly that. This was a tight circle. They had years of history and unswerving loyalty. She felt a touch of envy, but she didn't resent it.

Quinn was there to do a job. So she picked up her camera and began capturing a moment few people were allowed to see. If they vetoed her using the images, so be it. But she felt compelled to preserve with pictures something she didn't understand yet, felt to her very soul.

Their voices blended perfectly. They were four people becoming one. As the song reached its end, Quinn thought she saw a sheen of tears in Zoe's eyes, but it was gone before the last note faded.

"I love you." Zoe dropped her head onto Ryder's shoulder.

"I know. And every day I am grateful for it." Ryder, his eyes closed, brushed his cheek against Zoe's hair. It was a brief, poignant moment. One that Quinn would never forget.

"Is this the sappy portion of this farce?" Dalton grabbed Ashe's discarded bourbon, taking one long swig before setting it back on the table. "I love all you guys."

"I feel you, man." Ashe punched Dalton on the arm. "To the depths of my bowels."

"That's lovely." Zoe gave Ryder a worried glance, nodded when his eyes met hers, then rolled to her feet. "I can always count on you jokers to reduce a moment to bathroom humor."

"It wasn't me," Dalton protested.

"Not this time."

"I will admit—"

Whatever Dalton was about to say was interrupted when someone pounded on the door.

"Twenty minutes," a brusk voice called out.

"That's our cue." Ashe watched as Ryder put away his old guitar. "Better?"

"I'll meet you on stage."

Ryder's hazel eyes moved from bandmate to bandmate. When his gaze met Quinn's, he lingered for a second, causing a shiver of sexual awareness to shoot down her spine.

Holy crap, Quinn thought. One second she was worried about Ryder's state of mind, the next she wanted to rip his clothes off. *How messed up was that?*

As if reading her mind, Ryder's lips curved into a half smile that seemed to say, *I know exactly how you feel.*

"I say we rock Chicago like they've never been rocked then get the hell out of town," Dalton said.

"Best plan ever." Ashe clapped Dalton on the back. Draping his other arm around Zoe, he opened the dressing room door.

When Quinn started to leave with them, Ashe shook his head.

"He wants to be alone," she whispered.

"Ryder doesn't know what he wants. We need to get ready. Do me a favor and stay with him."

Ashe's tone told Quinn as much as his words. Dalton nodded. Zoe frowned, but she didn't protest.

"I won't leave him alone," Quinn promised.

The door closed quietly behind them.

"You're making a mistake. We shouldn't be alone."

Quinn gasped. She hadn't heard Ryder walk across the room. But his voice and the feel of his breath brushing against her ear told Quinn where he was.

Slowly, she turned to face him. "I don't have anything to do until the concert starts. Want to keep me company?"

"Don't placate me, Quinn." Ryder crowded her until her back was against the door. "I'm not a little boy."

"No argument here." Quinn tried to make it sound like a joke, but her words came out in a breathy rush that sounded more sexy than humorous.

"You want me. I've made no bones about how I feel." Ryder moved as close as possible without touching her. "If you hadn't set a wall of morality and ideals between us, we could be sharing a bed by now."

"That's an arrogant assumption." *True*, but arrogant.

"Normally, I respect a person's boundaries. Especially a woman's. But I'm on the edge, Quinn." Ryder's gaze dropped to her lips. "On a good day, you are a temptation I find hard to resist."

"You wouldn't force me." Quinn had no doubt about that.

"Who said anything about force?" Lightly, but with intent, Ryder touched her cheek with his index finger. Quinn leaned into his caress without a second thought. Ryder gave a low, satisfied laugh. "See? One touch and I can see the pulse at the base of your throat fluttering like mad. There's a lovely flush on your skin. Protest all you want. Your body doesn't lie."

"I'm not protesting."

"Jesus, Quinn." The green flecks in Ryder's eyes almost glowed. "You shouldn't have said that."

Quinn braced for Ryder's kiss, expecting it to be hard and desperate. It was all that, but what she hadn't expected was that her need would be as out of control as his.

It was a kiss like nothing Quinn had known. A wild intensity surged through her blood. She felt fierce. Strong. Invincible. She threaded her fingers through Ryder's dark, wavy hair, pulling him closer—if that were possible. They were fused together, the heat unbearable and beautiful all at once.

How long it lasted, Quinn couldn't have said. Seconds? Minutes? Hours? All she knew was that when Ryder lifted his head, it hadn't been long enough.

"I should go." But Quinn's feet felt cemented in place.

"You should run and never look back," Ryder corrected, his voice was low and husky.

"We both know that isn't going to happen." Reluctantly, Quinn stepped away. Picking up her forgotten camera, she took a shot of Ryder's face. It was perfect. Passionately beautiful. Nobody would ever see it but her.

"I would hate to hurt you, Quinn."

"Then don't."

Amazed by her response, Ryder laughed. "You make it sound easy. It isn't."

"I know." She opened the door, then paused. "We have another week to decide if we want to take this any further."

"I know what would be best for you."

"So do I." Reaching out, she touched his hand. "Something tells me your answer is different from mine."

THE CONCERT IN Chicago hit a high note for the tour. It was the kind of performance that those who were lucky enough to have tickets would talk about for years to come. Fans who had seen Ryder Hart before swore there had been something different about him. He *always* reached their emotions. But that night, he tore at their soul.

Every night was an exhausting experience. But tonight, everyone involved was worn out. They were taking the band's private plane to Los Angeles where they would end the tour with five sold-out concerts. There was little of the usual banter as they took their seats, waiting to be cleared for takeoff.

Ryder entered the plane after everyone else. He didn't look Quinn's way. He didn't look at anyone.

"I'll be in my room. Unless it's an emergency, I don't want to see or talk to anyone."

Nobody commented. Ashe continued his game of solitaire. Dalton was doing something on his phone. And Zoe put on her headphones then adjusted the volume on her iPod. Closing her eyes, she settled her head on the back of her seat.

"That's it?" Quinn asked. "The man poured everything he had into his performance tonight. Shouldn't one of you make sure he's okay?"

"Ryder needs rest, Ms. Abernathy." Alden didn't look at her as he spoke. He sat near the front, sipping from an insulated travel mug.

"But—"

"We have known him a long time. Do you doubt our concern?"

"No. Of course not."

"Then trust that we are doing what is best."

Supercilious asshole. Thinking nobody was watching, Quinn poked out her tongue at Alden's back.

"Did that make you feel better?" Ashe asked as he placed an ace of spades onto the table.

"Not really."

"Try adding a double-finger salute." When he saw Quinn's skeptical expression, Ashe nodded. "I understand, but trust me, it does wonders. But you have to do it with attitude." Ashe demonstrated. He whipped up his hands, his middle fingers flying high. For good measure, he finished by twirling his arms in a circle. The gesture was aimed at an oblivious Dalton.

With a sigh, Quinn copied Ashe—for good measure, she stood and stuck out her tongue. Ashe was right. It was satisfying. Unfortunately, Alden chose that moment to look over his shoulder. Ashe burst out laughing. Quinn, her face red as a beet, mumbled a quick apology to Alden before rushing to the bathroom.

Quinn locked the door. Turning on the tap, she let the water run until it was as cold as possible, splashing it on her burning cheeks. Every time she let herself get goaded into something, it always backfired. It was forgivable behavior for a ten-year-old. However, she was pushing thirty. She should have known better.

Looking at herself in the mirror, Quinn felt her lips twitch. *The hell with it*, she thought, chuckling. Yes, she was embarrassed that Alden had caught her flipping him off. But she wasn't sorry. It had felt good. When she thought of the look on Alden's face, she let out another round of laughter—this one louder and longer.

Deciding she was recovered enough to face the frowning Alden, Quinn patted her face with a towel. She took some gloss from her pocket and dabbed a touch onto her lips. As she left the bathroom, she glanced toward the back of the plane. Ryder's room was at the end of the aisle.

The fact was, the room didn't belong to any member of the band. It was there if someone wasn't feeling well or simply felt the need for some privacy. Most of the time, they stayed together in the main cabin. *Tonight*, it was Ryder's. No questions asked.

Quinn knew she should respect his wishes. And she wanted to. Honestly. But she had witnessed him firsthand before, during, and after the concert. The others might not have reason to worry, but she did. Alden had been right about one thing. She didn't know Ryder as well as the rest of them. Until she was certain he was doing all right, she wouldn't rest.

Taking a deep breath, Quinn raised her hand and tapped lightly on the closed door.

"Ryder?" There was no answer. "Ryder? All I ask is that you let me know you're fine. I promise after that I won't bother you again."

For a moment, Quinn didn't think that Ryder was going to respond. Then she heard the lock turn. When the door opened, she couldn't see anything. The room was dark, and Ryder stood out of her view.

"Come in."

Quinn hesitated. Ryder's voice sounded like sandpaper—*worn-out* sandpaper. "I don't want to disturb you." She slapped her forehead with the palm of her hand. "But that is exactly what I've done."

"As long as you're already here…" The door opened wider.

Cautiously, Quinn stepped into the room. She had to question the wisdom of this move—on both sides. But she kept walking. What could happen? The door closed with an almost eerie click. It rattled her more than if he had slammed it.

"Tell me you're okay and I will leave you to rest."

"I'm okay."

Quinn didn't budge. The words were the right ones. However, Ryder sounded like crap. The only light in the room came from the screen of an open laptop. It was near the bed—not close enough to illuminate Ryder clearly.

"Let me see your face."

"I'm not suicidal, Quinn. That has never been my problem." With a resigned sigh, Ryder turned on the overhead light. It was a shock to her eyes, but Ryder fixed that by dimming the brightness to a pleasant glow. "There. Satisfied?"

"Not even close." Quinn stepped closer. "You look like you've been through the ringer. Twice." She felt his forehead.

"Jesus, Quinn. I'm tired—not sick," Ryder protested, but he didn't move away from her touch.

"Did you take some aspirin? And plenty of water?" Worried by his pale complexion, Quinn took his hand and led him to the bed. "Sit." When she saw he was about to protest, she softly added, "Please?"

Ryder sat. "This is ridiculous."

"Aspirin?"

"In the bathroom cabinet."

Quinn retrieved the pills. "And water?"

"I have a bottle by the bed."

She handed Ryder three tablets and the water. Tapping her foot when he hesitated, Quinn held his gaze until he gave in and downed the aspirin.

"Finish the water. You need to replenish the fluids you lost on stage."

"I do that during the performance," he told her, draining the bottle.

"I noticed you didn't take as many breaks as usual tonight. Dehydration can land you in the hospital. Is that what you want?"

"Did you drop out of medical school as well as law school? What is with the good nurse routine?"

Quinn hid her smile. Annoying Ryder hadn't been her goal, but she would take it. The color was back in his face, and there was renewed energy in the tone of his voice. Her job here was almost done. Leaning close, she brushed her lips over his forehead, then let her lips linger for a moment.

"Definitely no fever," she said as she drew back.

When Quinn would have moved away, Ryder caught her hand in his.

"Kiss me again. It won't take long for the heat to rise."

"If you can hit on me while looking like death warmed over, I know you're feeling better." Quinn tried to pull away. Reluctantly, Ryder let her go. "That line needs some work. Rising heat? Really?"

"I'm not at my best. Try me again tomorrow."

"One week, remember?" Quinn teased. "In seven days, you won't need a line. I will be a sure thing."

"I haven't made up my mind about that," Ryder said.

His eyes drooped. *Finally,* Quinn thought. *He's ready for what his body needs most. Sleep.*

"Yes, you have." Quinn pushed him back onto the bed. "We will be lovers, Ryder Hart. It's our destiny."

"You don't believe in that crap."

"Not even a little. *I* determine my future." He let her arrange him so his head was on the pillow. "Since it is my choice, I choose sex. With you."

"What if I say no?"

Removing his shoes and socks, Quinn pulled the covers up to Ryder's chin. "Will you?"

"Probably not." He smiled when Quinn gently tugged on his ear. "Kiss me good night."

"Please?" Quinn urged teasingly.

"Please."

Quinn meant to keep it light and friendly. However, Ryder had more energy than she anticipated. But the time she pulled away, both of them were breathing heavily.

"That was…" Quinn struggled to find the proper words. *Wow* pretty much covered it.

"Yes, it was."

Quinn waited until Ryder closed his eyes, then turned to leave.

"Thank you, Quinn."

Ryder's voice was groggy, but his words sent a warm burst of pleasure through her.

"Anytime."

Closing the door behind her, Quinn realized she meant it. *Any time.* She had to be careful. Fun and games—with a helping of friendship thrown in—was one thing. But she would be a fool to think there could be anything more. The second she let herself forget that, she would be in trouble.

You'll know when it's time to walk away, Quinn assured herself. She didn't fall easily. She didn't cling. Or dream of rose petals and forever after. And she certainly was not going to fall in love with Ryder Hart.

CHAPTER EIGHT

THE DRAMA OF Chicago seemed a distant memory on the last night of the tour. Ryder had returned to his old self—or at least the one that Quinn had gotten to know. Admittedly, it was a small sample size. But if she could believe Zoe—plus Ashe and Dalton—most of the time, Ryder was a well-adjusted, happy person.

When his demons caught up with him, it could be ugly. And frightening to witness. But when he shook them loose, he recovered quickly. Thank God.

"The show in Chicago may be the stuff of legends, but I'm content with great over legendary. It's easier on the nerves."

Ashe unpacked his saxophone while Quinn took pictures. Of the group, he was the most comfortable with her impromptu shots. Zoe rarely put up with it. Dalton tended to tense up—though he was better than when she first joined the tour.

As for Ryder, he couldn't take a bad picture—something Quinn would have sworn was impossible. However, she checked the digital shots every night and the man never looked bad. Some were better than others. None were perfect. And that was Quinn's goal. Perfection was boring. And there was nothing boring about Ryder Hart or his band.

However, Ryder came close. It didn't matter if he were a sweating mess after a concert or catching a nap on the bus. His good looks and sex appeal made every shot magazine ready. He made her job easy—something she didn't plan on sharing with her employer.

"Do you ever get tired of looking at life through the lens of a camera?"

Surprised by the comment, Quinn stopped before she took the shot.

"This is my job, Ashe. My livelihood. And my passion. But I don't live with a camera glued to my face."

"That's good. There is a lot to see when you look with both eyes." He nodded toward the stage. "Ryder, for example."

Quinn glanced to where Ryder was talking with one of the lighting technicians. Whatever he said had the other man laughing.

"Do you want to give me a hint as to what I'm supposed to see?"

"He's a good man. One of the best."

"I'm sure he is." Quinn was afraid she knew where this was going. She decided to stop Ashe before he crossed over into potentially embarrassing territory. "I like Ryder. I like all of you."

Ashe didn't get the hint. "And we like you."

"Even Zoe?"

"Even Zoe," he laughed. "Much to her surprise. It's different with Ryder."

"Ashe—"

"Calm down. I'm not saying he's in love with you."

"Good." Quinn's heart rate had spiked. Relieved, it began to lower. "Tell me what you *are* saying."

"Ryder never takes a break. In all the years I've known him, his idea of a vacation has been songwriting or recording. Or working with other artists. I love the guy like a brother, but he's become a bit of a bore. He needs to cut loose. With you."

"What makes you think I have that kind of influence?"

"Maybe you don't. But would it hurt to try?"

"I'll think about it."

Satisfied that he had planted the seed, Ashe took out a new reed for the mouthpiece of his sax.

"I can't believe you gave Quinn that *poor Ryder* routine," Dalton said, shaking his head. He carried his drumsticks in one hand and a cup of coffee in the other. "Ryder has no problem leaving work behind. Last winter. In Figi? By the time we left, he had closed down every bar and nightclub in town."

"I wanted to give Quinn a little nudge."

"Quinn isn't the problem in this equation. Ryder is the one dragging his heels. For some unfathomable reason."

Ashe sighed. "Our friend has something called a conscience."

"A conscience? What's that?" Dalton asked, tongue in cheek. There had been a time when he ignored his. But maturity and the influence of a few good friends had turned him into one of the good guys. At times, Dalton found himself on the fence as to how he felt about that.

"*You* know. Most of the time." Ashe swung an arm over Dalton's shoulders. "Ryder needs a nudge—and you are just the man to give it to him."

"Short of dynamite, how do I move a mountain?"

"The green-eyed monster, my friend."

Dalton's eyes widened. "No. Absolutely not. I like my pearly whites. The last thing I need is for Ryder to knock them down my throat."

"It won't come to that," Ashe assured him. "Probably. All you have to do is express interest in the lovely Quinn. Ryder won't knock your teeth out over that."

"Says you," Dalton grumbled. However, they both knew he would go along with Ashe's plan. Dalton owed Ryder everything. He would never be able to repay his friend, but he would never stop trying.

"Now is a good time to start. A few well-chosen words should get Ryder thinking."

"Before the show?"

"Yes." Ashe gave Dalton a hefty shove. "And be subtle."

Behind his back, Dalton flipped Ashe off. But he kept going. Ashe watched as Dalton struck up a conversation with Ryder. *Casual*, Ashe thought. *That's good.* He grinned when he saw the expression on Ryder's face change. Not exactly angry. But not pleased.

"Good, boy," Ashe said to himself as Dalton walked away, leaving an annoyed, thoughtful Ryder in his wake. "If that doesn't give you the kick you need, nothing will."

"Talking to yourself again?" Zoe asked. She was dressed and ready for the show.

"I'm a fascinating conversationalist."

"Since when?"

"Smartass." Ashe gave Zoe a brotherly hug. "Come on. It's our last night. Let's go be brilliant."

"Aren't we always?"

Picking up his sax, Ashe ran his fingers up and down the keys in an impressive display. "No argument here."

THE LAST PICTURE she took, on the last night of the tour, turned out to be Quinn's favorite. The four band members, Ryder, Zoe, Ashe, and Dalton, stood at the edge of the stage, arms around each other. After a long tour, they were tired. But the audience didn't see it. They had treated their fans to the best they had to give.

Flushed with success, they took one last bow. Quinn caught the moment when Ryder said something only his friends could hear. Something that made them laugh. She couldn't be certain, but something told her *this* would be the cover of the magazine. The shot represented the band perfectly. Ryder might be the front man. But they were a team. Together. No matter what.

Quinn didn't stick around after the curtain fell. She had everything she needed to submit her story. In fact, she could have sent if off that afternoon. It was ready—and the pictures were some of the best of her career. But something had told her to hold off. It turned out she had been right to follow her gut.

Taking out her phone, she sent Ryder a text explaining that she had found a ride and would be at the hotel. As it turned out, getting a cab was an adventure. But she managed. Excited to begin, Quinn let herself into her room and got to work.

Quinn stretched her arms over her head. Glancing at the clock, she was amazed to see that it was almost dawn. As it always did when she immersed herself in her work, time flew by.

Typing in her editor's email address, Quinn took a deep breath before hitting send. She doubted the story would be published as is. However, she was confident it wouldn't need more than a few tweaks. It was good. Borderline great—if she did say so herself.

Yawning, Quinn pulled off her clothes and crawled into bed. She didn't feel particularly sleepy, but she needed to rest. Ryder wasn't leaving until tomorrow afternoon. She had given her conversation with Ashe a lot of thought. The band was at the end of a long, exhausting tour and Ryder needed a vacation. He hadn't asked her to go with him. However, if he did, she planned on saying no.

They had today. A few hours to enjoy each other. Good old-fashioned sex. Then goodbye. It was for the best. Quinn had to concentrate on her career, and there was no room in her life for Ryder Hart.

As for Ryder? He didn't need Quinn. Ryder had the world at his feet. That was more than enough for anyone.

"THE PROFITS FOR the tour are significantly above what we projected. Overhead came in under budget and concessions sales were through the roof. The exclusive stadium t-shirts might become collectors' items. They sold out. The online version is getting close. Though we can get more of those printed."

"That's great, Alden. Have the report sent to everyone. I know that Dalton doesn't bother, but Ashe and Zoe like to go over the numbers."

"Mmm." Alden made a note so he wouldn't forget. "Now that you've added to everyone's sizable wealth, what are your plans? Besides getting into the studio next month."

"That's it." Ryder double checked the closet before zipping up his suitcase. "I am going to sleep late and eat whatever I want."

Alden scoffed. "How long will that last? A week at the most."

"A week is good." Depending on a certain photographer, he might stretch it to two. "What about you? The Bahamas? I know you prefer the Caribbean."

"I haven't decided. Perhaps I'll do a staycation. The renovations are finally complete on my house. I should take some time to enjoy it."

"Sounds like a winner. After months on the road, home is a nice concept."

One that Ryder had yet to fully grasp. He had a house purchased when Alden had insisted it was a good investment. And it had been—according to Alden. It was worth almost twice what he paid for it. Tucked up in the Hollywood Hills, Ryder had been there exactly twice. Once to approve Alden's choice, and again when he had to decide where he wanted to put the swimming pool.

Ryder assumed the pool was finished—Alden showed him pictures. But he couldn't work up the enthusiasm to see it in person. Perhaps it was time to cash in on his investment before the market made its inevitable periodic downswing.

"I want to sell my Hollywood Hills place."

"What?" Caught off guard, Alden almost choked on his own spit. He coughed, sending Ryder an appalled look. "Why? It's a beautiful home."

"It's a beautiful *house*," Ryder corrected. "I've never lived there."

"But—"

"And I never will, Alden. Los Angeles is fine to visit, but it isn't where I see myself. After spending most of my life as a nomad, I want to try settling in one place between tours. Apartment living has gotten old."

Ryder had apartments in Los Angeles, New York, and Miami. Between touring, recording, and everything else involved in being *Ryder Hart*, he rarely spent time in any of them. When he did, they felt cold and generic. Hiring an expensive decorator only went so far to make a place a home. Ryder hadn't figured out the exact equation. Whatever it was, it was time to find it.

"Wasn't that the point when you bought your house—five years ago?"

"I thought so." Ryder couldn't explain except to say, "I wasn't ready."

"What's changed?" Alden's eyes grew wide. "Don't tell me this is because of the photographer. You've only known her for two weeks, Ryder."

"It has nothing to do with Quinn. I've been thinking about this for some time. I decided to wait until after the tour to mention my plans."

"If not Los Angeles, where?"

"I like New York. Or Seattle. They have a great music scene there."

"If you like the rain," Alden sneered.

"I do, as a matter of fact. Seattle isn't set in stone, Alden. I told you, I haven't decided."

"Then hold onto the house until you do. What's the hurry to sell?"

"You appear to be more attached to the place than I am. Should I get Shayla to find a realtor?"

"There is no need to trouble your assistant. I'm certain the realtor who sold it to you will be more than happy to take the listing. There will probably be multiple offers before you get back from your vacation." Alden stood. "I suppose that's it. Unless there's something else, I'll be going."

"It was a stellar tour, Alden." When Alden would have shaken his hand, Ryder laughed, pulling the man in for a hug. He knew why Alden hesitated. But it did neither of them any good to tiptoe around it. They had been friends a long time. He wasn't going to start holding back his affection because Alden couldn't get past his feelings.

"Right." Awkwardly patting Ryder on the back, Alden cleared his throat. "I will see you in a few weeks."

"Take care, Alden."

"Always."

Alden opened the hotel room door just as Quinn was about to knock.

"Oops," Quinn laughed. "I almost rapped you on the head."

"Hello, Ms. Abernathy."

"Will it ever be Quinn?"

"I doubt it. I spoke to your editor this morning. It seems your submission was satisfactory."

"So I understand." Quinn wondered if Alden planned on barring her from the room. "You will get an advance copy for approval."

"I would hope so."

"Is that Quinn?" Ryder called out from the bathroom.

Quinn heard Alden's sigh. He moved aside to let her enter. "Goodbye, Ms. Abernathy."

It sounded so final, as though Alden expected this to be the last time their paths crossed. Perhaps it would be. Quinn decided to leave it open ended. Partly because she didn't know if this was the end. But mostly because she knew it would rankle Alden.

"See you around, Mr. Christopher."

To Quinn's satisfaction, Alden's mouth tightened. She closed the door behind him before she broke out laughing.

"I like the sound of that."

Quinn looked Ryder up and down. It didn't matter how many times she saw him, it always made her glad she was a woman who liked men. Especially one who looked like Ryder Hart. "Hello, handsome."

"Hello, beautiful."

Ryder didn't move toward her. And for now, she was happy where she was.

"Have you had any thoughts about us?" Seeing no need to be subtle, Quinn cocked her head in the direction of the bed.

"When it comes to us," Ryder repeated her gesture, "that's all I *have* thought about. In graphic detail."

"I like that." Quinn's clothes and other personal items were packed and waiting in her room. But when she wasn't home, she never left her camera unattended. Setting the case on the floor, she removed her jacket. "I would love to hear all about it."

"Do you like dirty talk?" Ryder circled her, getting a little closer with each pass.

"I might. If the right man did the talking."

"Dalton?"

"I beg your pardon." Appalled, Quinn's eyes narrowed. Whatever she had missed, she didn't think she would like it.

Ryder laughed. "Before the concert last night, Dalton hinted that he had his eye on you."

"That is news to me."

"I suspect Ashe was behind it. He knew I hadn't decided if this," he motioned toward the bed, "was a good idea."

"And what? He thought if it seemed as though Dalton were sniffing around, it would turn you into a jealous fool?"

"Something like that. I knew what was up right away. Not that I didn't believe that he could be interested in you," Ryder quickly assured her. "But I know my friends. There is a line we don't cross."

"You don't poach each other's women?"

"Never."

Quinn liked that they thought of her as Ryder's woman. Temporary as the title might be.

"Their machinations didn't work?"

"Nope."

"Where does that leave us?"

"Here." Ryder pulled down the covers on the bed. "If it's what you want."

"I made it clear what I wanted." Quinn moved until she and Ryder stood only inches apart. "My editor loved my pictures. We fiddled with the layout for a couple of hours this morning until we were both satisfied. That means," she ran a finger over the top button of his shirt. "As of twelve-thirty this afternoon, I am officially off the job."

"That's all I've been waiting for."

CHAPTER NINE

RYDER COULDN'T REMEMBER the last time he wanted something—anything or anyone—as much as he wanted Quinn. Perhaps it was the anticipation. Two weeks was not a long time. However, Ryder was not used to waiting. When he desired a woman, she was his. Any woman. Any time. That wasn't his ego talking, it was fact. Part of it was him—the way he looked. But mostly it was the musician thing. Ryder had learned long ago that women liked a man who played an instrument. When he did it on stage *and* sang? From the time he played his first gig until today, finding a willing sex partner had never been a problem.

In Ryder's often misspent youth, he wasn't picky. He used condoms and took his chances. He had been damn lucky—all things considered. No transmitted diseases and nobody showed up pregnant. Though one woman tried a paternity suit just after he hit it big. Thank God for DNA testing. Ryder could have sworn on a stack of bibles that he had never slept with the lady—which was the truth. However, nobody could argue with science. He was not the child's father.

Sex used to be a way to make himself feel better. A way to connect with another human being. Ryder was no longer a randy, needy teenager. When he took a woman to bed, it was about desire. Instead of a quick fuck in the parking lot of a seedy bar, he took his time. There was finesse, style, and skill that he had deliberately cultivated. No more wham, bang, thank you, ma'am.

Ryder considered himself to be a mature, thoughtful lover. So why did he want to rip Quinn's clothes from her body and take her with all the skill of an untried virgin?

"Is there a problem?" Quinn asked.

"No." *Yes*. But it was difficult to explain without fear of scaring the crap out of her.

"I feel a little desperate." Slowly, Quinn unbuttoned his shirt. "I feel as if I've been waiting for this moment a long, long time."

"Two weeks." Ryder took a deep breath. Quinn's fingers brushed against his chest, making him swallow. If the lightest of touches made him burn, how would he last?

Quinn's lips curved into a smile. "I promised myself I wouldn't do this. That lasted about a day. Then I told myself it was okay to lust after you. Why should I be any different than every other woman in the world."

"Not *every* woman." Though Ryder liked knowing Quinn thought so.

"Close enough. It could be intimidating." Quinn's smile grew wider when she finished her task, folding back the ends of Ryder's shirt to reveal his bare chest. "That would be worth tackling a thousand buttons." She met his gaze. "What was I saying?"

"It could be intimidating?"

"Right. I don't shy away from a challenge. I plan on making this memorable for you, Ryder Hart. No matter how many women come after, you *will* remember me."

"I don't doubt it for a second."

The pleasure his words gave her sparkled in Quinn's lovely blue eyes. Ryder gave into his need to touch her. But he did so tentatively, placing his hands on her hips.

"You could kiss me," Quinn said, leaning closer.

"*You* could kiss *me*."

"Or…" she began.

"We could kiss each other."

The second their lips met, Ryder wondered what the hell he had been waiting for. Quinn tasted like heaven—and felt even better. With his tongue, he traced the outline of her mouth. He didn't ask for her to open; she did so on her own with a welcoming sigh.

Ryder loved kissing—another thing he had learned the joys of as he grew older. There had been a time when any kind of foreplay seemed like a waste of time. Now, he savored the pleasure of a woman's soft lips against his. And Quinn's? He could have gone on kissing her for hours.

Maybe another time. Today, Ryder wanted more. He craved everything.

Impatient to feel her skin against his, Ryder pulled Quinn's top over her head.

"That is a very pretty bra."

"Why, thank you." Quinn traced the top of a lilac-colored lace cup. "It's new."

Ryder's finger joined Quinn's, following right behind. "How new?"

"I bought it yesterday," she whispered, her eyes following the path of his finger.

"Were you thinking about me?"

"Yes."

Lord, Quinn's honesty made his blood heat. She didn't play coy or bat her eyes. She told him straight out that she purchased the sexy underwear with him in mind. In Ryder's opinion, there was nothing sexier than the truth.

Ryder slipped his hand up Quinn's side, sliding to her back. "May I take it off?"

"This morning when I put it on, I was hoping you would."

Years of playing the guitar had made Ryder's fingers nimble. With one hand, he easily unclasped her bra. He smiled when Quinn let out a happy sigh. The teasing banter had calmed him a bit. The urge to take her hard and fast had lessened—though not by much.

Easing the straps off Quinn's shoulders, Ryder kissed her neck before returning to her mouth for a long, heated kiss. His hand cupped her breast, the nipple hard against his palm. Ryder squeezed gently, flicking the straining peak with the calloused pad of his thumb.

"You like that?" he asked when Quinn gasped. Before she could answer, he did it again. "The guitar strings make the tips of my fingers rough."

"Another reason women go crazy for musicians."

Ryder chuckled. Quinn had a quick mind, and he found it damn sexy. Along with her taste. And the feel of her breasts. And her smile. Hell. Quinn was sexy top to bottom—inside and out.

"Let's find out what else drives you crazy."

Ryder licked the side of Quinn's neck—that sweet spot just below her ear. When she gasped, Ryder did it again, adding his teeth to the mix. Quinn grasped his shoulders, her fingers biting into his flesh. *Oh, yes. A sweet spot indeed.*

Falling to his knees, Ryder looked up. The view was spectacular. Quinn's flushed face, her lips parted slightly. The underside of her breasts that were topped by dark crimson nipples. Ryder nuzzled her belly button before laying a line of kisses just above the waistband of her pants.

Quinn's fingers slid into his hair, lightly massaging his scalp. This time, it was his turn to groan. When he looked up, her blues eyes met his. Bright. Blazing. And yet, strangely tender. Ryder swallowed. Something changed in that instant, though he couldn't have said what it was. It was fleeting. Dancing out of his grasp before he could fully comprehend what had happened. Then Quinn smiled, and he stopped worrying about anything else.

"You should be naked," she told him in a matter-of-fact manner—as though she spoke those words every day.

"Funny. I was thinking the same thing about you." Ryder unbuttoned her pants. "Do your panties match your bra?"

Quinn's lips twitched. "Will it be a major mood killer if they don't?"

"At the moment, this mood could survive anything. Even granny panties."

When Ryder began to lower her zipper, Quinn stayed his motion.

"What if they are big and white and made of that slippery satin?"

Ryder laughed. "Since I'm not having sex with your undies, I couldn't care less what they look like."

With a provocative wink, Quinn let him continue. Slowly, Ryder moved the zipper down inch by inch until he found a scrap of lilac-colored lace.

"Disappointed?"

"I think I can muddle through."

In one quick motion, Ryder had Quinn's pants at her ankles. Without prompting, she kicked them and her flats to the side with an impressively smooth move.

"Beautiful," Ryder murmured.

"My panties?"

"You. All of you."

Quinn put her hand under his chin, tipping his face toward hers. "Right back at you."

There it was again. That odd feeling Ryder couldn't identify zipped along the base of his spine. Gone in an instant. Perhaps it was never there. Rather than dwell on something he couldn't name—or control—Ryder turned his full attention to Quinn. With one finger, he toyed with the lace at the top of her leg.

"Mind if I rip these off?"

Quinn took in a quick breath. However, when she spoke, her voice was steady, light, and teasing.

"I would rather you didn't. They *are* new. Besides, I wouldn't have anything to match my bra."

"Very practical." Before Quinn could react, Ryder tore the lace in two, tossing the scraps over his shoulder. "I'll buy you a new pair. With a bra to match."

"Damn straight you will." But there was no heat to her words. If anything, the arousal in Quinn's voice had deepened.

"This is pretty." Ryder touched the tiny tuft of hair between her legs.

"I had it done after I bought the underwear. It's a heart." Quinn paused as though waiting for his reaction. "It was a silly whim. Was it too much?"

"Words fail me." He outlined the pattern with his finger. "Instead, let me show you what I think."

Ryder replaced his finger with his mouth, his lapping at the heart—then moving lower. When Quinn gasped with pleasure, her legs wobbling slightly, Ryder steadied her with his arm. The move was satisfactory for both of them, keeping Quinn upright and providing Ryder with a better angle to explore and sample.

"Let me guess," Quinn sighed when he moved lower. "Years of singing have made your tongue nimble." She let out a long, *mmm*. "And dexterous."

"And talented?"

"Oh, yes."

Ryder could tell by the change in Quinn's breathing that she was close to toppling over the edge of reason. Her fingers tightened, tugging at his hair. Her legs trembled. And the little cries of pleasure. *Hell, yes.* Those little cries were driving him crazy.

"Ready to fall?"

Quinn didn't answer with words. However, her gasp and the way she pulled him closer told Ryder everything he needed to know. Adding the thrust of his fingers to the rhythm of his tongue, Ryder didn't push Quinn. He toppled her with a sexy, concentrated shove.

Ryder kept her safe as Quinn cried out his name and rode wave after wave of pleasure. He made certain her high stretched on and on until there was nowhere else to go but down. However, Ryder made the fall an easy one. Standing, he gently lifted Quinn into his arms. Her eyes were closed, her breathing ragged—slowing. Ryder knew he had made it good for her. But it was the look on her face that made him burst with pride. Happy. Glowing. Spent. Quinn had the look of a woman who was utterly and completely satisfied.

Pulling back the covers, Ryder lay Quinn on the bed. Her smile widened as she stretched her arms over her head. Slowly, her eyes opened.

"That was nice."

"Nice?" Ryder paused in the middle of unbuckling his belt.

"Very nice."

Ryder was about to question Quinn's sanity when he noticed her lips twitch. *The little stinker*. She was lying there like a gorgeous limp rag—thanks to him—and she wanted to tease the beast? The very hard, very horny, beast? If the woman wanted to play with fire, he would be more than happy to make her burn. *Again. And again.*

Deciding it would be more impactful to let his actions speak for themselves, Ryder finished undressing. He knew what he looked like. Part genetics, part hard work, his naked body was an impressive sight. From the way Quinn's eyes widened, he could tell she agreed.

"Like what you see?"

"Yes."

"Do you think it's nice?" To emphasize his question, Ryder waggled his dick at Quinn.

"You could use that thing to hammer a nail." Quinn rose to her knees. "But I have a better idea."

Quinn took him in her hand and tugged. Not too hard—just enough to get him to her edge of the bed.

"I may have downplayed how much I enjoyed your talented mouth."

"You don't say." Hoping he knew where this was headed, Ryder smoothed Quinn's hair back from her face. "Want to elaborate?"

"You were spectacular." Quinn gave his erection a lingering kiss, ending with a swipe of her tongue. "Beyond amazing. I saw stars. I glimpsed heaven. The only bad part was that it had to end."

Between every other word, Quinn lavished him with kisses. Ryder loved every second. Then she took him into her mouth. She may have glimpsed heaven, but he swore he stood smack in the middle. Unfortunately, if she kept that up, it was going to be a short visit.

"Quinn." Ryder hated to interrupt, but he had no choice. "If you keep doing that, I'm going to explode. Now."

"Explode. Now, " Quinn told him. "We can go around again. And again. Unless you have someplace else to be?"

"No." Ryder threaded his fingers through her dark, silky hair. "We have all the time in the world."

QUINN RESTED, BUT she didn't feel like sleeping. She could feel the comforting thump of Ryder's heart under her cheek. The clock was out of her line of sight—much to her delight. Time was irrelevant. As far as she was concerned, there was no night. No day. She wanted what Ryder had said to be true. At least for a little while longer. Unfortunately, they *didn't* have all the time in the world. However, she wanted *this* time—these precious moments—to last as long as possible.

Being with Ryder had been better than her dreams. And that was saying something. For two weeks, Quinn's dreams had built the anticipation to epic proportions. Somehow, Ryder had surpassed epic. What would be the word? Homeric? It was sort of the same thing, but her body was satiated and her brain fuzzy. Wonderfully so. Homeric would have to do.

Quinn hadn't lost track of how many times she came. Six— thank you very much. Ryder's stamina was the stuff of legends. If a friend had bragged that a man had Ryder's staying power, Quinn would have rolled her eyes and called bullshit.

There had to be other men capable of such feats. Ryder was special—but he wasn't a freak of nature. Yet, Quinn had never heard of another such man—outside of flowery fiction. And she knew why. It was like discovering gold. One little whisper—even a hint— of multiple orgasms and women would be dropping out of the woodwork, trying to poach her claim.

Laughing silently, Quinn was glad Ryder couldn't hear her thoughts. Comparing him to a gold strike? She was going to keep that one to herself.

Ryder ran his hand over her back, coming to rest on her butt. Quinn had just enough energy to wiggle it in appreciation.

"I need food," he patted his flat stomach. "And a shower. You pick the order."

"You've worn me out. Food means room service. Which means using the phone." Quinn made a feeble show of reaching toward the nightstand. "Nope. Can't do it."

"*I* could move."

Quinn could hear the smile in Ryder's voice. Her lips curved in response.

"My body is draped over yours—most comfortably. If you move, I move. Sorry. I can't sanction that."

"Hold on." Holding her in place, Ryder shifted. Quinn would have protested, but he had the phone before she could summon the energy.

"Impressive."

"That's what you said after your… fifth orgasm?" Quinn merely hummed in appreciation, causing Ryder to laugh. "What are you hungry for?"

"Well…" Quinn reached between Ryder's legs. She found the twitch of response encouraging—and a little flattering.

"Good, God." Ryder swatted her hand away. "I'm only human, woman. I need fuel before I can pleasure you again."

Quinn didn't tell Ryder that she was as worn out as he was. Food sounded good. A shower sounded better.

"Do you want a steak?" Ryder asked, picking up the receiver. "I'm having a steak."

"With sautéed mushrooms and French fries."

"Salad?"

"I don't think so," Quinn snorted.

Ryder put in their order. After consulting Quinn, he added a slice of apple pie and a piece of cheesecake for dessert. Hanging up, he surprised her by jumping from the bed and swinging her into his arms.

"I thought you were running on fumes," Quinn laughed, wrapping her arms around Ryder's neck.

"Just the thought of food has given me a second wind." He headed toward the bathroom. "We have thirty minutes. Want to bet how many times I can make you cry out my name?"

"Why bother?" Quinn whispered into his ear. "Once? Twice? I win either way."

"Three times?"

Slamming the door behind them, Quinn pinched Ryder's butt. "Don't get cocky."

Ryder reached into the stall, turning the multiple jets on full blast. "Is that a challenge?" he asked, pulling her close.

"I would be happy with one, Ryder."

Quinn learned fast that Ryder Hart had a competitive streak in him a mile wide. She hadn't issued a challenge, but he took it as one.

"Three it is."

Quinn's laughter turned to moans the second Ryder led her into the shower and dropped to his knees. If the man was that determined, who was she to argue?

CHAPTER TEN

IN HER ENTIRE life, Quinn could not remember anything tasting better than the meal in front of her. The steak was perfectly cooked. The French fries crispy brown. Even the broccoli—which she had no say in ordering—was fresh and tasty.

Quinn chewed a piece of the tender meat. A good meal was fine. What made it great was the company. Ryder sat across from her in nothing but a dark blue robe. His hair, damp from their shared shower, curled around his ears, the ends brushing the collar of his robe. A woman could go a long way before she found a more appealing dinner companion.

"Stop smirking."

"Me?" Ryder gave her a not so innocent look. "What would I have to smirk about?"

"You are perfectly aware." Quinn wanted to sound exasperated—truly she did. But it was difficult when the reason for Ryder's expression had made her feel so good.

"I admitted that you are a sex god."

"And…" Ryder urged.

"Nobody has ever given me so much pleasure in such a short amount of time." Quinn could have said, *nobody has ever given me so much pleasure*—period. But why should she feed Ryder's already sizable ego? She suspected he knew the truth. That was good enough.

"I counted three orgasms. Four was in reach, but the food arrived."

"Thank you, Ryder."

To emphasize her appreciation, Quinn transferred half of her French fries onto Ryder's plate. He didn't know it, but for a woman who loved a good fry, that was quite the gesture of gratitude.

"With complete sincerity, I can say, the pleasure was mutual."

"Is this your usual routine?" Quinn inquired.

"Crazy sex in random hotel rooms?"

Quinn shrugged. "That is most people's idea of a rock star's life. But it isn't what I meant."

"I have some pretty crazy stories I could tell you."

Now he wanted to share? After two weeks of, *my personal life is off limits*, Ryder wanted to talk about his sex life? It was possible he was teasing. However, Quinn didn't want to hear it. Now, or ever. If she hadn't been planning on cleaning her plate, she would have tossed the rest of her meal in his lap.

"I'm certain your many exploits could fill a book."

"Well…"

"Save that for when you're old and ready to write a tell-all biography. I wanted to know if your life was this?" Quinn motioned toward their meal. "Hotels? Room service? The life of a nomad? I know from experience that traveling on business—even rock-star business—isn't as glamorous as it sounds. Does it grow old?"

When Ryder didn't answer, Quinn sighed.

"I understand I have broken rule number one. No questions. I thought you might bend a little since we've spent most of the day naked. I know very little about you, Ryder—outside of gossip and your official biography. You've been inside of me. Doesn't that entitle me to a little post-coital Q & A?"

"I agree." Ryder sat back, a thoughtful smile on his face. "The reason I hesitated is that you used the term nomad. I found it ironic. I had described myself the same way just this morning."

"Is that good or bad?"

"Finished with that?" Ryder pointed to her plate.

Surprised to see that she had indeed polished off every scrap, Quinn nodded. Ryder cleared the small table they used to dine. It was near the window, giving them a view of the city skyline as they ate. He stacked the dishes before picking up their dessert.

"A fork for you." The apple pie smelled fantastic. However, cheesecake was a weakness that Quinn didn't mind admitting. Guessing her dilemma, Ryder smiled. "I thought we could share."

Quinn didn't wait for him to sit. "Mmm. Extra creamy," she sighed. She held a bite of the cheesecake out for Ryder to sample. "Isn't that luscious?"

"You seem easily distracted by food."

Not the least bit insulted, Quinn sampled the pie. It was good. But she went back to the cheesecake. "And sex. Don't forget the sex."

"That isn't likely." Ryder seemed happy to watch Quinn, taking a bite whenever she fed it to him.

"It doesn't work unless it's good. The food *and* the sex. You can't distract me with a mediocre pizza or boring sex."

"Good to know."

Quinn took a sip of water, her gaze meeting Ryder's. "Are you laughing at me?"

"Maybe. A little. But not in a bad way."

Deciding she could live with that, Quinn offered Ryder more cheesecake. When he shook his head, she set down the fork. It didn't happen often, but she was full. Both her stomach and her libido were wonderfully satisfied. For now.

"Okay, nomad man, tell me your tale."

For a moment, Quinn thought that Ryder had changed his mind. Getting him to talk about himself was a big step. Perhaps he was ready. However, after a little while, he began.

"I have been on my own since I was sixteen—by choice. The foster care system and I didn't see eye to eye."

Quinn knew the basics of Ryder's background. His mother left soon after Zoe was born—never to be heard from again. His father was a troubled man. He drank. Did drugs. Though there was nothing on record, it was suspected that Ryder had suffered parental abuse. How extensive? Only Ryder could say. It was a subject strictly off limits.

When Ryder was thirteen and Zoe ten, their father committed suicide. The rest, like all aspects of his life, was sketchy. To Quinn's surprise, Ryder had handed her a piece of the puzzle.

"You ran away?"

"Ran. Was pushed. I suppose it depends on your perspective—and who you ask. The last couple who took me in tried to sell their story to the tabloids. They painted themselves as saintly do-gooders. Loving. Caring. I, on the other hand, had been a nasty handful. They tried to show me love and compassion. I rewarded their efforts by trashing their home before disappearing. They searched. Called the police. But until they saw my picture in a magazine—all grown up and famous—they had lived with the constant worry that I had met a tragic ending."

"I don't recall reading that story." To prepare for her job following Ryder and his band, Quinn had scoured the internet. As the saying said, *forearmed is forewarned.* She would have remembered a story like the one Ryder had mentioned.

"That's because it was never published. Alden slipped them a few bucks and made them sign a non-disclosure agreement."

"At your request?"

"No." Ryder pushed back from the table. He threaded his fingers through his hair until his hands cupped the back of his head. When his eyes met Quinn's, a hard edge had entered his gaze. "That was Alden. If I had known what he was doing, I would have stopped him. I don't give a shit about what people say about me. I never have. I'm a musician, not a saint. There isn't much that could tarnish my image. Just the opposite. Chicks love a bad boy."

It was a cynical outlook. And oh, so true.

"If you don't care, why all the secrecy?" Quinn frowned. "The first thing you made clear when you agreed to let me photograph you and your band was that your past was off limits. No questions. None."

"I told you it was up to Dalton and Ashe. If they wanted to talk, I had no problem with that. As for me?" Ryder hesitated. "My past is tied directly to Zoe's. To protect her privacy, it is easier not to say anything."

"What about Zoe? Does she avoid interviews to protect you?"

For some reason, Ryder found Quinn's question amusing. "You would have to ask her."

Quinn chuckled. It was a fascinating maze filled with twists, turns, and dead ends. Ryder. Zoe. Dalton. Ashe. They were such mysteries. Deliberate or not, it added to their public appeal. The foursome was talented, young, attractive, and kept their private lives just that—private. Not an easy accomplishment in this day and age of twenty-four-hour news cycles where there was an easy buck made by anyone peddling half-truths and innuendo.

"You protect them all, don't you?"

"With my life—if necessary.

It was said with such a calm conviction that Quinn knew Ryder wasn't exaggerating. He meant every word. A shiver ran down Quinn's spine. She didn't know how she felt. Unsettled? Disturbed? But there was an emotion she recognized immediately. Jealousy. What was it like to have someone that committed to keeping you, and your secrets, safe? Sadly, Quinn doubted she would ever know.

"I think we got off the subject."

"So we did." Ryder took Quinn's hand, leading her to the sofa. He sat, settling her by his side with his arm around her shoulders—holding her close. "I don't often ramble. I guess you bring it out in me."

"Is that good or bad?" Quinn asked as she relaxed against Ryder.

This was nice. Almost normal. It would have been easy to forget that she was sitting next to one of the most famous musicians in the world. Quinn was too smart to let that happen. She knew this would end—and soon. However, no matter what tomorrow brought, for tonight, Ryder belonged to her. How many women could say that?

"Good. I live too much inside my head. The songs. The music. It's profitable. However, it is not always comfortable. You make me laugh. And want."

Ryder kissed her slowly. It wasn't a prelude to anything. Simply a kiss to be enjoyed for what it was. With a sigh, Quinn sank in. She wanted to have a lasting memory of Ryder's taste and touch and feel.

"Where were we?" Quinn asked Ryder as he pulled back.

The smile Ryder gave her could only be described as a smirk. A sexy smirk, to be sure. It was the sexy part that made her smile in spite of herself. She didn't want to add to the man's cocky attitude. But what could she do?

"I was about to tell you that I'm tired of the nomadic lifestyle."

"Right." Quinn snuggled closer, her hand resting on his hip. "Tell me more."

Needing no further prompting, Ryder explained to Quinn about the home he had bought but never lived in. The apartments that acted more like temporary hostels than actual homes.

Whether he knew it or not, he was giving Quinn an insight she hadn't expected. Ryder Hart had never lived in a real home. A haven away from the world. His childhood had been filled with abandonment, abuse, and the knowledge that he wasn't wanted—any place.

"I'm ready for a home. The problem is *making* one."

"When I was a little girl, I believed the myth that a home meant a mother and a father. They never fought or cheated or left."

"Or hit," Ryder mumbled to himself.

Though it made her want to cry, Quinn had a feeling that Ryder wouldn't appreciate it if she wept for the little boy he once was. Instead, she took his hand and linked her fingers with his. Silently, she told him that if he needed her strength, here it was.

"My parents argued all the time. They didn't try to hide their problems behind closed doors. And maybe that was good. I don't know. I do know they were miserable together. Mom remarried—happily as far as I know. My father remarried. Divorced. Remarried. I have no idea if this one will stick."

"Hardly *Leave It to Beaver*."

"That show was always a myth." Quinn leaned back so that she could look Ryder in the eyes. She reached out, smoothing back the lock of wavy hair that had fallen over his forehead. "I think home is where you want to be. My father didn't want to be with my mother. She made a home with her new husband. He's still looking."

"What about you?"

To Quinn's relief, there was nothing but interest in Ryder's hazel eyes. No lingering sadness. No pain.

"I think of my little apartment as home. I'm comfortable there. My neighbors are friendly."

"Comfortable would be nice. I've never had that." Ryder sent her a self-deprecating smile. "Poor me. Fame. Fortune. Adoring fans. What do I have to complain about?"

"I didn't hear a complaint. I heard you wishing for a little peace and quiet."

"That would be nice." Ryder sighed. Then a slow smile lit his face. "What are you doing when you leave here?"

"Laundry."

Laughing, Ryder brought her hand to his lips. It was such a sweet, natural gesture. He had an innate charm that couldn't be learned. If she weren't careful, she could lose her head—and her heart. It was a good thing they would be parting ways tomorrow. The last thing Quinn needed was to start wanting something that could never happen. That would be a major complication and nothing but folly.

"I'm taking a vacation. Sand and sun. Mountains and trees. It doesn't matter."

"Sounds like heaven."

"I'm glad you think so," Ryder grinned. "Come with me."

Quinn stared at him for a second, making certain he was serious. When he stared back, his gaze never wavering, she realized he meant it. *Well, crap.*

"I'm afraid my bank account is on the lean side these days. But I appreciate the invitation."

"This isn't Dutch treat, Quinn. I'll pay for everything."

"God, no." Quinn jumped to her feet. "I pay my own way."

"That's admirable. But what's the harm in letting me treat you to a few days of carefree fun?"

"Would you agree if our situations were reversed?"

"Hell, yes." Ryder laughed. "I always thought I would make a terrific gigolo."

"The equivalent of a male prostitute? What would that make me if I agreed to go with you?"

"A friend—and lover. Jesus, Quinn. How did this conversation take such a bizarre turn?" Ryder shook his head, clearly puzzled.

"I'm sorry, Ryder. Money is a bit of a sore spot with me."

"Really? I never would have guessed."

"Jeez." Quinn paced back and forth. "My father used money to keep me in line, dangling it like a carrot. Here is your reward, Quinn. Go to law school and I will pay for your education. Promise to join my firm and that new car is yours. When I rebelled by dropping out of school, he cut off his financial support."

"You survived."

"Better than that. I thrived."

Ryder looked her over. "I can see that." He stood, sweeping Quinn into his arms. They began to sway to a silent rhythm. "I'm not asking for anything in return, Quinn."

Quinn laughed when Ryder spun her in a circle.

"Nothing?" she asked provocatively.

"I don't want to buy your body. Or your time. I want you to give both freely—because you enjoy our time together as much as I do. Forget the money for a moment. If all things were equal—financially speaking—would you say yes?"

Would she? Quinn swayed in Ryder's arms, thinking hard about his question. It was dangerous on so many levels. But, oh, so tempting. *Forget the money*? Okay. Ryder wasn't using it to manipulate her. It would be fun to take a trip that had nothing to do with work and simply relax.

"You want to say yes." Ryder began to hum a slow, sultry tune. They danced, their bodies perfectly in tune as though they had known each other for years, instead of weeks. "Would you like separate rooms?"

"If I go, I want to be with you. Two rooms? Separate beds? That *would* be a waste of money."

Ryder nuzzled Quinn's neck with his lips. "Why are you hesitating? Two weeks with nothing to worry about except which bikini to wear."

Quinn tilted her head, giving him better access. "What makes you think I own a bikini?"

"Even better. We'll get a bungalow on a private beach and spend all day naked. No tan lines."

Ryder described paradise, and Quinn wanted to quibble about money and her pride? If she said yes, all she had to worry about was Ryder stealing part of her heart. Honestly, that had already happened. If she said no, there was no doubt in her mind that she would regret it for the rest of her life.

Why *was* she hesitating?

"Ryder—" Quinn groaned when her phone rang. She knew the ringtone. *What Have You Done For Me Lately*? "That would be my father."

Ryder pulled her closer, his wandering lips finding the curve of her ear. "Let it go to voicemail."

"I would." Reluctantly, Quinn slid from Ryder's embrace. "Unfortunately, my father doesn't take a hint. He will call again. And again. And again. If I turn my phone off, he'll send the police."

"You're kidding?"

Quinn smiled at the disbelief in Ryder's tone. The phone stopped ringing. She had just enough time before the next call to explain. Though she didn't think Ryder would understand. Quinn had lived with her father's massive ego all of her life, and she had yet to figure him out.

"Michael Abernathy, aka my father, never takes no for an answer. When I don't answer his call, he considers it a personal affront. The police thing only happened once—just after I left law school. However, it taught me to call him back. When he gets in a mood, there is no telling what he will do."

Ryder tensed, his eyes narrowing. "Is he abusive?"

"No," Quinn assured him. "Dad is pushy. Opinionated. And doesn't hesitate to freeze me out when I don't follow his dictates. But he seldom raises his voice. And never hits anything but a tennis ball."

As witticisms went, the tennis ball reference was pretty lame. However, Ryder didn't call her on it. He relaxed, obviously trusting that she wasn't covering for her father.

"There he is again," Quinn said, picking up her phone.

"Do you want some privacy?"

It was sweet of Ryder to ask, but Quinn shook her head. Her conversations with her father were sometimes frustrating, but nothing was said that she would mind if Ryder overheard.

"Hello, Dad."

"Do you know what day it is?"

As always, her father began every conversation without a greeting.

"Sunday?"

As though Quinn hadn't spoken, her father barreled forward. "It is two days until Cora's birthday. When are you arriving?"

"I—"

"Tomorrow would be best. It will give you time to visit with your Aunt Pinney and Uncle Titus."

Quinn didn't know where to start so she jumped into the middle.

"Pinney and Titus are not my aunt and uncle. They are friends of yours I haven't seen since I was eight—and I didn't like them then. I doubt that will have changed."

"They've talked of nothing else since they found out you were coming."

"Really?" Quinn was slightly appalled. "Pinney and Titus need to get out more."

"Cora wants to talk to you."

"No! Dad, don't you dare—"

"Quinn. I can't wait to show you all the changes I've made to the house." Cora's sugarcoated, little girl's voice made Quinn wince. "Michael tells me you'll be here tomorrow."

"That is still up in the air. Would you put my father on, Cora?"

"What did you say to Cora? She ran out of the room in tears."

And the drama queen strikes again. Unconsciously, Quinn massaged her temple. Ryder moved behind her, took away her hand, his fingers magically making her threatening headache disappear. With a grateful sigh, Quinn leaned back. Solid and warm, Ryder's body was there to support her.

"I have plans, Dad."

"Aren't you finished photographing that ridiculous rock band? I don't know what all the fuss is about. Ryder Hart," her father snorted derisively. "He has nothing on the singers of my generation. Give me David Lee Roth any day."

Quinn made a silent prayer, hoping her father's voice wasn't as loud as it sounded to her. When she heard Ryder chuckle, she knew her prayer had gone unanswered.

Covering the phone, she whispered, "Sorry about that."

"I'm a Van Halen fan." Ryder's warm breath against her ear made Quinn shiver. "Though I preferred them with Sammy Hagar."

"Quinn?" Her father sounded impatient. But what else was new?

"I'm going away for a few weeks."

"By yourself?"

"No. With a friend."

"Your friend can't wait," Ryder whispered.

"I'm not a young man, Quinn."

98

"Fifty-seven is hardly ancient, Dad."

"My cholesterol is high. My blood pressure could be better. Who's to say it won't catch up with me sooner than later?"

Quinn took a deep breath, counted to ten, then slowly exhaled. It didn't help. Her father, the manipulative bastard, had won.

"I will see you tomorrow."

"Text me your flight number. I'll send a car."

Knowing better than to push his luck, her father hung up without a goodbye or a kiss my ass. Actually, that would have been Quinn's parting shot.

"He's good." There was a trace of admiration in Ryder's voice.

"He should be. He's had a lifetime of practice." Quinn put down her phone. "I'm sorry, Ryder. It looks like you'll be flying solo on your vacation after all."

"Why?"

"You heard. I get to spend a few days with my father, his third wife, and my fake aunt and uncle. The birthday party from hell falls during the yearly Popcorn Festival. Cora is always queen."

"The thirtysomething popcorn queen." Quinn gave Ryder props for saying it with a straight face. "She never loses?"

"Her father is mayor. *And* grows a lot of popcorn. They used to have a pageant, but eventually, nobody else entered."

"Where does your father live?"

"Minnow, Indiana. It's about twenty miles from Indianapolis where my father's law offices are located." Quinn flopped onto the sofa. "This is going to be torture."

"Okay," Ryder flopped down beside her. "You've talked me into it."

"Into what?" Quinn asked cautiously.

"Going with you to Minot, Indiana."

"Minnow," she corrected automatically. "And what are you talking about?"

"You made it sound irresistible. Cora the popcorn queen? A town named after a fish used for bait? And I have to meet Aunt Pinney and Uncle Titus."

"Have you lost your mind?" Balling up her fist, Quinn tapped Ryder on the side of his head. "I *have* to go. Why would you subject yourself to this?"

"It solves our problem. You host me in Minnow. After that, I treat us to a getaway—any place you like."

"I'll be staying with my father."

"I'll get a hotel room."

"That won't be necessary. It's a big house." Realizing what she had said, Quinn's eyes widened. "Ryder, this is not a good idea."

Ryder didn't seem to share her misgivings. Pulling her close, his lips brushed hers. "I've never been to a popcorn festival. Or *any* festival with a food-related theme."

Quinn savored the feel of Ryder's kiss. It almost made her forget what she had agreed to. "You can still change your mind."

"I could. But I won't."

"I warned you."

"Come on." Ryder took Quinn's hand, leading her toward the bed. Taking her in his arms, he jumped onto the mattress. "Do you have any objections to us taking the private jet?"

"No," Quinn sighed, sinking into the bliss of Ryder's kiss. "We'll be able to escape at a moment's notice."

"You sound certain that will be necessary."

"Knowing Cora and my father? It's inevitable."

CHAPTER ELEVEN

QUINN UNDERSTOOD ABOUT double standards. She had taken a stand about Ryder paying her way—though she caved rather quickly. In theory, she should have objected to taking his private jet. It was expensive. Elitist. It was also convenient, comfortable, and—yes—practical.

Ryder Hart was a superstar. Fans mobbed him wherever he went. Quinn had witnessed the chaos just the whisper of his name could cause in a crowd. She shuddered to think what it would be like in a crowded airport. The security. The flashing cameras. Ryder downplayed those incidents. But Quinn imagined it was a relief when he could travel in peace.

"That's a pensive look," Ryder said, taking the seat opposite her.

"Am I a hypocrite? I want to pay my own way, but I *love* this jet."

"If it will make you feel any better, give the money you would have spent on a plane ticket to charity."

Quinn felt a wave of shame that she hadn't thought of that herself. Her head had been filled with ideas of a new lens for her camera or an upgrade of her photography software. For her, the amount of money wasn't life changing. But for someone in need, it could make all the difference. There was a shelter for battered women that she had donated to in the past. As soon as they landed, Quinn would transfer the money.

Unaware of his influence on her, Ryder strummed his ever-present guitar. Another thing Quinn had learned about him was that he was rarely without the instrument. Sometimes he simply played. Most of the time, Ryder jotted down notes. Quinn woke that morning to find him sitting near the window of his hotel room. Bathed in the light of the rising sun, his head was bent over the guitar, his fingers in motion. Next to him was his phone, recording every note.

They were more alike than Quinn had realized. Ryder and his guitar. She and her camera. Without disturbing him, Quinn slipped from the bed. She forgot she was naked. All she could think about was capturing the man and his music.

The bag was exactly where Quinn knew it would be—never far from her sight. She took her camera, removed the lens cover, and focused on Ryder. For a second, she became lost in his beauty—his utter concentration. Shirtless and wearing only a pair of faded jeans, the sun made his dark hair glow—shining with a touch of red and gold. Ryder's profile was perfectly outlined. His head was tilted in her direction. His eyes were closed. And his lips moved slightly as though he sang along to the tune he created.

Quinn's breath caught in her throat. He was so beautiful. Inside and out. Bringing the camera to her eye, she took the first picture. Then another. And another. She circled Ryder, catching him from every angle. However, she kept her distance, not wanting to disturb him.

Who knew how many shots she took or how much time passed? Then, without warning, Ryder lifted his head, looking her way. Quinn caught the moment before she finally lowered her camera. The look in Ryder's eyes took her breath away. Intense—almost wild. His gaze never wavering, Ryder set aside his guitar. He stood and held out his hand. Mesmerized, Quinn left her camera on the table. Not a word was spoken. None were necessary. She walked into Ryder's arms, her mouth meeting his.

What happened next wasn't sex. It was more. A coming together of two souls. At least that was how it felt to Quinn. She couldn't say if Ryder were affected the same way. They hadn't spoken of it. Hours later, Quinn was still a little shaky. And Ryder? His smile was easy, his manner matter-of-fact. If anything had changed, Quinn feared it was only on her side.

Quinn shook off her wandering musings. She had made a promise to herself, and she wasn't going to break it. Ryder was a temporary situation. Her flight from reality. If it lasted a few weeks or blew up in her face tomorrow, Quinn would have no regrets. It was about living in the here and now.

"Are you certain you brought enough clothes?"

Quinn's eyes narrowed. She knew sarcasm when she heard it.

"It was your idea to stop in San Francisco," she reminded Ryder.

"I know," Ryder sighed, plucking out a three-chord lament. "You would have been happy making do with what you already had with you."

"All I needed was a laundromat and a supply of quarters."

Quinn laughed at Ryder's horrified expression. All things considered—the money, the adulation, the worldwide fame—he was surprisingly down to Earth. However, he liked the perks that came with his lifestyle. It seemed public laundry facilities were near the top of Ryder's *hell no* list.

"If you've ever spent the night in one of those places, it will make you avoid them like the plague," he had explained. "I saw a man urinate on an entire row of chairs. Then for good measure, take a dump in a dryer."

Since Ryder's tone was light, Quinn laughed. However, it wasn't her first reaction. There was a time when Ryder had been homeless. What he had seen—what had happened to him—made her want to weep for that boy. And it made her admire the man he had fashioned himself into.

"As long as you insisted, I saw no reason I shouldn't bring something for any contingency. Cora is an expert with the social curve ball."

Unable to resist, Quinn took Ryder's picture. He had such an expressive face. Ever changing and oh, so photogenic. Quinn could have made a fortune from the photos she had taken today alone. But she had no plans for them to see the light of day. This morning especially. Those were too private—too personal. She would file them away. *For her eyes only.*

"Your stepmother sounds like a piece of work."

"Cora was my father's secretary—while he was married to wife number two." When Ryder lifted an eyebrow, Quinn nodded. "I know. The ultimate cliché. The affair wasn't the only reason for the divorce. However, it was the final blow. Dad married Cora because he hates to be single and by the luck of the draw, she was the last mistress standing."

"In other words, there were others before Cora?" Ryder pushed the button on the intercom.

Quinn shrugged. "Before. During."

The air hostess arrived. Deena Branch was the same pretty, red-haired woman who Quinn had met during the tour. She was efficient, professional, and seemingly unimpressed by her famous employer. Notepad in hand, she took down Ryder's request for water and a fruit plate. "What would you like, Quinn?"

"Nothing. Thank you."

Though it had been awhile since lunch, for once Quinn wasn't hungry. Thinking about her father and his many peccadilloes had a way of ruining her appetite.

"Bring enough for two, Deena. Did the cookies arrive?"

"They did, Mr. Hart. Just before takeoff."

"Bring them, too."

"Cookies?" Hungry or not, Quinn couldn't resist asking.

"There's a bakery down by Fisherman's Wharf. They make something called a Caramel Pecan Dream."

"*Peirson's?*"

"That's the place. Do you know it?"

Did she? Quinn would go out of her way for the smell alone. The cookie Ryder was talking about was one of her favorites.

"I may be able to force one down."

Ryder smiled. She wasn't fooling him. The man had seen her eat. He knew as well as she did that one would not be enough.

"Continue what you were saying about Cora."

"There isn't much to tell. Cora is pretty. Ambitious. My father thinks that she's a piece of harmless fluff."

Deena returned. Thanking her, Ryder took the plate of cookies, handing one to Quinn.

"But…?" he urged.

"Cora is smart. Smart enough to have landed a big fish for a husband. And smart enough to know her chances of holding onto him for long are slim. Dad will stay married—someday. When he's too old to care about the chase. But that day is not now."

"I take it your sympathy does not lie with your stepmother." Ryder took the top off a bottle of water before offering it to her.

"Thanks," Quinn smiled at his thoughtfulness. "This marriage has lasted five years. I'm not the only one who knows it is quickly approaching its sell-by date."

"You don't get along?"

"I tolerate her. She hates my guts."

Ryder paused between bites of melon. "Then why does she want you at her party? I got the impression Cora was the one pushing for your attendance."

"Cora likes to think that her marriage to my father is a major thorn in my butt. What better gift to herself than the chance to dig that thorn a little deeper?"

"Does your father know her motives?"

Quinn bit off a piece of the cookie. "I might as well show up wearing a big, red bow."

"Fuck this." Ryder balled up his napkin, throwing it to the ground. "I'll have the pilot keep going. New York? Miami? London is a go, though we will need to stop and refuel."

"I promised my father I would be there." Quinn was touched by Ryder's vehement response. "I'm a big girl, Ryder. Cora thinks her claws are sharp, but the truth is, they have all the scratching power of a newborn kitten. Besides, this visit will satisfy my father for the foreseeable future. The next time I see him, Cora will likely be a distant memory."

"Is there such a thing as a normal family?"

"No. Just varying degrees of screwed up."

The sadness Quinn felt was more for Ryder than herself. *Her father*, for all his narcissistic bombast, veered toward sainthood when compared to Ryder's.

"Indiana it is." Surprising her, Ryder took her hand, pulling her onto his lap.

"You still have the option of sparing yourself. Drop me off in Indianapolis. I can meet up with you in few days."

Ryder began unbuttoning the front of Quinn's shirt. "You already texted your father that you were bringing a guest."

"Mmm," Quinn sighed as his mouth kissed the hollow at the base of her throat. "He won't care. In fact, I doubt he read the text."

"You're stuck with me."

Ryder slid his fingers through her hair until his hand cupped the back of her head. His kiss was deep, thorough, and arousing. By the time he pulled away, Quinn's breath was coming fast.

"Putting up with having you around will be a hardship," Quinn sighed, her eyes sparkling. "But if I must, I must."

MINNOW, INDIANA WAS a lovely town. Clean streets were lined with neatly trimmed trees and well-tended patches of weed-free beds of brightly headed flowers. Though Quinn's memories were few, she had lived here until her parent's divorce.

Belinda Abernathy took Quinn and the large monetary settlement that her cheating husband had been required to pay out, to California. Along with the monthly alimony payments and child support checks, she proceeded to settle in a small town quite similar to Minnow.

It was an irony Quinn found amusing. But wisely, she kept that to herself. She loved her mother dearly, however, when it came to Michael Abernathy, she had no sense of humor. Or perspective. Their divorce had become final over twenty years ago. They never spoke and had little contact of any kind. Yet her ex-husband was a wound that never seemed to heal. Belinda hated the man. Hated that Quinn had anything to do with him.

Quinn had spoken to her mother that morning. However, she did not mention that she was on her way to Indiana to see her father. It was best for Belinda's sanity—and Quinn's.

"So this is small town America." Ryder looked out the window as though he was observing alien lifeforms. "I always wondered what it was like to live in Mayberry."

Quinn laughed. She loved the way Ryder pulled references out of the blue. "You won't find Barney Fife or Opie strolling *these* sidewalks."

"It looks so…"

"Wholesome?"

Ryder scoffed. "I doubt it. I can guarantee you that there is some kinky stuff going on behind those closed doors."

"How do you know?"

"Some of my biggest fans come from towns like this one. The stuff they put in their letters would curdle your yogurt."

Intrigued, Quinn tugged Ryder's hand until he looked her way. "Give me a for instance."

Leaning close, Ryder whispered three words in Quinn's ear.

"No."

"Yes."

Quinn glanced at the driver who had picked them up at the Indianapolis airport. She would have loved to question Ryder further, but some things were better left unsaid—until later when there was nobody to hear.

The black Cadillac slowed to a halt at the end of a wide cul-de-sac. The driveway leading to the house wasn't long. However, Quinn knew the backyard was huge. Cora liked to tell anyone who would listen about the amount of outdoor space. The swimming pool and tennis courts dwarfed anything owned by their neighbors. Though Cora used neither, she had bragging rights. Apparently, that was what mattered.

"Did you see the first season of *American Horror Story*?" Ryder nodded toward the house. "Avoid the basement."

Quinn was still laughing as she rang the doorbell. Ryder was right. Soon after their wedding, Michael had purchased the house at his new bride's request. The first time Quinn saw it, she knew there was something odd, but couldn't put her finger on what it was. Now, she knew.

The door flew open, and there stood Cora.

"Quinn. You made it."

"Hello, Cora. Happy birthday."

"That isn't until tomorrow, silly." Cora air-kissed in the direction of Quinn's face. "Don't make me thirty before my time."

It was all Quinn could do not to roll her eyes. For Cora, thirty was a sticking point. She had been stuck there for the last three years.

"You don't look a day older than when we met."

Which was true. Cora was petite. In heels, she barely reached Quinn's shoulders. With her long, bleached-blond ringlets and propensity to giggle, Cora looked and acted like a woman ten years younger. Why Michael Abernathy wanted that, Quinn didn't know. The less she thought about it, the better.

"And you look...," Cora batted her false eyelashes, looking Quinn up and down. "Well traveled."

Quinn knew that was an attempted dig. Since it was the best that Cora could manage, she hid her smile and nodded. She let Cora enjoy her moment. Quinn thought of it as an extra birthday present.

"Come in." Cora motioned for Quinn to follow. "Did you ask the driver to bring in your bags?"

"I..."

"I hope you don't mind taking the green room. It's not the one you had the last time you visited, but I didn't think you would mind something a bit smaller. My parents are coming. They need the extra space."

Quinn waited to see if Cora had more to say. When nothing came, she shook her head.

"That will be fine, Cora. Dad told you I was bringing a guest, didn't he?"

It was obvious from her expression that this was the first time Cora had heard of it. Quinn should have known. It was how her father operated. In one ear and out the other—unless it was something he deemed important.

"If it's an inconvenience—"

"Not at all." Give Cora credit, her recovery time was stellar. "What is the situation between you and your... girlfriend?"

"Are you asking if my lesbian lover and I want to share a room?"

"Well? Do you?"

Cora's eyes practically danced with glee. In her world, same-sex relationships were something to be ashamed of. Quinn was extremely grateful that she didn't live in Cora's world.

"I'm afraid I'm not a lesbian. Can I still share Quinn's room?"

The expression on Cora's face when she saw Ryder was one for the ages. Thank goodness Quinn's camera was never far from her hands. Pulling it from the bag slung over her shoulder, Quinn focused and snapped the shot. Christmas card material, no doubt.

"Is that...? Are you...?"

"Ryder Hart. And you must be Cora."

In a daze, Cora took Ryder's outstretched hand. "I am," she gushed. "And you are Ryder Hart."

"I apologize for crashing your birthday celebration, Cora. I completely understand if you don't have room in your lovely home."

Quinn stood back and watched a master at work. Ryder knew how to charm. She already knew that. In seconds, he had Cora eating out of his hand. Of course, it didn't hurt that he was a world-famous rock star. Or that Cora was obviously a fan.

"Oh, no. There is plenty of room." Cora kept Ryder's hand grasped in hers long past the introductory stage of their meeting. "The blue room has a wonderful view of the backyard."

The blue room. The one Cora had given to her parents. Quinn wondered how Cora's parents would feel about getting kicked out to accommodate Ryder Hart.

"Blue looks good on you," Ryder smiled at Quinn.

"My room is green."

"There is no need to crowd you into the same room." Cora reluctantly let Ryder reclaim sole ownership of his hand. "Besides, the blue room has an attached bath."

"The truth is, Cora," Ryder lowered his voice in a conspiratorial tone. "When Quinn told me she was coming here, I invited myself. I know that's pushy, but I wanted to be with her. I'm sure you know how it is when you can't stand the thought of being away from someone—even for a few days. If you give us separate rooms, I will have to sneak in with Quinn every night. Then sneak out in the morning."

"Oh." Cora's high spirits seemed to deflate.

"Perhaps Cora has a moral objection to us sharing a room."

When Ryder's surprised gaze met hers, Quinn shrugged. She didn't know why she had said it. The words came out before she could stop them. To Cora's credit, she didn't take the chance to keep Ryder's virtue intact.

"Naturally, I have no objection." Cora plastered her best hostess smile on her face. "I'm certain you will both be very comfortable in the blue room. I'll have your luggage taken up."

"Thank you for being so understanding." Ryder gave Cora his most dazzling smile.

With a sigh, Cora nodded. "We are having drinks on the lanai."

"Ryder and I will join you in a few minutes, Cora, after we freshen up."

Since Quinn had been there before, Cora left them to find their way to their room.

"Wait a second," Quinn said when Ryder would have started up the stairs. She looked at the bottom of her shoe, then did the same to the other.

"Is there a problem?" Ryder looked puzzled.

"Just checking to see if I had stepped in any of the bullshit you dished out."

"It wasn't bullshit; it was natural charm," Ryder informed her.

"Please." Quinn laughed as they walked up the huge *Gone With the Wind*-inspired staircase. "The only reason the crap didn't pile up is that Cora ate it up with a spoon faster than you could dish it out."

"Your stepmother is an *interesting* woman."

"And a big fan of yours. With the slightest encouragement, she could be yours." Quinn turned left at the top of the stairs. At the end of the hall, she opened a set of French doors. "I would have found her overt fawning humorous if she weren't married to my father."

"It was a bit much."

"You handled her perfectly." Quinn shut the door before walking into Ryder's waiting arms. "Thank you. And I'm sorry."

"Please. You had no way of anticipating Cora's behavior." Ryder kissed Quinn's cheek. "Compared to some of the female fans I've encountered, she was nothing."

"Right now you should be sipping a Mai Tai and rubbing on sunscreen. Cora is nobody's idea of a vacation."

"I wanted to spend time with you." Ryder looked her in the eyes. "I want to get to know you, Quinn. Here. On a beach. It doesn't matter where we start."

"We scratched the itch. Now you want more?"

Quinn held her breath, waiting for the answer that might change her life.

"I guess I do." Ryder looked a bit bemused. "How do you feel about that?"

"Does that go both ways?" Quinn had to ask. "Are you going to let me in, Ryder?"

Ryder ran a hand over the stubble on his face. He paced, stopping to look out the window. "You can ask me anything, Quinn."

"Will you tell me anything?"

"I don't know." Taking a deep breath, Ryder turned toward her. Slowly, as though gathering his thoughts, he exhaled. "I've never met anyone like you, Quinn. You have questions and damned if I don't want to give you the answers. But I've guarded my secrets for so long. There are things nobody knows."

"Not Zoe? Or Dalton?"

"Or Ashe," Ryder finished for her. "It's—"

"Trust." Quinn nodded. She understood how hard that could be. "It's a Catch-22. I can swear I'll never betray you. But how can you be certain unless you trust me with your secrets?"

Taking Quinn's face between his hands, Ryder rested his forehead against hers. "I want to trust you."

"Let's start slowly. I'm an open book." Quinn put a warm kiss on Ryder's left wrist. Then turned her head, kissing the other. "Ask me anything. Just to break the ice? The touch of polyester against my skin gives me the willies."

Ryder smiled. When Quinn looked in his eyes, she found them filled with warmth and humor. "It could be dangerous to arm me with that kind of information."

"I trust you not to use it against me."

Understanding, Ryder nodded. Baby steps. Quinn didn't expect him to reveal everything in one emotion-packed rush. She didn't expect anything. But she hoped he would start to let her in. How much was ultimately up to him.

"Remember the night we met?"

"How could I forget?"

"My knee hurt like a bitch, and you asked what happened?"

Quinn nodded. Reaching up, she gripped Ryder's hand. He was about to take step number one, and she wanted him to know that she was a safe place for him to land.

"It isn't an old war wound."

"No? Really?" Quinn teased.

Ryder's lips twitched, but a smile wasn't coming. He swallowed.

"It was caused by a baseball bat."

"Your father?"

Ryder nodded. His eyes searched hers—looking for what, Quinn couldn't have said. She wanted to say something deep and meaningful and comforting. She wanted to be wise and insightful. She wanted to find the words that would heal Ryder's wounds and take away his pain.

The last thing Quinn wanted was for tears to well up in her eyes or to let loose with a string of the foulest words that had ever passed her lips. However, what she wanted and what actually happened, didn't always coincide.

"Sorry." Quinn wiped her eyes. "I have never reacted that way in my life."

"Don't apologize." To Quinn's amazement, Ryder was laughing—hard. "When it comes to swearing, I thought I had heard it all. However, you managed to put together some truly unique combinations."

"Oh, God." Cheeks burning, Quinn turned away. "I asked for you to tell me something personal and when you do, I cry and curse."

"And made me laugh." Ryder slid his hands around her waist, pulling her close until her back was flush with his chest. "In a million years, I wouldn't have thought that was possible."

"I wanted to comfort you."

"You did," Ryder whispered against her ear. "In the best way possible. Thank you."

RYDER WATCHED QUINN from across the patio. He refused to call it a lanai. If they had been in Hawaii, that would have been different. However, this was the freaking Midwest, and he knew a pretentious load of crap when it was dumped at his feet.

As if sensing his gaze, Quinn looked Ryder's way and smiled. A burst of warmth shot through his body, settling in the vicinity of his heart. *Damn.* Unconsciously, he rubbed his chest. Something had happened between them in that bedroom. There had been a shift. A change inside of him. But Ryder wasn't ready to figure out what it was.

One thing Ryder did know. Quinn was in his life. Not for today or the next few weeks. She had become important. He could count on one hand the number of people he called a friend. It was a small, tight group. Ryder had thought the number finite. Set in stone.

It had taken someone special to change his mind. And in a short amount of time. It had taken Quinn.

Ryder shouldn't have been surprised. His friendship with Dalton and Ashe happened in a flash. A meeting of like-minded musicians. One gig and that had been it. A band was born. Zoe had been an easy addition. She was his little sister. And soon his friends thought of her the same way. They had ten years of ups and downs. Hardships and triumphs.

This thing with Quinn was new, but, just as with Zoe, and Dalton, and Ashe, Ryder knew in his soul that she would be his friend for the rest of his life.

"I thought about pursuing a singing career. My father pushed me toward secretarial school."

Cora had been speaking non-stop for what seemed like an eternity. Ryder wasn't required to respond beyond the occasional nod. Absently, he did just that.

"Who knows, we might have recorded a huge hit song together." Cora twirled a lock of blond hair around her finger. "Not that I regret my decision. I love Michael. And he adores me."

"I'm certain that Michael's gain was the music industry's loss." Ryder decided if he were going to escape, this was the moment. "Excuse me, Cora. I need to speak to Quinn."

"She has you all the time," Cora said with a pout. She reached for him with her long, pale-pink claws, but he backed away just in time.

"You know how it is. We can't keep our hands off each other."

Cora stomped her foot as she watched Ryder hurry across the lanai and slide an arm around Quinn's waist.

"Actually," she muttered, "I have no idea how it is. But I would love to find out."

"What was that, cupcake?" Michael joined her, a glass of single malt in one hand and a lit cigar in the other.

"You know those are bad for you," Cora said automatically. Michael only had a small part of her attention. Her interest lay with Ryder Hart.

"A few puffs and a sip or two. Where's the harm?"

"Fine, honey." Cora patted Michael's hand.

Michael frowned. He liked to complain when Cora nagged him about his health, but the truth was, he expected it as his due. He paid the bills. She fawned. That was their unwritten deal. He followed her gaze. *Ryder Hart. He should have known.*

"He's just a man, Cora."

"He's gorgeous." Realizing who she was speaking to, Cora gave her husband her breathiest laugh. Brushing her breasts against his arms, she sighed, "But you are the most handsome man I've ever met."

"Mmm."

"And sexy." Cora wrapped herself around Michael. But her gaze stayed on Ryder. "Wait until I get you alone," she purred. "You won't have any doubt about how I feel."

CHAPTER TWELVE

"NOW I CAN breathe."

To prove his point, Ryder filled his lungs.

"It smells like stale beer and rancid sweat. With an overlay of *Pine-Sol*."

"If you added cigarette smoke, you would have the fragrance of my youth."

Quinn shook her head in mock sympathy. "Damn the government for making smoking in bars illegal."

"I'll give you that one."

Quinn looked around the crowded tavern. She couldn't help feeling a little apprehensive. They were one, *Oh, my God, it's Ryder Hart*, away from a stampede.

"Relax. Nobody is going to recognize me." Ryder pulled the faded *Colts* cap lower on his forehead. "I blend right in."

When Ryder had suggested they skip dinner with her father, Cora, and the gang, Quinn hadn't argued. She hadn't relished a long, drawn-out meal of Cora drooling over Ryder and her father glaring at her. Somehow, his wife's overt interest in another man had become Quinn's fault.

"Would you bring candy to a diabetic?" Michael had asked the second he maneuvered Quinn off the lanai and into his office.

"No." Quinn thought for a moment, trying to decide what her father was getting at. "Are you saying Cora is a sex addict?"

"Of course not."

Her father poured himself a drink from the bottle of whiskey he had hidden behind a copy of *Lost Weekend*. Quinn gave him props for his sense of irony.

"Then what are we talking about? Cora is having a fangirl moment. Nothing will come of it."

"Cora has no self-restraint. When she wants a man, she won't take no for an answer. I should know."

Quinn snorted. "Like you said no."

"This isn't funny, Quinn. That rock star is going to ruin my marriage. And it will be your fault." Michael's eyes narrowed. "Was that your plan all along?"

Choosing to ignore what they both knew was a ridiculous accusation, Quinn decided to play the adult and use reason.

"For argument's sake, let's say you're right about Cora. If she throws herself at Ryder, I can assure you, he won't catch her."

"Don't be so naïve. Cora is a beautiful woman."

"But not irresistible."

"You aren't a man. Or a sex-crazed musician. Ryder Hart will eat Cora for dinner and spit out her bones. Leaving me to clean up his mess."

"That makes absolutely no sense." Quinn watched her father drain his glass then reach for the bottle. "Slow down, Dad. How much have you had to drink?"

"Not nearly enough." But to his credit, Michael left the glass empty. "What are you going to do about the mess you've made, Quinn?"

It was clear that her father had Ryder pegged as a hedonistic sex maniac and Cora as his next victim. Telling him otherwise was not working.

"I will take Ryder out to dinner and explain the situation. We'll leave in the morning."

"That would be best." Michael held his arms out, beckoning to Quinn. Thinking of Ryder, Quinn reminded herself that there were far worse fathers in the world. Yes, she had been saddled with a self-absorbed twit. But Michael Abernathy wasn't all bad. Sometimes, like when he hugged her, Quinn actually believed he loved her.

That was how she found herself in a less-than-stellar bar on the outskirts of Minnow, Indiana in the company of an incognito rock star. Even her best friend would never believe it.

"I see a bandstand." Ryder craned his neck to get a better view. "Do you think there will be live music?"

"Damn straight," a man from the next table answered Ryder's question. He had a handlebar mustache and somewhere under all his tattoos, Quinn imagined there was skin the same color as his pasty white face. "It's Popcorn Festival week. Mickey does things up right every night."

"Mickey?" Ryder raised his voice to be heard over the crowd.

"The owner. That's him behind the bar."

"I wonder if the band will let me sit in for a song or two?"

Quinn could see how excited Ryder was at the idea. Back to his roots, so to speak. After years of playing stadiums and arenas to huge crowds of adoring fans, he wanted to take it down to the ground again. If only for one night.

"I'm sure they would be thrilled." Quinn leaned closer. "But do you think it's a good idea?"

"It's the best idea I've had in a long time." Ryder captured her lips with his. "Besides that."

"Then I say you should do it."

And damn the consequences. What was the worst that could happen? A stampede? A riot? Busted chairs? Broken bones? Fire? The police? Blaring headlines that would have Ryder's manager tearing his hair out?

"What's so funny?" Ryder asked when she laughed aloud.

"I have a vivid and colorful imagination."

He wiggled his eyebrows. "Me too."

Ryder ordered two more beers from the passing waitress.

"I'll be right back."

"Hey." When he saw that she was headed toward the door, Ryder stayed her with his hand. "The bathroom is that way."

"If you're going to do this, I need my camera."

"Maybe they'll tell me no."

Quinn smiled. Ryder grinned back. *Ya, right.* "I need my camera."

"I'll go with you."

This time, it was Quinn who stopped him. "Don't bother. I'll only be a second."

Ryder kissed Quinn's fingers before taking her hand in his. "I'll go with you."

"I appreciate it. But someone will probably grab our table while we're gone."

Unconcerned, Ryder shrugged. "There's always another table. If not, we'll sit at the bar."

Chances were that Quinn would have made it to the car she had borrowed for the night from her father, retrieved her camera, and returned to her seat without incident. However, it was a rowdy crowd. And the parking lot was dark. Having Ryder by her side made her feel safe and protected. After looking out for herself for so long, it was nice to have someone to lean on. Even if just for a little while.

Surprisingly, when they entered the bar, Quinn saw that their seats hadn't been pilfered. At the next table, the tattooed man gave them a thumb's up, letting them know he was responsible.

"Thanks," Ryder said. "We appreciate it. Let me take care of the next round for you and your friends."

"Much obliged." The other men at the table lifted their bottles of beer, saluting Ryder.

The crowd was content to play the jukebox for the next hour, dancing and drinking to the selection of country classics. Then the band arrived. Locals, they were well known, getting shout outs as they set up their instruments.

"I love this part," Ryder told her, his eyes locked on the band. "The anticipation. The adrenalin will be building. It's easier to get jacked up when you have a large crowd."

"What was it like when you were starting out?"

Ryder smiled. "Scary as hell. All I wanted to do was play guitar and sing. My dreams were small. The idea was to make some money, put it in the bank, and have a place for Zoe to live."

"You were sixteen? That means Zoe was thirteen. Was she planning to run away like you did?"

"Zoe had a good home—comparatively. I made certain of that."

"How?"

It was hard for Quinn to imagine what it had been like. Her parents had divorced, but there was always someone there to take care of her. Ryder had taken on that responsibility for himself and his sister at such a young age. And succeeded.

"Zoe and I were separated after our father killed himself. Separate foster homes. Luckily, she was only a bus ride away. I visited as often as I could. There were three other kids in the house—close to Zoe's age. She liked them. And the couple who looked after them were nicer than most."

"That's good."

"Zoe was quiet. Introverted."

"*Zoe?*" Introverted was not the word Quinn would have used to describe Ryder's sister.

Ryder shrugged, a smile playing around his lips. "She's come out of her shell. But back then, I was worried that she wouldn't be able to stand up for herself and would get pushed around. I didn't care where they put me as long as I could keep an eye on Zoe."

"Is that why you ran away? Because you were going to be sent someplace too far away from Zoe?"

"I had worn out my welcome with the greater Chicago-area foster system. I think the word they used was unmanageable." Ryder took a sip of beer. "I disappeared a lot, and that didn't sit well with my various foster parents."

"Disappeared to visit Zoe." It wasn't a question. Quinn knew the answer.

"The last family—the ones that tried to sell their story to the tabloids? He thought he could control me by smacking me around. That didn't go over well with me."

"Did you report him?"

"I knew how the system worked, Quinn. It's slow—at best. The case workers mean well but there aren't enough. Money and manpower were tight. I was on my own."

"So you left."

Quinn knew how the story turned out. Ryder sat beside her—strong, healthy, and successful. Not to mention amazingly well adjusted. However, she couldn't help but worry about the sixteen-year-old boy he once was. It couldn't have been easy.

"If I had stayed, I would have hit him back, Quinn. I was bigger and stronger than he was. It wouldn't have turned out well."

There was so much Quinn wanted to ask. Where had he gone? How had he found food and shelter? However, she could feel the tension radiating from Ryder's body. He had talked long enough about that part of his life.

"Tell me about your first gig."

Quinn knew she had hit the right button when Ryder grinned.

"I lied about my age. The bar owner gave me a meal and a few bucks under the table. I wasn't exactly a hit. But I *was* cheap. Word got around, and I started picking up more and more work, all the while polishing my performing skills."

"And the rest is history?"

"With plenty of bumps in between." Taking Quinn's hand, Ryder threaded his fingers through hers. "That's the most I've ever said to anyone about those days."

"I won't make you sorry that you confided in me, Ryder."

Ryder didn't speak for a moment, his eyes locked with Quinn's. Finally, his gaze never wavering, he kissed the back of her hand. "I know."

Two words. Yet they touched Quinn to her soul. Ryder was not a man who trusted easily. This was a moment she would treasure forever.

"How is everybody doing this evening?" The voice from the bandstand rang out, getting an enthusiastic response from the crowd.

"Some of you know us. But for the rest of you, we are *Lightning Strikes*."

The band jumped into a fast tempo song that Quinn couldn't identify. Not that it mattered. It was all about pulling the audience in from the first note. Ryder grinned, tapping his foot and bobbing his head. Quinn laughed. He looked like a little boy in the middle of the best Christmas morning ever.

"Want to dance?" Ryder asked, practically yelling the question.

Quinn hesitated. She couldn't leave her camera unattended.

"My butt is in this chair for the duration." Their friend at the next table told her. "My name is Rudy, by the way." He held out his hand.

"Quinn." She didn't introduce Ryder. He had a first name you didn't hear every day. So far, he hadn't been recognized, but there was no reason to push their luck.

"I'll watch your bag."

"I appreciate that. But—"

Rudy took something from his back pocket and set it on the table. It was a badge.

"Officer Rudy Rayburn, at your service."

So much for judging a book by its cover. It was Quinn's fault for not looking past the tattoos and the bushy mustache.

"Thank you, Rudy."

"No problem." He motioned Quinn closer. "I'm a big fan, by the way."

Quinn looked from the policeman to Ryder and laughed. Rudy was full of surprises. It was apparent he hadn't shared his discovery with anyone else. She gave Rudy a quick kiss on the cheek and to her amazement, he blushed.

"What was that about?" Ryder asked her.

"I'll tell you later."

Holding her hand, Ryder zig-zagged across the room to the postage stamp-sized dance floor. It was already full of bouncing, gyrating bodies. Unconcerned, Ryder pulled Quinn close. She didn't

122

know if his moves had a name, but there was an innate grace to his steps.

"You're good," Quinn called out.

"It's all in the rhythm."

One song flowed into another. Quinn couldn't remember the last time she danced—except by herself when she got her first paying job as a photographer. She became sweaty and breathless and loved every second. When the next song started, it was slow and romantic. *This* one she recognized. It was one of Ryder's. He slid his arms around her waist. Quinn automatically put her hands on his shoulders.

"I wrote this when I was nineteen, in love for the first time, and convinced that it would last forever. It was my first song to hit the charts. If I recall, it barely broke the top twenty," Ryder said, then began to hum along with the music.

"Not bad." Happy, Quinn sighed, resting her cheek on Ryder's chest as his chin nuzzled the top of her head. "Did she break your heart?"

"It lasted three passionate weeks before we broke up by mutual consent. So, no. My heart remained in one piece."

Not every woman had a hit song written in her honor. Quinn wondered what it would be like to be immortalized for all time? Did Ryder's first love smile when her song came on the radio? Or did she lament the fact that she had been too young and foolish to realize what she had let slip away?

"I danced to this at my senior prom."

"Jesus. Really?" Ryder laughed. "If it played in the background while you lost your virginity in the backseat of some rube's borrowed car, I don't want to know."

"His name was Anton. He was an exchange student from Russia. I thought he was exotic and deep. We made out to *Livin' on a Prayer*." Quinn shook her head at the memory. "My virginity was safe until my sophomore year of college."

"Practically a prude."

"How old were you your first time?"

"Fifteen."

"Was she older?"

"Infinitely." Ryder chuckled. "By a whole three months. We fumbled our way through it."

"You don't fumble anymore."

"I'm glad you noticed."

After another song, the band took a break. Ryder escorted Quinn back to the table.

"I hate to leave you alone." Ryder had spotted the lead singer of the band going out a side door. "Maybe you should come with me."

Quinn shook her head. There was protective and then there was unreasonable. Ryder skirted the edges of the latter. "I can take care of myself. Besides, I have Minnow's finest at the next table. If there's any trouble, Rudy will help."

"I'm on it," Rudy called out.

Having gotten the lowdown from Quinn, Ryder nodded, shaking his hand. "I appreciate it, man."

"Do you mind if I make a request?"

"Name it."

"Sing *Leaving the Past Behind*. It's my wife's favorite."

"You got it." Ryder looked around. "Is your wife here?"

Rudy laughed. "My Katie has been serving your drinks all night, son."

Chuckling, Ryder left Quinn with a kiss and a promise.

"I'll sing *Leaving* for Katie. But the rest will be for you."

MUSICIANS WERE UNPREDICTABLE creatures. Ryder knew. He had dealt with them from half-empty dives to packed arenas. Hell, when it came down to it, *he* could be as bad as they came.

Call it ego. Testosterone. The old, *I peed on it first* syndrome. Whatever the reason, musicians were territorial about their gig and their band. That was why Ryder approached the lead singer of *Lightning Strikes* with his ego in his back pocket. Though they were close in age, their situations were worlds apart. Ryder didn't want to come across as a big shot out to slum it for a night.

As it turned out, Marsh Jenner was a fan. A mega-fan. For a second, Ryder was afraid the man was going fall to his knees and cry out, *I'm not worthy*. To save them both the embarrassment, Ryder grabbed Marsh's hand and shook it vigorously.

"You're my hero." Marsh kept pumping away until Ryder gently disengaged. "We play covers of your shit all the time."

"You did a great job on *First and Only*."

"Really?" Marsh threw his half-smoked cigarette on the ground. "Man, I am glad I didn't know you were out there when I was singing. I wouldn't have gotten through it."

Ryder knew how Marsh felt. It could be surreal meeting a musician you admired. The afternoon he had spent with Willie Nelson would go down as one of the greatest experiences of his life. It had nothing to do with rock or country. There were legends and then there was Willie—an artist who crossed all music lines.

"I don't want to tread on your time. Would you mind if I sat in for a set?"

Marsh's mouth opened then closed. The only sound that escaped was a high-pitched squeak.

"Is that a yes?"

March nodded.

"Great." Ryder clapped him on the back. "It means a lot to me."

QUINN SIPPED HER club soda wondering what the reaction would be when Ryder stepped onto that tiny platform. Surprise followed by bedlam?

The drummer came out first, followed by the rest of the band. Ryder, his hat still pulled low, picked up an electric guitar, plugging it in before he strummed the strings. Nobody in the crowd paid attention. They continued talking and drinking, unaware that a superstar was only a few feet away.

"I want to get closer to the stage," Quinn informed Rudy as she took her camera from the bag. "In a few minutes, getting up there will be impossible."

"I called a few of my buddies on the force for back-up. Just in case things get out of hand. They are milling around." Rudy lowered his voice. "Undercover."

Though Rudy's tone was light, she knew he had been smart to take precautions. There was no way to anticipate what a sober crowd would do when Ryder revealed himself. This bunch had been drinking steadily since they arrived. It could turn into a love fest. Or it could go south in a hurry. Either way, Rudy and his friends were ready.

"I'll go with you," Rudy said, following closely behind Quinn.

Rather than argue, Quinn felt a rush of gratitude. The world had some nasty characters in it, but there were more good guys than bad. Rudy Rayburn was proof positive. Turning, she took a quick picture. She knew without looking at the result that it would be a keeper. Quinn made a mental note to get his wife's email address so she could send Katie the photo.

"Look at him." After snapping a few shots of Ryder, Quinn lowered her camera. "He is practically bouncing with excitement."

Rudy shook his head. "It's crazy. The man plays all the time. What's so special about tonight?"

Quinn shrugged. It wasn't something she could explain even if she weren't pledged to keep Ryder's confidence to herself. Only Ryder understood the importance of getting back to his roots. She was glad that she was here to witness the moment.

"We are back." When the lead singer tapped the microphone, the crowd quieted a bit. But not much. "We have a rare treat for you tonight. As you know, every now and then, a guest will sit in with the band. This was unexpected. He was in the crowd and asked if he could join us for a few songs."

The announcement didn't cause a stir. Not even a ripple. *Just wait*, Quinn thought.

Without further introduction, the band began to play. Quinn exchanged grins with Rudy when they recognized *Leaving the Past Behind*. Taking the lead, Ryder stepped up to the microphone.

"A new friend of mine asked if I would sing this for his wife. Katie? Are you out there?"

A small rumble as a few people began to realize who was on stage.

"Here she is."

Through an opening in the crowd, Rudy's wife popped. The pretty brunette looked confused. Frowning, she walked up to her husband.

"What is going on?"

Rudy put an arm around her and kissed her cheek. "Just wait."

Ryder played the opening chords one more time.

Katie gasped. "Is that...? Holy crap."

Ryder removed his hat and tossed it to Katie. If Rudy weren't standing there to hold her up, Quinn thought his wife would have melted onto the floor. Ryder speared Katie with his gaze.

"This one is for you, Katie."

Ryder sang the first few words and Katie screamed. Loudly and repeatedly. Quinn had to give Rudy credit. He only winced one or twice.

Quinn had flipped the button on her camera from portrait to video. She filmed the entire serenade. Just as he played the final note, to everyone's surprise, Ryder jumped off the stage and kissed Katie—full on the lips. Before anyone could make a grab for him, he was back behind the microphone and onto the next song.

There were no words to describe the energy and joy that filled that room for the next hour. The numbers of bodies grew—which wasn't a surprise. Texts and phone calls flew to family and friends. If they were within driving distance, chances were they tried to get to the bar.

However, Rudy and the other police officers present did not have to step in and handle an out of control mob. Quinn didn't know if it were partly the shock of seeing Ryder Hart in their little corner of the world or the magic of the moment. Whatever forces were at work, they kept the crowd well-behaved and, for the most part, courteous. Quinn lost track of the times someone jostled her from behind. But there was no ill intent involved. Everyone was into the music. Bouncing, swaying, and dancing was to be expected.

Ryder looked as though he could have played all night. Sweat dampened his shirt and caused his hair to curl more than usual. He was the epitome of the cool, sexy rocker. Every woman in the room wanted him. Every man wanted to be him. And Quinn had it all captured on her camera. Now and then, she would take her eye away from the viewfinder and enjoy the show. As a fan. And as the woman who—lucky her—would share his bed tonight and for the foreseeable future.

"One more song and then I have to call it a night."

Protests were shouted, but there was no heat to them. They had known from the beginning that tonight would have to end. The time had flown, and it was hard to let go.

"I want to thank the members of *Lightning Strikes* for letting me jam with them." The crowd let out a loud cheer. "Tonight reminded me of why I do what I do. It isn't the money. Though that isn't bad." His comment got the expected burst of laughter. "What made me fall in love with music is the pleasure it gives. To me, and to you. Thank you. It has been my pleasure."

Everyone knew Ryder's final song. A sing-along anthem about giving the world the finger when it tried to hold you down. The last words blasted through the bar. Out of nowhere, Rudy and his team formed a wall in front of the stage, blocking anyone from getting to Ryder.

Rudy pushed Quinn toward him, who grabbed her hand and headed out the back.

"Aren't you going to stick around and bask in the adulation."

"That kind of adulation can land a man in the hospital."

They exited into the rear parking lot. Quinn took a deep breath of the cool, fresh, evening air.

"How did this get here?" she asked when she spied her father's car.

"I had Rudy move it before the set started." Ryder had her in the passenger seat and himself behind the wheel in record time. The engine turned over without hesitation. "Damn, that was fun."

Peeling out, Ryder headed down a side road. He was still burning energy and Quinn could feel the heat radiating from his body. He smelled of clean, sweaty man. It was odd, but all she could think about was licking every inch of his hot, salty skin. Quinn glanced at Ryder. Okay, maybe it wasn't that odd. Damn, he was sexy.

"You know what I need?" Ryder asked, the street light illuminating his wide grin.

"Tell me."

"Sex."

"Thank God," Quinn groaned.

Ryder's head whipped around. "You too?"

"I was afraid you were going to say a hamburger."

"That too. After."

Ryder pulled the car into the first dark alley they passed. It was crazy and reckless. And Quinn loved it. She felt like a teenager. Not the good girl who had never put a step wrong. But the bad girl she suppressed because she had been too afraid to let her out.

"I know you made out in the back of a car. Ever gone all the way?"

"Never."

Taking Quinn's camera bag, Ryder set it on the floor. She expected him to get in the backseat the usual way. Out one door and in the other. But Ryder was full of surprises. He flipped the button on the side of her seat, sending them backward.

"Smooth," Quinn said with a gasping laugh. "Did you learn that in your wild youth or is it new to your repertoire?"

"That was a first." Ryder pulled Quinn's shirt over her head. "You inspire me."

"Does this mean no backseat?"

"We'll get there. Think of this as foreplay."

Quinn sighed when Ryder's mouth closed over hers. Foreplay, her ass. He wasn't teasing. It was the kiss of a man ready for the final act. To show him that she was on the same page, Quinn slid her fingers through Ryder's hair, tugging him closer.

"Nope." Panting, Quinn stayed Ryder's hands when he tried to remove her bra. "Shuck the pants. I want this hard and fast, guitar boy."

"I need bare breasts."

Before Quinn could blink, Ryder flung her bra behind him. His tongue swiped at her nipple as he magically dealt with his jeans.

"God, you are good."

"I want that for my ringtone."

"Now? Really?"

Ryder took his phone from his pocket, hit a few buttons, then held it near Quinn's mouth.

"Say it again."

"Fuck you."

"Let me inspire you." Ryder bent his head, taking her straining nipple into his mouth.

"You are crazy." Quinn arched her back, pushing toward Ryder.

"Say it," Ryder spoke without raising his head. His teeth joined the fun and Quinn caved.

"God, you are good," she moaned, louder than she had intended. But there was no denying it. Ryder had a talented mouth. And tongue. And what he could do with his teeth? Pure bliss.

"There you go."

Ryder removed his jeans, then did the same with Quinn's. He moved between her legs, the tip of his hard penis brushing against her.

130

"Condom," Quinn cried out before she lost all reason.

"I'm on it."

Fast and efficient, the packet was opened, and the latex applied. Then, with one push, Ryder was inside of her.

"Hard and fast," he asked, the strain in his voice evident.

"Yes." Quinn lifted her legs, wrapping them around Ryder's waist. "Please. Now."

Ryder clasped Quinn's hands with his, raising them over her head. His eyes locked with hers.

"Do you feel that…" he asked. "The connection?"

The connection of their bodies or their minds? Quinn felt both. It was wild. Beautiful. Quinn felt the urge to cry.

"Yes, Ryder. I feel it. I feel everything."

Ryder moved his hips and Quinn met his every thrust. Again and again. She didn't want it to end, but there was no stopping the burst of pleasure that shot through her body from her center. Out to her toes. Up to the top of her head. Ryder cried out her name, his mouth finding hers. They rode the pleasure together. To the very end.

"I DON'T WANT to go back to that house."

"It sounds good. However, blood is just returning to my brain. Give me a moment to process what you said."

Laughing, Quinn smoothed her hand down Ryder's back. They hadn't moved, nor did she want them to. She would have been happy to stay right there, in his arms. Unfortunately, potential disaster loomed. And the blood flow to her brain was just fine.

"Cora will try something. If only to get a rise out of my father. I feel loose and wonderful. But when I think of returning to all that drama, I start to tense up."

Ryder gave her a series of soothing kisses. First on her forehead, then on each eye, the tip of her nose, and finally her mouth. As stress relievers went, it was damn effective.

"You don't know that Cora will hit on me. And if she did, I wouldn't act on the offer."

"I trust you completely."

"You do?" Ryder sounded surprised. And pleased.

"Yes. But saying no to Cora will only set in motion another problem. She'll be insulted. And my father will be upset because she's upset. And all of it will be my fault because I put temptation—namely you—in Cora's path."

"That is fucked up reasoning."

"That is my father."

"You don't want to go back?"

"Nope."

"Not even to say goodbye?"

Quinn sighed. "I think my father already took care of that."

"Then we won't go back."

"But—"

"Our luggage is in the trunk. I put it there before we left. Just in case."

As gestures went, it might not have been grand, but it was pretty damn close. Quinn threw her arms around Ryder's neck, peppering his face with kisses.

Ryder slid down Quinn's body, leaving a warm trail with his lips. He ended up with his knees on the car floor, her legs spread to accommodate him. Leaning close, he blew a puff of air on her sensitive flesh. Smiling, Quinn brushed her fingers through his hair.

"If that is a *thank you*," he said, kissing the inside of her thigh. "Here is my *you're welcome*."

CHAPTER THIRTEEN

DECIDING WHERE TO spend the next two weeks had been relatively easy. Quinn named three places. Ryder did the same. They put the destinations in a hat and pulled out the winner.

Ryder and Quinn were on the private jet. One call had set the pre-flight arrangements in motion and by the time they arrived at the airport, the wait for takeoff had been surprisingly short. Now that they were in the air, all that remained was deciding on their final destination.

"This isn't set in stone." Ryder watched as Quinn reached her for her floppy sun hat. It had been that or a fedora Ryder had acquired a few years ago while in New York. He wore it once before leaving it on the plane. And here it had stayed.

"Weren't these places you wanted to go?"

"Yes." Ryder laughed when Quinn flashed the paper at him, too fast for him to read. "However, this was a fun way to choose. If deep down you are disappointed, pick again."

"I want to go someplace where we can play, and you can relax. Private but not too isolated." Quinn looked at the scrap in her hand. "Aruba."

"Look at this."

Taking out his phone, Ryder pulled up a website. The resort had plenty of options for the budget conscious or those looking for a place to hide away from crowds—and fans.

"Is that bungalow over the water?"

Instead of taking the phone, Quinn snuggled under his arm to get a better view. She smelled so good Ryder briefly lost his train of thought.

"Ryder? The bungalow?"

"Meals are delivered. Or we can go to one of four restaurants. If you feel like sightseeing, there are plenty of options. We can scuba dive, deep sea fish, laze on our own private beach. There is a dance club. And—"

"Sold." Quinn covered his mouth with hers. "Are you part owner of the resort? Or simply a fan?"

"I took the band there two years ago for Christmas. We had a great time."

"Is that the only time you've been there?"

"If you are asking me if I've taken another woman there, the answer is no."

"I didn't ask." Quinn poked her tongue out at him.

"Not in so many words." Ryder teased.

"I…" Quinn sighed. "Fine. I was curious. Now I know. Please shelve the subject permanently."

"I don't mind a touch of jealousy, Quinn."

In fact, Ryder liked finding out that Quinn's feelings for him ran deeper than a few good fucks and some laughs. It had always been enough. Plenty. Ryder had never wanted more. However, Quinn was different. She made him think of where they would be beyond the next two weeks. Beyond Aruba.

Did Ryder want a relationship with Quinn? *Yes. No. Maybe.* He chuckled to himself. *That was clear—as mud.*

"I wouldn't say jealous," Quinn said.

"No?"

"A touch."

"A touch is just the right amount. Anything more gets sticky."

"Tell me about it." She took a drink from the bottle of water the air hostess had given her before takeoff. "My mother was jealous of my father. My father is jealous of my mother's happy marriage. Cora is jealous of everybody. I try not to follow in my family's footsteps. And yet, here I am."

"If I thought you were anything like Cora—or your father—we wouldn't be here."

Ryder could tell that his words pleased Quinn. Unable to resist, he placed a kiss on her smiling lips.

"Where would we be?" she asked.

"You? San Francisco, I imagine. Me?" Ryder shrugged.

"Trolling for a new bed partner?

Ryder caught the teasing light in Quinn's eyes.

"Hey, I haven't trolled since I was a teenager."

"No need when you're a certified rock god. The groupies fall from the trees."

"*I don't sleep with groupies.*" Ryder started the familiar refrain, Quinn finished it. "Smartass," he growled, pulling her onto his lap.

Ryder's lips were magic, leaving a trail of electricity in the wake as he kissed Quinn's neck. "I don't believe *sleep* was the word you used."

"But accurate. I used to fuck groupies—in my misspent youth. But I never slept with them. I rarely *sleep* with anyone."

He slept with her. Quinn didn't let herself linger on the dangerous thought. However, this time, the shiver that coursed through her body was caused by more than Ryder's expert touch. Whether he knew it or not, he had placed Quinn in rare company. She let herself believe she was special. What woman didn't want that—no matter how temporary the relationship.

Thank you, Quinn whispered to Ryder. Though she said it in her head—and never planned to raise the subject aloud—it was no less sincere. She would hold this time with him dear for the rest of her life. A precious memory. A vignette. Bittersweet. Beautiful.

Not because of his fame. Quinn and the rock star? She didn't care about that. It was the man she was slowly growing to know. The man she admired as well as desired. He could be a plumber. A lawyer. A ditch digger. Or a deep sea diver. Those were jobs. Quinn knew without a doubt that she would have been drawn to Ryder—the kind, caring man—no matter his profession.

Quinn could hear the advice her mother had given her years ago. *Outside trappings are nice, but it's a man's character that counts.*

Outside, Ryder Hart was gorgeous. Top to bottom perfection. Quinn should know, she had explored every inch with unrestrained delight. However, impossibly, he was more beautiful on the inside. The protective brother. The fiercely loyal friend. A man of integrity with a shadowed past. She wept for the little boy he had been and cheered the man he had made of himself.

Yes, Ryder Hart was the real deal. And if Quinn weren't careful, she could lose her heart to a man who had no use for it.

"Are we off to Aruba?" Ryder asked, blessedly unaware of Quinn's guarded thoughts.

Aruba. Ryder. And their moment out of time. Quinn could live with that. She couldn't protect herself from him. If she declared their affair over—here and now—what good would it do? The feelings were already there. She had a choice. Leave and make herself miserable for ending things before she had to. Or embrace the moment—the hell with tomorrow. Or next week. Or a month from now.

Quinn wanted to be with Ryder. If that meant dealing with the eventual emotional fallout, so be it. A chance like this didn't come along every day. In fact, it might never come again. They were young, free, and they wanted each other. Desperately. It was enough. It had to be.

Wrapping her arms around Ryder's neck, Quinn brushed her lips against his and smiled.

"Aruba sounds like heaven."

ARUBA TURNED OUT to be a dream. No, that wasn't right. A dream had a hazy quality to it. No matter how real it seemed, there was always the feeling that everything that was happening was just out of reach. Frustratingly unreal. This was happening. Every beautiful, memorable moment.

Fun in the sun didn't begin to describe the week. Quinn enjoyed every second, not letting herself feel the slightest twinge of guilt. Yes, it was Ryder's money that paid for everything. From the elegant, richly appointed room, the scrumptious meals that looked like little works of art. *Lifestyles of the Rich and Famous*. Not her world even when her father paid for everything. This was uncharted territory for Quinn, and she found it was not a hardship to fall into its seductive lure.

A perfect example was the bathing suit she donned that morning. The tiny scraps of bright red material had been waiting on the king-sized bed when they arrived. When Quinn sent Ryder an enquiring look, he had merely shrugged, stating that it was his vacation. He had the right to look at her in the swimwear of his choice. As arguments went, that one was thinner than tissue paper. However, Quinn didn't make a fuss. It *was* his vacation.

There was nothing to the suit, but Quinn would have laid even odds it cost more than a month's rent on her apartment. Checking the label, she let out a silent whistle. Okay, make that two months. Her lofty principles said that she should protest. Still, it was her vacation too. If he wanted her in the beautiful bikini, and if she wanted to wear it, she couldn't think of a single reason not to.

"Red looks good on you." Ryder swam up to where Quinn floated aimlessly in the impossibly blue water. "You should wear it more often."

"Are you saying that red *suits* me?"

Admittedly, it was a lame pun. However, Quinn's brain, like the rest of her, was in sand-and-surf mode. Lame was the best she could manage.

"I will excuse your groan-worthy comment, just this once because you look so incredible, the water is in danger of turning to steam. But watch it. Next time I won't be as lenient."

"Please." Deliberately, Quinn used her hands as paddles, pushing herself through the water. Away from Ryder. "What are you going to do, you big pussycat?"

"You're right," he said with an exaggerated sigh. "I'm all talk and no action."

Quinn quickly discovered that Ryder was a dual threat. Talk *and* action—he made it a wonderfully sexy mix. She was particularly fond of his action. They had drifted toward the shore, making it easy for him to stand, grab Quinn, and hoist her over his tanned, powerful shoulder. Rather than fight the pleasure-filled inevitable, Quinn relaxed and enjoyed the view of Ryder's fine, firm trunks-covered ass.

What happened when they reached the beach left them gasping for air—with big grins on their faces.

"This is why I love a private beach." Ryder took a deep, calming breath.

"Sex in the open air?"

Naked and fantastically satiated, Quinn rolled onto her back. Her brand new—outrageously expensive—bathing suit was somewhere in their general vicinity. The top had gone in one direction, the bottoms in another. She had been so distracted by what his hands and mouth were up to, Quinn had no idea when Ryder had shucked his trunks. Or where they ended up. Nor had she cared. And she was fine with that. In her opinion, Ryder could stay naked for the duration of their time in Aruba. Who in their right mind would argue?

They lay side by side, the hot sand feeling like the best spa treatment ever. The heat seeped into Quinn's bones—deep and delicious. Her little finger brushed against Ryder's. Though she didn't feel like moving, she needed the connection with him now that his body had left hers.

"You have to admit it is one of life's little pleasures."

In Quinn's opinion, it—this—was only a pleasure with the right person. She couldn't picture doing what they had just done, with anyone but Ryder. Not that she was going to share that piece of wisdom. Instead, she kept her response light.

"I have sand in my hoo-ha."

Ryder snorted. "Since I have become very fond of your hoo-ha, I promise to help de-sand you—later. Right now, all I want to do is lie here and let the world pass by slowly—gentle and serene. No concerts. No writing deadlines. No songs to record. Nobody clamoring for my time. Just the sand, the sun, the sea, and you."

A woman could live her entire life and never hear the right man say something so off-handedly sweet. Ryder had no agenda or ulterior motive. She was already sleeping with him. And Lord knew, there were plenty of guys out there who became aloof oafs as soon as they sealed the deal. Ryder was not one of them.

A little part of Quinn—the unreasonable optimist—wanted to believe he spoke from the heart. However, she had promised herself she wouldn't go down that road. Her feelings were one thing. Ryder was having fun. He enjoyed her body and her company. Nothing more. She wasn't going to start hoping for the impossible.

"What do you say we have dinner at that little Mexican place the bellhop told us about when we checked in? A cold beer and a ton of guacamole sound like heaven."

"Add some tamales to the mix and you've got a deal."

"I love an easy woman."

When Quinn opened her mouth to protest that statement, Ryder stopped her with his hand on her lips. He had the good grace to wince.

"I heard the words as I said them. It didn't come out the way I intended. I retract my statement with a sincere apology."

"I knew what you meant."

"You were going to give me hell."

"Naturally." Eyes sparkling, Quinn kissed Ryder's palm before lacing her fingers with his. "As a woman, it is my duty to call foul when the situation arises. You saved us both the trouble."

"I bet you are something when you get on your soap box."

"I *am* a lawyer."

Ryder smiled. Then, just as Quinn realized what she had said, he had the same realization.

"You *are* a lawyer? I thought you dropped out before you finished."

Quinn sighed, flopping back onto the sand.

"Well?" Ryder urged, leaning over her. "What's the deal?"

"Fine." Quinn tugged Ryder's arm until he lay beside her. If she had to confess, she didn't want to do it with him hovering over her like an avenging angel ready to pass judgment for her misdeeds. "I have a quirk."

"Is that anything like a kink? Because I can live with that."

Despite herself, Quinn snickered. Ryder had a quick mind and a quirky sense of humor. At least she thought he was kidding.

"Get your thoughts out of the bedroom for two seconds."

"It will be difficult." Ryder slid a hand along her thigh, though his touch was comforting—not provocative. "Go on. I'm listening."

"I can't start something and not finish it. Not that I'm obsessive. I can walk out in the middle of a movie or start a book and not hit the final chapter. However, if it's a biggy? It is impossible for me to walk away."

"Law school was a biggy?"

"Huge. It preyed on me that I had gotten so close to the finish line. I could see it—tantalizingly close. I should have known better than to think it wouldn't bother me." Quinn closed her eyes, raising her face to the warm, soothing light. "I could have completed my degree without the intention of practicing law. People do it all the time. It didn't take much soul-searching to figure out why I quit."

"Your father."

"Ding, ding, ding," With each ding, Quinn tapped Ryder on the hand. "Give the man a prize."

Ryder lifted her hand to his lips, then brought it to his chest without letting go. "What made you decide to go back?"

"It was never a question of would I or wouldn't I. Though I will admit that I fooled myself into thinking I could walk away without looking over my shoulder in regret. That lasted six months."

"Not bad. When did you start getting antsy? Month three? Four?"

"How did you know?"

140

"I suffer from a similar trait." Ryder chuckled. "An unfinished song is my bugaboo. Even if it will never see the light of day. Even if it turns out to be the worst thing I've ever written. I can't leave it alone until it's done. Sometimes it turns out to be a good thing. I took a piece of music that I thought was pure crap and it became *Night Wanderer*. Lemons to lemonade."

Quinn felt a little catch in her throat. God, she loved that song. Soulful and poignant. It made her sad and happy at the same time.

"I would call you a genius, but your ego gets enough stroking."

"My ego," Ryder waggled his eyebrows, "loves all the stroking it can get, *honey*."

Quinn didn't rise to the bait. Honey, her ass. Ryder never called her that unless he was teasing. "Again with the sexual innuendo?"

"I'm a man. I love sex."

"I'm a woman. So do I. But I can carry on a conversation without referencing the act, or a body part involved."

Moving a little closer, Ryder rubbed his arm against hers. "I'm a pig. All men are."

"So true." Though so far, Ryder was proving to be a big, lovely, unexpected exception to the rule.

"Tell me the rest of the story."

"Well, *Paul Harvey*." Ryder snorted. The fact that he got the reference was another reason they had clicked so quickly. "The inevitable happened. I couldn't ignore that little voice in the back of my head urging me on."

"I know that little voice well."

Quinn nodded. Of course, he did.

"The most important thing was to get my degree without my father finding out. It was one thing to have him bug me to finish school. If he knew I was an accredited attorney, he would have been on me night and day to move back to Indiana and join his firm."

"I know this is your story. But you keep throwing in pertinent details—rushing over them. You are accredited? As in legally, you can practice the law?"

Surprised, Quinn realized that was exactly what she had been doing. She liked to tell a linear story. Beginning. Middle. Ending. Ryder had a strange influence on her. Her mother would call him a *brain muddler*. It wasn't a complimentary term. However, Quinn wondered if, in her case, that was a bad thing. She could be a little rigid. Not anal—but set in her ways. If Ryder shook up the status quo, she could live with that. Especially when his *muddling* was accompanied by kisses—and so forth.

"I found a school that had no affiliation with my father. Not as easy as you might think. He keeps his ear to the ground so he can recruit the best and brightest. Fresh, eager newbies are the bread and butter of a large firm. They work for peanuts and are so grateful just to have the job, they don't complain about the horrible hours or overload of grunt work."

Quinn had been destined to be one of the masses. She knew her father well enough to understand that he would have balked at giving her preferential treatment. Not that she would have asked. If she had chosen the law as a career, she would have wanted to learn from the ground up. One of the masses, so to speak. Luckily, she came to her senses before it was too late.

"Peanuts. Does that make them monkeys?"

Quinn nodded. "Intelligent, but ultimately slaves to their master. If they work hard and are trainable, there is a ladder to step up. Slowly. The rungs are miles apart. I get hives just thinking about it."

Ryder kissed Quinn's shoulder. Such a small gesture, yet blissfully comforting.

"Once I chose the under-the-radar law school, the rest was easy. I graduated. Took the California bar exam. And poof. I was a lawyer. Then I went back to hustling to further my photography career full time. Did that cover everything?"

"One more thing. Why photography?"

"Why music?"

"Question answered."

Ryder rolled until his chest covered hers. The smile on his face took her breath away. Like the sight of a sunrise. Or the first snowfall. Where was her camera when she needed it?

"Passion can't be picked out of the ether. You feel it," Ryder took her lips in a long, slow kiss. "Or you don't."

Quinn's moan originated from her core. Soft, yet emotion packed. Her eyes locked with his, she took Ryder's growing erection in her hand. "Oh, I feel it."

"The question is, what are you going to do about it?"

While seeming to ponder his question, Quinn absently ran her hand up and down his cock. She had ideas. Too many to count. From the wild to wacky to the downright dangerous. In the end, she went with the tried and true. Why tamper with something that had worked since man—and woman—began to walk upright? Hell, probably before that.

Smiling slyly, a promise in her eyes, Quinn leaned down and took Ryder into her mouth.

Air hissed through Ryder's teeth. He slid his fingers into her hair, anchoring her in place. *There you go*, she thought, thoroughly enjoying the taste of him. He was happy. She was happy. Try as one might, *nothing* could beat a classic.

CHAPTER FOURTEEN

"STOP STARING AT my mouth."

"I wasn't." Ryder protested calmly.

Ryder's eyes zeroed in as Quinn took a drink of beer. *Well, shit.* He *was* staring. It wasn't his fault that the bottle was the same general shape of his dick. About as long, but nowhere near as thick. Seeing her put it in her mouth took him back to the beach. Had it only been an hour ago? As Quinn raised the bottle again, he felt his body heat. Damn, when had he morphed into the horn dog of his youth? Ryder chuckled silently. Easy answer. Thirty seconds after he met Quinn.

Quinn returned the beer to the table. Without a trace of annoyance, she sent Ryder a smile. "I don't mind. I'm glad you enjoyed my... efforts. If we were alone, you could add a little color commentary. A woman likes to know how she can improve her technique—as long as the criticism is constructive. But your gaze leaves little doubt what you're thinking about."

"Nobody has any idea what is going on in my lascivious brain," Ryder assured her.

"Lucky for you."

Ryder laughed. He knew he was right. For now, nobody cared who he was, why they were there, or what they had gotten up to on that beach two miles down the coast. However, for Quinn's peace of mind, and his own, Ryder gave the room a surreptitious glance. Nope. The crowd was interested in two things. The food on their plates and the booze in their glasses. Happily, they had received barely a glance since entering the restaurant. Not that Ryder had been particularly worried about drawing attention. Quinn had been the one to express her concern.

Since their arrival, he and Quinn hadn't left their bungalow to do more than a stroll on the beach and wander through the small town a few miles away. Ryder wore a hat and dark glasses—his usual incognito attire. Having dinner in a crowded restaurant was a different matter. Though it was mostly frequented by locals, the occasional tourist wandered in. Quinn had the idea that wherever he went, hordes of rabid fans followed.

To be fair, Quinn wasn't that far from the truth. It was a fact. His face. His voice. His music. The public persona he had spent years perfecting. Where he went, they followed closely behind. From Iowa to Indonesia. Tallahassee to Timbuktu. Early on, he could still get away with playing the *regular guy*. However, there was never a rhyme or reason to when he would be recognized.

One day he walked down the streets of New York by himself. No entourage or security. For three hours, he didn't hear a single, *Oh, God. It's Ryder Hart*. Eventually, he was recognized, but the freedom of those three hours had been bliss.

On the other hand, on a visit to Istanbul, he decided it would be fun to visit one of the street markets. Hat and glasses covering his famous face hadn't helped him that morning. Five minutes. That was the ETA. *Estimated time of attack*. One person called out his name and he had been mobbed. If it weren't for an alley and a kind shopkeeper, Ryder might still be fighting off his *loving* fans.

That experience had changed Ryder's approach to the outside world. He hadn't become a recluse, locked away in a room like Howard Hughes collecting bottle after bottle of his own urine. What he *had* become was much more pragmatic. Ryder Hart was famous—worldwide. Walking around as though that was not the case was unrealistic and irresponsible. His friends—his bandmates—relied on him. Not just as their lead singer and founding member, but as the group's bedrock. It sounded egotistical, but it was no less true.

Ryder had no doubt they would survive without him. However, why test that theory? He had found other ways to exert his personal freedom without putting anyone he loved in the position of having to worry about his wellbeing.

Naked sex with Quinn on a secluded beach in Aruba was a perfect example.

"Lucky for me, you have the most beautiful, luscious, talented mouth it has ever been my privilege to enjoy." Ryder wasn't certain, but he thought he saw a tinge of pink riding high on Quinn's cheeks. The woman was filled with surprises. "And FYI? Don't change a thing. You were perfect." He carried her hand to his lips. "You, *all* of you, are perfect."

Quinn's smile took Ryder's breath away. Bright. Happy. It showed him what spring should look like. Blazing with beauty and the hope of what was ahead. If he were a different man—one who wasn't too damaged to think a woman like Quinn could be his forever—he would tell her every thought about her that entered his head. Tell her—everything. The problem was, if he did that, the bright and happy would fade faster than the last note of a heartbreaking ballad.

"What's the matter?" Quinn asked. "A second ago, you were smiling."

"And now? What do you see, Quinn?"

Ryder searched Quinn's eyes, curious if any of his inner turmoil spilled over. He hoped not. Most of the time, his hidden anger and bitterness stayed exactly where such shit-assed thoughts belonged— deep, deep in his bowels. However, he had to release the ugliness every now and then. It was why he insisted on booking Chicago— the last place on Earth he would step foot, except when they were on tour.

And *Flowers On the Wall*. Between the town and the song, it was the only time Ryder allowed himself to wallow. Not too long. Just enough to blow off steam and keep himself sane. Or at the very least, sane enough.

"I see the pain that I would do anything to take away."

To Ryder's amazement, Quinn brushed away a tear. It should have appalled him. Sympathy in any form angered him. He was a strong man. A survivor. No, he had done more than survive. He had thrived. It didn't matter that the demons lurked—sometimes in the shadows, sometimes nipping at his heels. The world saw a strong, confident man. And ninety-nine percent of the time, that was exactly who Ryder Hart was.

"I'm a waste of your tears, Quinn." Rather than harsh and distant as Ryder expected, his rebuke was soft. Almost tender. Another tell that Quinn was beginning to mean more to him than was wise. "Save them for lost puppies and Hallmark commercials."

"Fuck you, Ryder." Quinn angrily swiped at her cheeks. "And I don't cry over lost puppies. I find them homes."

"I don't need a savior."

"Yes, you do. But it won't be me," Quinn assured him. "I know a lost cause when I see one."

Quinn pushed away her half-finished tamales.

Ryder wanted to apologize for ruining her meal. But for the life of him, he didn't know what had happened or how to fix it. One second, they were teasing and flirting. The next he found himself wandering down a lane of memories he wished would fall into a giant sinkhole.

If Ryder said he were sorry, Quinn would expect an explanation. That wasn't going to happen—for her sake as well as his. Instead, he remained stoically resigned. She was pissed—rightfully so. And there was nothing he could do about it.

"Where are you going?" Ryder asked when Quinn shot to her feet.

"I have a choice. Dump my food in your lap or splash some cold water on my face. Luckily for those expensive linen pants, I also have to pee." Quinn turned toward the back of the restaurant and the bathroom. Pausing, she said over her shoulder. "This could take a lot of water. Don't expect me back anytime soon."

Ryder watched Quinn walk away with an increasingly heavy heart. Her flowered dress that swirled so prettily around her shapely legs. The happy colors were another sign of the spring she represented. He knew she was coming back, but something told Ryder that she was walking out of his life.

QUINN LOOKED AT her reflection in the mirror. If it were as old as it looked, chances were it had hung over the equally ancient sink for a long, long time. Her face blurred in the wavy glass like something she would see in a funhouse at the carnival.

Quinn sighed. That was appropriate. Carnival. Ryder had certainly taken her on an emotional rollercoaster. What had happened? The change in him was so quick. Quinn racked her brain trying to figure out what had set him off. What had been the trigger? Something she said? Or didn't say?

It didn't matter anymore that she had made a special effort to look her best. The dress was new. Something she had splurged on when she finished a photo shoot last spring. Temptation called her name all the time when it came to clothing and shoes. It was a siren's call she usually ignored. However, when she saw the yellow silk dress with the flirty skirt and the thin shoulder straps, walking away wasn't easy. The light blue peonies that dotted the material made her smile. She would have resisted, but she made a fatal mistake. She looked at the price tag.

The gesture was meant to be the final nail in the dress' proverbial coffin. True, the cost had been dear. But it was *on sale* dear. Knowing it was a mistake and promising herself a month of nothing but Ramen noodles and peanut butter, Quinn gave in. The dress hung in her closet, unworn. She did take it out to admire. Touching the flowers. Holding the material to her nose as though she could take in their sweet scent.

When she donned the garment for the first time, Quinn had felt a thrill. It didn't matter that Ryder had no idea of the sacrifices she had made to get to this moment. She felt sexy and confident. That was all that mattered. And when she walked out of the bedroom and saw the appreciation in his gaze, Quinn knew the lack of variety in her diet had been worth every boring bite.

Splashing another handful of icy water on her face, Quinn took a paper towel from the dispenser. When had she become such a girl? Obsessing over a man, even one as fine as Ryder, was something she

148

never did—not even when she *was* a girl. Yet here she was, obsessing because—boo hoo—a man had hurt her feelings. How pathetic was that? Quinn should have stayed in her seat and had it out with Ryder then and there.

One thing was for certain, hiding in here wasn't giving her any answers. Determined, she took two things from her purse. Powder for her nose and gloss for her lips. Her cheeks needed no extra color. They were rosy with unvented frustration. Pulling her shoulders back, Quinn reached for the bathroom door. Ryder could glare. He could try to give her the silent treatment—good luck with that. But he would not get away with shutting her out. Whatever the problem, she couldn't fix it unless he told her what was wrong.

Filled with righteous indignation, Quinn marched back not certain what she would say. It didn't matter. The table was empty, and Ryder was nowhere to be seen.

"Excuse me." As he rushed by, Quinn stopped the tall, dark-haired man who had taken their dinner order. "The man who was with me. Do you know if he is in the bathroom?" She couldn't imagine Ryder leaving her here.

"Are you Quinn?" Surprisingly, the man had a New York accent.

"That's right."

"Your friend left."

So much for her imagination. Normally vivid and unrestrained, it had let her down like a lead balloon.

"How long ago? Did he say where he was going?

"Just now. And no. But he asked me to make certain you got back to your bungalow safely."

Well, whoop dee-fucking-do. It was exactly the kind of thoughtful gesture that Quinn would have appreciated—another time and another place. Right now, she wanted to kick him in the ass. Then something penetrated her red-misted self-involvement. Something familiar. It was music. But not just any music. A song on the jukebox. She listened closer. No. It couldn't be. They were in

Aruba. In a small-town bar. It was the last place she would expect to hear *Flowers On the Wall.*

"Did Ryder play that song?"

"Your friend? Nah. One of the locals plays it all the time."

"All the time." Quinn clenched her teeth. What were the chances? She didn't know the song's significance, but she had seen enough in Chicago to know it wasn't good.

"Why?" Quinn muttered. Was it a freaking cosmic joke? If so, she wasn't laughing.

Thinking Quinn was talking to him, the man scratched his head. "Huh?"

"How did my friend seem before he left?"

"How should I know? I came down here to get away from my family's shit. I sure as hell don't want to get tied in yours," he mumbled. When Quinn's eyes narrowed threateningly, the waiter held up his hands. "Jeez, why are women so bossy? All I know is that he bought two shots of tequila, slammed them down bang, bang, and left. West. But don't worry. He paid me five hundred dollars to walk you home."

Tequila? That couldn't be good. Whatever Ryder was going through, like his friends gathering around him when he needed them, Quinn wasn't going to let him go through this alone.

"Come on." Quinn grabbed the man by the arm and headed out the door. "What is your name?"

"Alvin." When Quinn turned in the opposite direction he expected, Alvin tried to pull back, but he was no match for her. The man was tall and wiry, but Quinn had the power of a worried, determined woman on her side. Even in heels, Quinn easily hustled Alvin out of the restaurant. "Hey. I'm supposed to take you home."

"Too bad."

"But what about the five hundred?"

Money, Quinn sighed with frustration. *It truly made the world go around.* If that was all it took, then she could play the game.

"Help me find my friend and you can keep his money. And I'll pay you five hundred more."

That was all the incentive Alvin needed. He rushed down the street, Quinn close behind. Ryder wanted to handle this on his own? Fight his own fight? *Too bad, Mr. Hart.* Almost twisting her ankle on the uneven sidewalk, Quinn quickly removed her shoes. Barefoot worked. She didn't know what kind of shape Ryder would be in when she found him, but she wouldn't stop until she knew he was safe.

Hurrying to keep up with the suddenly swift Alvin, Quinn crossed her fingers and said a silent prayer. *Please, let him be all right.*

CHAPTER FIFTEEN

THE TEQUILA SANG in Ryder's blood. It had been a long time since he had indulged in anything stronger than a beer or two. It had hit him fast—but not hard. Two shots. Enough to give himself a buffer but not enough to send him over any cliffs.

Ryder had almost forgotten alcohol's power. How it loosened his body and eased his mind. Booze could turn an introvert into the life of the party. Or, in the case of his father, create a monster. Some people could handle a drink or two—or three. Some should never take the slightest sip. Bennett Hart had fallen into the latter category.

It wasn't that Ryder's father came apart after one drink. Or two. However, one or two was never enough. They led to three. Then four. Around five, Bennett switched on the old turntable, set it on repeat, and removed the record from its beat-up cover. A forty-five. It wasn't the only music he owned. But it was the only one played when he was drunk.

Over and over and over again.

The road in front of him wasn't blurred. Ryder didn't stumble as he walked toward the beach—the one far, far away from the idyllic one he and Quinn had romped on for the past week. *Quinn.* He shouldn't have left her in that restaurant, but she was safer with an unknown waiter than with him in his current state of mind. Hell, Ryder wondered if she should be around him at all. He had nothing to give her—nothing beyond a few weeks of fun.

There was a mantra he and his bandmates stuck to. *Fuck 'em and flee.* It was crude but accurate. Though Quinn knew the score—though she understood how things worked—she deserved better. The problem was, Ryder didn't have better to give.

By the time he reached the edge of the water, that instant buzz from the tequila had worn off. Ryder should have taken the whole bottle. He sighed, letting the ocean breeze rush over his heated face. Cool. Tipping his head back, Ryder stared into the clear, moonlit sky. He knew that alcohol was only a temporary fix. Problems never disappeared. They lurked in the corner, ready to jump at you the next morning. They didn't care about your pounding head or your roiling stomach. If anything, your problems rejoiced. Now, everything had an extra layer of shitty and the few hours of respite were a distant memory.

Ryder had tried drinking. He experimented with drugs. It didn't take him long to realize that they were false prophets. There was no salvation in the bottom of a bottle, only ruination. Drugs made you sloppy and stupid. Ryder gave up on them before he turned sixteen when he had a true, life-changing revelation.

There was only one way to maintain his sanity. Only one source of goodness and light in the world. Music. It had saved Ryder's soul and made him a very wealthy man. He had a good life. Great. Yet it was a song that could cut the legs out from under him.

The irony of that was not lost on Ryder. A damn good song at that. But all it took was the first few chords and Ryder was back in that tiny trailer. Scared. Helpless. The swing of his father's arm as he wielded his belt over and over again, matching the beat in a kind of sick, syncopated duet.

It had hit Ryder hard and fast. Though the worst had worn off, he couldn't go back to Quinn like this. He felt jumbled. Unsteady. Unpredictable. It was the last one that worried him. There was no fear that he would do her physical harm. Never, not even in the middle of his hardest drunk, had he ever raised a hand to a woman. Perhaps that had been the point of those drunken benders. A test to see how much of his father was in him. To his relief—and joy—he found out there wasn't much.

However, Ryder could say some stingingly bitter things when provoked. During the early days with Dalton and Ashe, they had gotten into a couple of shouting matches that came close to breaking apart the band. Ryder knew how to push their buttons, and they knew his weak spots. It made for some volatile times. Luckily, the three of them never held a grudge—not over a few words. They were friends. Brothers by choice. And incredibly young. For the most part, the arguments ended as they matured. The friendship and the brotherhood grew stronger. It was an unbreakable bond that had survived the ups and downs of an industry that had no patience for anything but success.

Dalton, Ashe—and Zoe—had been there through the early struggles. They celebrated together the astronomical high they were currently riding. And they would be there when the inevitable cool off occurred.

Zoe understood Ryder's demons. Ashe and Dalton knew what they were. If he went off the rails, they gave him some leeway, taking whatever he said with more than a few grains of salt. Quinn wasn't prepared to deal with his shit. Until he was certain none of it would fall on her, he had to stay away.

The sea looked so different at night. A stand-offish inky black instead of an inviting deep blue. But the dark depths didn't scare Ryder. He knew trouble when he saw it. Under that deceptive surface was nothing but smooth, calm water. And it called his name.

Whipping off his shirt, Ryder kept his gaze locked on the moon's reflection. He made it his goal. Not far from shore. A brief swim there and back. Tossing the last of his clothing into the pile, Ryder took one step forward. The water was wonderfully cool, lapping at his ankles. This was what he needed. There and back. Hopefully, he would leave the rest of his waning tension in the saline depths and be ready to return to Quinn.

Lovely Quinn. Ryder didn't realize that it was the thought of her, not the water, that calmed his soul and lightened his mind. He wasn't ready to delve into those feelings so his subconscious refused to acknowledge their existence. Not tonight. Not when he felt raw and vulnerable.

Taking a deep breath, Ryder blindly plunged in.

Quinn reached the beach just as Ryder disappeared under the dark water. Heart pounding, she waited for him to surface. And waited. And waited.

"Holy shit, did he kill himself?" Alvin took a step back. "I've never seen a dead body."

Quinn had the same fear, but she wasn't going to say it. Not to Alvin, nor to herself. Saying something made the possibility real.

"He didn't kill himself."

However, if that were Ryder's intent, Quinn didn't plan on standing around watching. She threw her shoes away, running toward the shore. She had her dress over her head seconds before her feet touched the water.

"I can't swim," Alvin called after her.

Quinn didn't give a shit. She could.

RYDER TIMED HIS ascent perfectly. Breaking the surface of the water so close to his original destination, he forgave himself the few inches of difference. Moonlight bathed his face without the welcoming warmth of the sun, but no less inviting. The allure was just as potent and, at the moment, infinitely more soothing.

There was nothing like the caress of water against his naked skin. Except Quinn. Her touch couldn't be equaled. But all things considered, this was a decent substitute.

As he let the sea free his mind, Ryder had a thought—an idea that the more and more he pondered, made more and more sense. This—Aruba—might be the answer. He needed a place to live. A home where he could find the peace and quiet to regenerate after a long tour. A place where he could wander around in a pair of board shorts—or nothing at all—without the worry that his picture would wind up on the next edition of *TMZ*.

Hmm, Ryder smiled—he actually smiled. It was definitely something to think about. The brush of something against his leg made Ryder frown. The body shooting out of the water almost stopped his heart.

"Are you suicidal or simply stupid? Tell me now so I can act accordingly."

"Quinn?" For a second, Ryder wondered if the tequila had been laced with a hallucinogen because he was definitely tripping. "What the hell are you doing here?"

"Me?" Quinn tread water with one hand while pushing her hair out of her face with the other. "Me?"

"Yes, you. You scared the shit out of me."

"Join the club, asshole. First, you play Houdini—nice disappearing act, by the way. Then I find you skinny dipping in a pool of ink."

"It's water." Ryder ran the water through his fingers.

"I'm aware, dickwad. My question stands. Suicidal? Stupid?"

"I will never kill myself." Even if Ryder had the desire to end his life, which he didn't, he would never do that to Zoe.

"Stupid it is." Quinn sent a shot of water into his face. Unlike last afternoon, there was nothing playful about her. "I could kick your ass, Ryder Hart. See that?"

Quinn pointed to the top of her head, but all Ryder could see was wet hair.

"Help me out. What am I looking at?"

"I don't know. I thought there might be a gray streak. Fright will do that, you know."

"Quinn?" Ryder patted her shoulder to make certain she was really there. This had taken a bizarre turn. If he were on drugs, it had sent him on one crazy-assed trip. *Thank God*, he thought when his hand encountered solid flesh. "What are you doing here?"

"Saving you. Or something to that effect."

"Do I need saving?"

That was a stupid question. Ryder needed it more than most. However, to save him, Quinn would get covered in the grunge of his childhood. He would not be responsible for dimming even a smidgen of the light that shined from her.

"How was I supposed to know this was a whimsical midnight swim?" In the moonlight, Ryder watched as a myriad of emotions traveled across Quinn's expressive face. "First, you left without a word. Then…"

"Then?" Ryder urged.

"I heard the song."

Ryder hadn't seen that coming. Somehow, he had forgotten that Quinn was witness to his Chicago self-flagellation. He didn't know whether to feel embarrassment or distress. As a man who had always liked to go big or go home, he wasn't surprised when both emotions rushed through him.

"I don't know what to say, Quinn."

"Yes, you do. Unfortunately, you don't trust me enough."

"That's—"

With a shake of her head, Quinn stopped Ryder before he could respond. What he would have said? He had no idea.

"It's your story to tell—or not." Ryder couldn't help but catch the flash of sadness in Quinn's eyes. "All I ask is that you don't do this," she motioned to the water, "again."

Quinn started back toward shore, her pace unhurried. Silently, Ryder fell in beside her.

"Hey. Is everything okay?" a voice called out from shore.

"You brought Alvin with you?"

"He was the only one who knew which way you headed."

Ryder sensed when they were close enough to stand. That was when he realized that Quinn was naked—at least from the waist up.

"Jesus, Quinn." Taking her by the shoulders, Ryder turned her away from Alvin's eagle-eyed interest.

"I'm certain Alvin has seen a woman's breasts before, Ryder."

"Not yours." Ryder knew how it sounded—especially under the circumstances. However, it didn't change the way he felt. The sight of Quinn's beautiful breasts was not for public consumption. "Stay here."

"Don't you care if Alvin gets a look at your bare essentials?"

"No." Ryder walked up the beach to retrieve his shirt. "The show is free, Alvin. At least my part of it. Ogle my woman, and I'll knock you on your ass. Understand?"

Alvin gulped. Without a word, he proved that he had learned a thing or two from growing up in New York. Wisely, he turned in the opposite direction as Quinn.

"Smart man."

"Your woman?" Quinn snatched the shirt from him, not in the mood to let him help. "Since when?"

"As long as we are here—together—you are mine. And I don't share. Not even the view."

"That is a chauvinistic heap of steaming crap."

"I won't argue. But it doesn't change the way I feel."

Grumbling, Quinn pulled on Ryder's shirt. It hit her at mid-thigh—not shorter than a lot of hemlines that passed his way every day. It would do until they were safely at the bungalow.

"By the way," Quinn said as she walked to the beach. "I need to borrow five hundred dollars."

QUINN HAD TAKEN her shower and was sitting on the deck when Ryder exited the bathroom. He would have suggested they share, however, didn't think Quinn was in the mood to have his hands on her at the moment. She hadn't spoken on the walk back except to veto his offer of motorized transportation. It wouldn't have taken long for Alvin to round up a car. *No, thank you.* Ryder gave points for politeness, but the tone of her voice was colder than a mid-December day at the North Pole.

Ryder raided the refrigerator, taking two bottles of water from the shelf, before joining Quinn.

"I paid Alvin." Ryder handed her the water. Quinn took it without looking his way. "It wasn't a loan, Quinn. If you try to pay me back, we will have words."

When Quinn didn't answer, Ryder frowned. From their first meeting, he couldn't recall her staying silent for long. She wasn't afraid to share her opinion. A silent Quinn made Ryder uncomfortable.

"Quinn. I—"

The sound Quinn made stopped Ryder cold. It sounded like something between a hiccup and a sniffle. The sound someone made when they were crying.

"I'm sorry," Quinn whispered, taking a shaky breath.

"Why?" Ryder dropped to his knees in front of her. Cupping Quinn's face with his hands, he wiped the wetness from her cheeks with his thumbs. "I messed up, not you."

Quinn leaned into his touch. The look in her big, dark eyes almost tore Ryder's heart out. How could she feel so much for him? What had he ever done to deserve her empathy?

"That song." Quinn kissed the palm of his hand. Ryder wondered why it felt as though her lips reached toward his heart. "I knew there was something wrong the second I heard it. All I wanted was to find you to make sure you were okay. And what did I do when I saw you? I yelled. Bitched, would be more accurate. That hadn't been my plan."

Quinn had no idea what her concern meant to him. Ryder had spent so many years where nobody cared if he lived or died—except Zoe.

"You came after me. That's all that matters."

"But—"

"I overreacted."

"Did you?"

Ryder saw the doubt. How could he blame her? There were times when he wondered if his childhood had become an insignificant blip. Horrible at the time but so much had happened since. So many good things to counteract the bad. Then something would happen—like hearing that song—and Ryder was reminded with a blinding punch to his gut that the past was never buried. Not when a little thing like notes strung together could bring a man to his knees.

"I left because it was unexpected. When I was younger, I would have found a hole to crawl into. Someplace dark and moldering to match my mood."

Another tear escaped down Quinn's cheek. "Sounds lovely," she said, her angry tone belying her words.

Quinn scooted over, silently inviting Ryder to join her on the padded bench. Grateful, he sat, his leg brushing hers. After his shower, Ryder had pulled on a loose pair of shorts. The temperature hadn't dipped enough to require anything else. Quinn had twisted her damp hair onto the top of her head in one of those messy, sexy knots every woman seemed to know how to fashion. Her white shorts were paired with a t-shirt that proclaimed her love for cookies. The dancing chocolate chips made Ryder's lips twitch.

"Nothing about those days was lovely."

"After your father…"

Ryder knew the moment had come. It was either tell Quinn everything or change the conversation. This moment felt big. Important. If he didn't do it now, he never would. But would it change everything? Would Quinn's perception warp when she heard the ugly, twisted details?

"How do you want to do this, Quinn?" Ryder lifted her legs until they draped over his. Instead of leaning back, Quinn cuddled close, resting her head on his shoulder. "We can forget about tonight—pretend it didn't happen."

"And forget about the elephant in the room? I don't think I can do that."

"It's not so hard," Ryder assured her. "I did it every time I went to school. Or swapped doing chores for guitar lessons with the retired teacher who lived a few blocks away."

"Was she nice? Did she serve you lemonade and brownies?" Quinn asked hopefully.

"She was a mean old harridan with a sharp tongue and no patience for sloppy playing." Ryder lifted her chin. "Don't look so desolate. Mrs. Finch made my life bearable. Without her and those lessons to look forward to, I don't know what I would have done."

"How old were you when you started?"

"Eight."

It had been so long since he had thought about it. At the time, music was the enemy. It meant pain. It meant slapping and whipping and kicking. The day Ryder found out there was more had been nothing but chance. If he had gotten to the corner of that street a few minutes earlier—or later—his life might have turned out very different.

"I was on my way home from school. I didn't like to be late because—"

"Because you were afraid to leave Zoe alone with your father?"

Ryder shook his head, smiling in spite of himself. "Have you heard this story?"

"I've seen the way you are with Zoe. You take your job as big brother seriously. It wouldn't have been any different when you were little."

"He never hit her." It was hard to control his shudder. Wondering when their old man would turn his wrath on Zoe had kept Ryder awake at night. "Why it never happened, I don't know."

"Don't you?" Quinn hugged Ryder's arm, letting him know she was there for him. "You made yourself into a target, didn't you?"

Ryder wouldn't let Quinn turn him into a heroic martyr. It hadn't been like that.

"I made certain Zoe traveled under the old man's radar. But if he had wanted to hit her, nothing I could have done would have stopped him." Not then. Ryder used to dream of the day when he would be strong enough to rip that belt from his hands and turn it on him. But his father never gave him a chance.

"Tell me about your epiphany."

"Epiphany, college girl? That's a mighty big word."

Quinn pinched his arm. Not too hard, but it had some bite.

"You can't play the uneducated card with me. I've seen the books you read. I've heard the way you speak." For emphasis, Quinn tapped the side of his head. "You have a good brain up there, Ryder. Besides, I don't have sex with stupid men. At least, not on purpose."

"When did you *accidentally* have sex with a stupid man?"

"That is a story for another time. Tell me about finding music."

Ryder settled them both, Quinn snuggled close. Funny, he never told this story. There had been one semi-drunken disclosure to Dalton and Ashe when they were high off a stellar performance. They passed around a bottle of cheap bourbon and talked about why they did what they did. Their beginnings had been different—very different. However, the love of playing. The passion of making a song soar. Those were the first things that bonded them as a band and as friends.

The public—his fans—didn't know. Outside of Zoe, and the guys, nobody did. Yet it felt right to tell Quinn.

"As I said, I was rushing home from school. I took the same way—the shortest from point A to point B. It was hot. I remember that so clearly. Late April and it felt like July. There was a man who was always on the same corner, playing for tips. He had an old guitar and a beat-up case that sat open. There was never more than a few bucks in there."

Ryder rarely gave the man a second look. He had more important things on his eight-year-old brain. Like if there were enough food in the trailer for Zoe's dinner. And if the old man had spent all his money on booze—again. Some fool playing for peanuts held no interest to Ryder.

That changed—quickly. Ryder stood, impatiently waiting to cross the street—the light at this crosswalk was always slow. The guitar guy sat under an awning, out of the direct sunlight, when he called out to Ryder.

"Hey, kid."

Ryder pretended he hadn't heard. He didn't talk to many people. Never strangers. Especially ones that sat around on the dirty city sidewalk all day.

"Skinny kid. You with the dark, shaggy hair."

The man raised his voice enough to get Ryder's attention—and the people closest to him. Several sets of eyes turned his way as if to access the musician's description. They saw a boy who was tall for his age. It was easy to see that he was too slender. What they couldn't know was that Ryder was always hungry. He ate when he could, but he made certain his sister ate first. The dark hair came from his father. Its tendency to curl? Who knew. Maybe the mother who left when Zoe was a baby? A distant relative? What did it matter? It was Ryder and Zoe against the world. He didn't know what genetics were, let alone care how they worked.

Ryder squirmed, wondering why the light didn't turn. He didn't like being the center of attention. The fewer people who noticed him, the better.

"Boy, has that changed," Quinn teased lightly.

Ryder smiled, his hand absently caressing her smooth, bare thigh. "I *have* become an attention whore."

"On stage," Quinn clarified.

His smile widened. This woman *got* him.

"What did the guitar man want?"

"To show me my future."

Not that the man, or Ryder, understood the significance of their brief meeting. But it changed Ryder's life. As for the man? Who knew. Ryder returned to the spot years later, but the man wasn't there. Not surprising. However, Ryder had hoped to thank the man. To let him know that he had saved an aimless boy—given him a dream.

"Hope."

"Yes," Ryder agreed with Quinn's simple yet profound interpretation.

Hope. A small word, but so often it could be the difference between giving up and finding something—no matter how small—to hold onto.

The man called out to him again, but this time, he spoke Ryder's language.

"I'll give you five bucks if you go across the street and buy me a mega bottle of water."

He was young and inexperienced, but Ryder knew when something sounded too good to be true. Five bucks? It was a fortune.

In spite of himself, Ryder drifted a little closer. "Why don't you go yourself?"

"This is my best time of the day. Lots of foot traffic. I underestimated how hot it would be. Hydration is key in my business, kid."

Ryder ignored the big word. He didn't know what it meant—nor did he care. Five bucks. The amount zinged through his brain. He could buy Zoe a hamburger off the dollar menu at Mickey D's. And the rest, hide from the old man. The money meant food, something that was always in short supply around the Hart residence.

He calculated the risk—almost none in broad daylight on a busy street. And the reward—huge. The answer was a no-brainer.

"I want the money upfront."

"I'll bet you do," the man laughed. "I'm taking a chance on you, kid. What if you take my money and never come back? No, buy the water, get the five bucks. That's the deal. Take it or leave it."

Ryder didn't have time to argue. He agreed. His long legs helped him complete the task in a flash and to his amazement, the man kept his word. Five bucks. Paid in crumpled one dollar bills. It was more money than Ryder had ever seen. To his embarrassment, he felt close to tears.

Then he heard the music and his tears were forgotten. Ryder was drawn to the melody and the rhythm. The syncopation unique to this man—though he had no idea what that was until years later.

"Like what you hear?" The man's fingers flew over the strings. "For a buck, I'll play you a song."

It sounded like a trap. Pay for a lousy song? If Ryder had *ten* dollars, he wouldn't waste it on something so ridiculous and unimportant. Clutching his money, Ryder slowly backed away, certain that at any moment, the man would attempt to snatch it from him. Then he turned and ran.

The money didn't last as long as Ryder would have liked, but it made a difference. However, the music. That stayed with him forever. It played through his mind. Sang through his blood. It became such a part of Ryder's life; he began playing records when his father was out. He knew what would happen if the old man found out, but he didn't care. He had to hear more.

"Music opened the world to me. Literally. I dropped my blinkers, the ones that took me from our trailer to school, and back. I began to look around. To listen. Songs are everywhere, Quinn. In the traffic. In the air. In our breath."

Ryder took Quinn's hand, laying it at the base of his throat. He drew air in, then let it out. In. Out.

"Feel that?"

"I do," Quinn nodded. "And it's unique to each person, isn't it?" When she brought his hand to her neck, she kissed the palm before laying it against her skin. "What do you feel?"

Holding her gaze, Ryder let Quinn's natural beat travel down his arm and into his body. His head began to bob. Slow. Steady. The melody—Quinn—came to him and he started to hum.

"Is that me?" Quinn asked in wonder.

"Sweet. Sexy. Complex." Not stopping, Ryder covered her lips with his, letting his impromptu song flow from him to her.

"That's me?" Quinn asked in wonder.

"That's how I see you."

The pleasure in her eyes made Ryder want to write a symphony. *Maybe*, he thought. *One day.*

"What do you call it?"

"I don't know yet."

Quinn was too easy. Like the woman, the title of her song needed more thought and consideration. And like this—what was happening between them—it needed fleshing out. This was the beginning. Ryder didn't know how it would end.

"How did you get your first guitar?"

"You are determined to hear the rest of this, aren't you?"

Ryder had hoped to talk Quinn into bed. He found the idea of exploring her body much more appealing than mucking through the shit pile of his childhood. Yet something strangely unexpected was happening. As he recounted the events, Ryder realized that there had been moments—small but memorable—that had been good. Even happy.

Taking Zoe for that hamburger had been one of those moments. Until now, he had almost forgotten. There was so little to laugh about in her short life. But seeing her face light up when she unwrapped that sandwich. Hearing her giggles when Ryder blew bubbles with his straw, making the Coke in his glass bubble like a mad scientist's lab experiment. He would have blown the entire five dollars if it meant giving his sister a rare chance to be a little girl.

"You want to know about my first guitar?" Ryder asked. His emotions for Quinn were bubbling like that newly remembered Coke, making it hard to think clearly of anything else. When she nodded, he closed his eyes for a second until he pictured the instrument and smiled.

"It was that good?"

"It was that bad." Ryder shook his head. "I found it in an alley. I cut through that place all the time. It smelled like... an alley, I guess. Old garbage and fresh excrement. There was always a drunk propped up against the wall and stray cats rooting around for something to eat."

Ryder hadn't meant to make it sound so Dickensian. If he added Fagan and the Artful Dodger lurking in the shadows, the portrait would have been complete—but inaccurate. It had been his life. Period. It wasn't scary or upsetting. It just was. He was grateful when Quinn didn't comment. She took his hand in hers. The gesture said more than words ever could.

"It doesn't sound like your typical guitar emporium."

Once again, Quinn made him smile.

"You sometimes find a gem in the least expected places. Or if not a gem, a warped, broken stringed facsimile. My hands actually shook when I picked it up."

There had been no doubt why the guitar had been thrown out. It was a piece of junk. The neck was broken. The wood scratched. But to Ryder it was beautiful. He picked it up, looking around—just in case—then rushed home with his newfound treasure.

Ryder hid the guitar under the rusty trailer where nobody— especially his father—would look. Some duct tape borrowed from a neighbor took care of the broken neck. After that, he was stuck. Having a guitar was one thing. Figuring out what to do with it was another. Ryder tried to imitate the street musician but quickly discovered his untried fingers wouldn't move that way.

Finding Mrs. Finch had been a fluke—the luckiest of Ryder's life.

"She lived near us, though the difference in her street and ours was like night and day. Pretty flowers grew in her yard. Her grass was green. Her windows were clean and shiny. I knew people lived like that, but I didn't know *them*. One day I saw a *Help Wanted* sign in her window."

Ryder figured he would earn enough money for guitar lessons. Little did he know, his lessons were waiting behind those clean, shiny windows. Mrs. Finch had been reluctant to hire someone so young, but the desperation—the *want*—must have been obvious. She took a chance. And Ryder made certain she wasn't sorry.

"Mrs. Finch let me bring Zoe after school."

"I think I'm in love with Mrs. Finch."

"She never asked why or what happened behind our battered trailer door. I don't think she wanted to know. But in her way, she looked out for us. She fed us cookies and taught me the guitar. Later, I taught Zoe."

Ryder laughed at his own joke. *Taught* Zoe? His sister was born knowing how to play the guitar. It hadn't taken her long to surpass him. Soon, she was showing him.

"A star was born." Quinn touched the callouses on Ryder's hand. "Is Mrs. Finch still around?"

"She was at the Chicago show."

"Really?"

"I leave tickets for her whenever we're in town. She comes. Watches. Then leaves. I've asked her backstage, but she never takes me up on it."

"She must be very proud," Quinn said. "Of you *and* Zoe."

"I like to think so."

Quinn didn't ask anything else, and Ryder was happy to hold her close. The air smelled sweet, ripe with night sounds unique to Aruba. A calmness settled over him. He liked talking to Quinn. He liked the way she listened, occasionally injecting a question to either focus his story or lighten a heavy moment. She seemed to understand that he wouldn't be pushed. His words had to come from a natural progression—or not at all.

"About my father." Ryder felt a twinge of tension enter his shoulders. "About *Flowers On the Wall*."

"Not tonight," Quinn whispered. Again, she seemed to understand. "Another time. When and if you're ready."

"Thank you, Quinn." Ryder kissed her forehead.

"Anytime."

Ryder lifted Quinn into his arms, heading inside. Tenderly, he undressed her, touching her soft skin reverently. So beautiful. So kind. Ryder went to his knees, placing his head over Quinn's heart. If he were a different man, he would wish for more than he deserved. Perhaps—if he were very lucky—she would give it to him.

"Do you want me?" he asked, looking into her eyes.

"Yes."

Smiling, Ryder stood. A woman like Quinn wanted him. For tonight. For tomorrow. For a little while. Did he deserve her? Probably not. But he would be a fool not to enjoy what she offered. For as long as possible.

CHAPTER SIXTEEN

QUINN KNELT ON one knee to get the perfect angle. She knew what she was looking for. Because her subject was incapable of taking a bad picture, it was the mood—the emotion she wanted to capture.

"I can't believe you took this from the plane," Ryder sat the fedora on his head at a cocky angle.

Quinn shrugged, snapping another shot. "I thought it might come in handy."

The truth was, the instant she saw the hat on Ryder's plane, Quinn had pictured him just like this. Dark pants, no shirt, and the fedora. The suspenders and the attitude came directly from Ryder.

"Why did you pack a pair of suspenders?"

"Don't you like them?" Ryder plucked at the black elastic as he would a string on his guitar.

Did she like them? They were sexy as hell. Starting at Ryder's waist, traveling over his bare chest, over his shoulders and crisscrossing his sleek back, the suspenders drew attention to everything good about his upper body. Quinn knew for a fact that Ryder had a firm body. She had kissed every luscious inch—multiple times. Muscle without bulk. His arms alone were enough to make a grown woman weep with want.

"I like them just fine. But why do you need suspenders in Aruba?"

"So you can take my picture," Ryder said in his best smartass tone. When Quinn lowered the camera, staring, Ryder laughed. "Aruba wasn't our first destination. Remember? I packed for Indiana and a week at your father's house. Hence, suspenders."

How could she have forgotten? Their brief layover in Quinn's hometown seemed like months ago, not days. Her father hadn't called or left a message. Not even a terse text—his specialty. Except for the bar and Ryder's impromptu jam with the local band, Quinn had put the visit out of her mind.

"Hence?" She smiled, calling Ryder out for what he would have called *fancy talk*. "Nice word."

"I may be uneducated, ma'am," Ryder tipped his hat in her direction. "But I can sound as highfalutin as the next guy."

"Yes, you can."

Ryder loved to joke that he was a high school dropout. The fact was, he had read more and seen more than any man she had ever known. He might not have a piece of paper lauding his intelligence. However, no one who met him would ever call Ryder Hart *uneducated*.

"Are we almost finished? I feel like a swim and…"

"And…?" Quinn prompted. She had known Ryder long enough to know what *and* meant. She just liked hearing him say it. In detail.

"I want to take that sweet dress off your delectable body."

"Go on."

Quinn raised the camera. She hadn't known it when they began, but this was what she had waited for. The look on Ryder's face. The glint in his dark eyes. That half smile on his lips. These pictures would burn up the paper they were printed on.

"I think I will start at the top. I crave your mouth."

Quinn let out a slow breath. Ryder had a way with words. He didn't want her mouth. Or desire a kiss. He craved. It was a good thing she was already on her knees. The way he looked at her made her legs turn to jelly.

"You like when I take your nipple between my teeth, don't you, Quinn?"

Quinn cleared her throat. "You know I do."

"What is better? My mouth on your breasts or between your legs."

"I have to choose?" As Ryder moved toward her, Quinn somehow had the presence of mind to continue snapping pictures.

170

"Is that what you want?" Reaching for her camera, Ryder carefully loosened her fingers. Quinn hadn't realized how hard she was gripping it. "Do you want both, Quinn?"

Quinn licked her lips as she watched Ryder toss the fedora across the room.

"I want everything," she whispered.

Ryder dropped to his knees, his body close enough for Quinn to feel the heat radiating from his tanned skin.

"Everything?" Ryder said, his lips brushing hers. "I think I can handle that."

THERE WAS SOMETHING about the breeze in Aruba just as the sun set. Quinn took a deep breath. As she stood on the porch of their bungalow, it was easy to imagine that nobody else existed. Just Ryder and her. She let out a private laugh. Them—and the waitress clearing away their dinner dishes.

Dazzled, Quinn watched the colors in the sky change as though swirling in her own personal kaleidoscope.

"Will that be all, Ms. Abernathy?"

"Yes. Thank you, Pella," Quinn said to the young woman who worked at the hotel.

Ryder had gone for an after-dinner run on the beach. Quinn didn't know how he could exercise right after he ate, but it certainly worked for him. Quinn preferred a long swim in the early morning.

"Would you like me to add croissants to your morning order? Our pastry chef makes them fresh every Friday morning. He is famous for—" Pella's voice broke. She sniffled once before tears started running down her face.

"What's wrong?"

Quinn put an arm around Pella's shoulders, leading her to the sofa. They hadn't spoken more than a few words since Quinn and Ryder arrived, but Quinn knew the young woman was a native of the island and was saving to go to college. In spite of his teasing, Ryder was someone who appreciated higher education. Quinn knew that he planned on leaving her a *very* generous tip.

"I'm sorry." Pella wiped at her face. When Quinn handed her a tissue, she sent her a watery smile.

"Tell me what happened."

"My best friend's father…" Pella hesitated, blowing her nose. "He…"

"Take a second. Is there something I can do to help?"

Pella sucked in a shaky breath. "No. It's just that her father has been out of work for some time and had health problems. This afternoon he took his own life."

"Oh, Pella. I'm so sorry." Quinn pulled Pella closer, lending her sympathy. But at the same time, Quinn's thoughts went to Ryder. She was grateful he wasn't here to be reminded of *his* father's suicide. "You should be with your friend."

"I'll go to her as soon as I finish my shift." Pella wiped her eyes before standing. "I'm sorry, Ms. Abernathy. I shouldn't have broken down like that. It suddenly hit me again."

"Don't apologize. Go back to the hotel and splash some cold water on your face." Her arm still around Pella's shoulders, Quinn led the young woman to the door.

"I need to get back. Thank you, Ms. Abernathy."

"Pella. If you see Mr. Hart, please don't mention this to him."

"I won't. I promise."

Quinn leaned against the bamboo post, watching Pella's retreating form. The world was a crappy place sometimes. So many bad things happened to good people. Whoever wrote the rules got it wrong way too often.

"Nobody cried when my father died. Not me. Not Zoe. I think there may have been a party, but no one was crass enough to invite us."

"You heard." Quinn turned. At the end of the porch, Ryder stepped out of the shadows. "I'm sorry."

Dressed in nothing but a pair of running shorts, Ryder shrugged. In his hand, he carried his shoes which he carelessly tossed onto the padded swing. Taking Quinn's hand, he walked into the bungalow.

"I'm going to take a quick shower."

"Ryder—"

"If it makes you feel better, I'll leave the bathroom door open, but believe me, Quinn. I'm fine."

"Are you?"

Ryder turned his head, his eyes meeting hers. "How do I look?"

"Calm." Quinn looked harder. Ryder's eyes were clear—no sign of pain or torment. Frowning, she reached out, dropping her hand when Ryder stepped back.

"The only good thing that bastard ever did was stick a gun in his mouth and pull the trigger. I came into this world on September fourth. But May twenty-second, the day my father died, was the day I was born."

Ryder must have sensed Quinn's confusion. Leaning over, he cupped her cheek, giving her a light kiss.

"What can I do?" she asked.

"You're here. That's all I need."

To Quinn's relief, when Ryder said his shower would be quick, he meant it. She poured him a glass of water, left it in on the living room table, and had just started to pace when there he was. His dark hair was damp, and his face flushed from his run and the warm shower. Without a word, she walked into his arms.

"Feel bad for Pella and her friend, not for me." But Ryder didn't argue when Quinn tightened her arms around his waist.

"I can do both."

Quinn felt Ryder rub his cheek against her hair, listened as he breathed in her scent. The simple actions soothed her nerves, and she realized that she needed his comfort more than he needed hers.

"It was never my father's suicide that haunted me, Quinn. Or the abuse." Ryder sighed. "Okay, that might be stretching it. I used to wake up in a sweat, thinking I could hear that song—convinced my father was outside my door."

"Come."

Quinn tugged Ryder's hand until he followed her to the bed. She climbed under the covers, patting the mattress, inviting him to join her.

Ryder ran a hand through his hair and sighed. "Quinn, I told you, I'm not upset."

"Then humor me. Besides, when have you ever objected to getting in bed with me?"

"I prefer you are naked when I do." But Ryder did as Quinn asked. His lips quirked when she arranged him on his side facing her, but again, he went along.

"Happy?" he asked when she was settled.

"On my way." Quinn laced her fingers with Ryder's. "Do you want to tell me what he did to you?"

"Do you want to hear?"

"No." Quinn knew it would rip her guts out. "But I'll listen if it will help."

"It won't. But thank you for offering." Ryder kissed the back of her hand. Then again, lingering. "I went to a shrink just after we hit it big. I had the money, so I figured, why not? It's what people do, right?"

"Did it help?"

"No," Ryder scoffed. Then after a little thought, he shook his head. "Maybe. Hell, I don't know. The dreams are gone, but they had started to fade on their own. I can't seem to let go of that song."

Quinn gently pushed a lock of Ryder's hair back from his face. It was getting so long, almost brushing his shoulders. It gave him an air of the vulnerable little boy. She wanted to hold him tight and protect him from the world even though she knew he neither wanted nor needed her to do so.

"What did the doctor say about that?"

"She said when I was ready, I would know." Ryder's laughed, the tone self-deprecating. "As you witnessed in Chicago, I'm not ready."

"You will be."

"How do you know?"

Quinn searched for something profound and wise. But she only had one answer.

"Because I believe in you."

Ryder's eyes widened with surprise, the spark of pleasure touched Quinn deep inside. Ryder's opinion meant a lot to her. If felt good to know he felt the same.

"You shouldn't. I'm not as solid a character as you think."

Quinn tapped Ryder's chest—just above his heart. "Feels pretty solid to me."

Ryder simply shook his head. "I didn't know I had a Pollyanna on my hands."

"I don't believe the world is perfect. I *know* you aren't." Ryder grinned, making Quinn's heart beat just a little faster. "However, there is nothing wrong with hoping for the best."

Ryder didn't answer. Instead, he turned onto his back, his eyes staring at nothing. Quinn could hear his steady breathing and the hum of the turning ceiling fan. She could tell there was more—something he wanted to tell her. She waited patiently, letting him say it in his own time.

"There is something about the day my father died." Ryder's voice was low, but steady. "I lied. To Zoe. To the police. To my shrink."

"Lied?"

"I told everyone that I found my father's body. That isn't the truth."

There weren't a lot of possibilities. If Ryder hadn't found his father, did that mean he…?

"I can practically hear your mind working." Ryder rubbed a hand over his face. "No, I didn't kill him."

"I wouldn't have blamed you."

Quinn's response was met with a bark of laughter. Ryder didn't turn his head, but she could see the trace of a smile on his lips.

"I thought about it a few times. Hell, sometimes it was *all* I could think about. I didn't know what would happen to me—I didn't care. But I couldn't risk leaving Zoe alone."

Always the protector. Quinn wondered if Ryder saw himself that way. She didn't think so. His love for his sister—his absolute commitment to keeping her safe—was absolute. Ryder wouldn't consider it anything out of the ordinary. But she was certain Zoe knew better. And so did Quinn.

"*Did* your father kill himself?"

"Yes. But he waited until I was there to do it."

Quinn gasped. Of all the things Ryder could have said, that was a complete shock.

"Ryder. That's..."

"Fucked up?" Ryder blew out a long breath before taking in another. "That pretty much sums up Bennett Hart's entire existence."

It was so unbelievably cruel, Quinn had trouble taking it in. Then she remembered what that man had done to his son. Why should she be surprised that a monster would be capable of one last monstrous act?

Ryder closed his eyes. When he spoke, his tone was matter-of-fact. "He left me something,"

Quinn felt a tingle up her spine. How much worse could it get?

"It couldn't have been good."

"Depends on your perspective. I walked into that trailer not knowing it would be the last time. My father sat in his chair, the gun in his lap. I thought it was for me."

As though she were watching it unfold, Quinn felt frozen in place, unable to move. She doubted she could if she tried.

"Bennett Hart was a man of few words. He told me the world was a horrible place and one day soon, I would figure out that it never got better. So his parting gift to me was a do-it-yourself guide to ending it all. Then he put the gun in his mouth and pulled the trigger. Goodbye, Bennett. Goodbye, nightmare."

And hello new one. Quinn didn't know what to do. Ryder was so calm he didn't need her anger. How could she rage against a dead man? She could hate Bennett Hart, but again, what good would it do? Ryder had moved on as best he could—once again protecting Zoe. He didn't want her to know. If it were up to Quinn, she never would.

"You can't un-see something like that."

"Let me hold you." When Ryder didn't move, Quinn forced the issue. She scooted close, wrapping herself around him like a human cocoon. "I know you're fine. I'm not. Hug me back, damn it."

"Bossy."

"You bet your fine ass."

Resigned, Ryder allowed Quinn to take charge. Though he didn't know it, it was exactly what he needed. The tone of Ryder's voice had belied the tension in his body. He felt like a shaft of metal—unforgiving and alarmingly cold. Reaching for the blanket, Quinn pulled it over them. Then she rubbed his arms and willed the heat of her body to transfer to his.

Quinn couldn't have said how much time passed. She didn't care, she wasn't going anywhere. If it took a day or a month of Sundays, she would stay. She wasn't moving. At some point, she became aware of the things around them. The room was bathed in moonlight. The smell of wildflowers perfumed the air. And Ryder's breathing had changed to a steady, shallow rhythm. Glancing at his face, Quinn let out a sigh of relief. He was asleep—just what he needed. Brushing her lips against his forehead, she said a silent thank you when she found the skin to be warm instead of icy.

Holding the secret of his father's death inside for so long had been hard enough. Letting it out had taken a toll neither of them expected. Quinn hoped Ryder was through the worst.

A sudden need came over Quinn—one she didn't want to control. Carefully, she eased away from Ryder until she could reach her phone. Checking him again, she kept a hand on his arm while she dialed with the other.

"Hello?"

"Hi, Dad," Quinn whispered. She didn't know what time it was in Aruba or Indiana. And she didn't care.

"Quinn?" There was a gruff edge to her father's voice—an air of impatience. Another time his, *why are you bothering me* tone would have bothered her. Tonight, Quinn's thoughts were elsewhere, and she barely noticed. Or rather, it didn't matter.

"Dad, I—" Quinn swallowed, trying to clear the lump that had popped up in her throat.

"Is everything okay?"

The concern in her father's voice was almost her undoing. Quinn swallowed again, looking at Ryder's sleeping figure. No matter what, even though he drove her crazy, her father was a good man. She lightly rubbed Ryder's arm. Quinn knew more than ever how lucky she had been. How lucky she *was*. She would never take it for granted

"Everything is fine. Great. Dad?"

"Yes?"

"I love you."

CHAPTER SEVENTEEN

THE NEXT MORNING, Quinn rolled to her side, reaching for Ryder. As her hand encountered nothing but a cold, empty space, her eyes flew open. Instantly awake—and panicked—she sat up. Had Ryder left? Had last night been too much? Did he regret opening up to her? Had he left for good? Those questions, and a dozen more, swirled around Quinn's head. Before she could check the closet or form a plan, Ryder strolled into the bedroom, carrying a large tray.

"Fresh-squeezed orange juice. Hot coffee. And croissants that would rival anything you'll find in Paris."

Ryder set the tray on the nearby table, sat on the edge of the bed, then pulled her close for a long, good morning kiss.

"You're in a good mood." Quinn didn't tell Ryder what road her thoughts had traveled before he returned. He was smiling. His eyes were bright and clear. That was all that mattered.

"I woke up full of energy and hungry as a bear." Ryder fed Quinn a bite of pastry before taking one of his own. "I took an early run. I had just gotten out of the shower when the waiter arrived."

"How late is it?" Quinn couldn't believe she had slept through all of that. Normally, it didn't take very much to wake her.

"A little after eight." Ryder smoothed back the hair from her face. "It's a beautiful morning, Quinn. Thanks to you."

"Me?" Quinn took a sip of juice. Mmm. Her favorite. "Thank Mother Nature."

"You know what I mean."

Quinn had wondered if Ryder planned to bring the subject up. Now that he had, she wasn't certain what to say.

"I listened."

Ryder shook his head, apparently not satisfied with the way she shrugged it off. "If it were as simple as that, I would have told someone years ago."

"Friends?" Quinn hoped that was true. When Ryder nodded, she could have sworn her heart sighed. "And lovers."

"Friends *and* lovers." Ryder digested the thought. "That's a new one for me."

"Me too."

"I like it."

Ryder sounded so pleased—like a little boy with a shiny new toy—Quinn couldn't help but laugh.

"Me, too."

The rest of the week flew by. Quinn was happy to let the sun-kissed days tick by at their own pace. However, she hated to see the nights sail by in the blink of an eye. It wasn't the sex—though that took her breath away and made her body sing—it was the long talks. For the first time, Quinn felt free to ask Ryder anything without fear of breaking the rules. His friends and Zoe were still off limits, but Ryder was an open book. Fascinating and never dull.

There was one subject that Quinn hesitated to broach. It was the night before they were to leave. Ryder sipped a glass of wine, Quinn had opted for iced tea, as they sat on the porch swing, his arm comfortably resting on her shoulders. The silence was peaceful, broken only by the creatures of the night and Ryder humming. They were so relaxed, so at ease. Quinn didn't want to spoil the moment by dragging up one more taboo subject. But she had to know.

"What happened to your mother?"

"I have no idea."

Ryder's response was so matter-of-fact. So dispassionate. Quinn found it hard to believe that he was that blasé.

"Your father never talked about her?"

"My father rarely talked about anything. She left." Ryder shrugged. "I was too young to remember her so she must have left soon after Zoe was born. I know it's hard to imagine, but sometimes mothers aren't maternal."

"I understand that, Ryder." At least theoretically. Once more, Quinn silently thanked her parents for doing the best they could. She promised herself to visit her mother as soon as possible. "Haven't you ever wondered what happened?"

"Honestly? I never think of it—or her." With his finger, Ryder lifted her chin, meeting her gaze. The look in his eyes was a little sad, but Quinn had the feeling he felt worse for her than himself. "Tina Hart—that's her name—gave birth to me. She may have been a decent mother for the next three years. Or not. Why she left was between her and my father."

"But—"

"You can't understand because you love your mother. I don't miss what I never had."

"What about Zoe?" Quinn knew she was close to crossing the line Ryder had drawn in permanent ink. There was a natural crossover between Ryder and Zoe's life. A few questions were bound to involve his sister.

"You would have to ask her." When Quinn let out a frustrated sigh, Ryder smiled. "Not because I refuse to answer. Because I don't know. Zoe used to ask about her, but she stopped after our father's death."

"Would you have a problem if Zoe tried to find her?"

Slowly, Ryder shook his head. "It is up to her. Maybe she's already tried." That made him frown. "I don't want her to think she would have to keep it to herself."

"Zoe is an enigma." To put it mildly.

"You haven't had the chance to get to know her."

"Does she ever drop her attitude?"

"Nope." Ryder sounded pleased—almost proud. "She earned it legitimately. Nobody takes down a mean girl like Zoe Hart. However..." Ryder lowered his voice to a conspiratorial whisper. "If you ever tell her this, I'll deny you got it from me. Inside? If she loves you? She is nothing but marshmallow fluff."

That was hard for Quinn to picture. Even around Dalton and Ashe, Zoe had an edge. She laughed at their jokes and smiled when she didn't think Quinn was looking. But fluff? Zoe? Quinn would never say so, but when it came to his sister, it was possible that Ryder wore big brother blinders.

"What are your plans after we leave paradise?"

As Quinn asked the question, it suddenly hit her. They were leaving *tomorrow*. It had passed in a blink of the eye. She had to prepare to say goodbye to Aruba—and Ryder. Two weeks. Fun and games. No strings. No commitment. No future. Those had been the unspoken terms. Terms that sounded perfect at the time. The problem was, she hadn't expected to care so much.

Quinn hadn't planned on falling in love.

However, Quinn knew a broken heart was a small price to pay for what she had gained. Every moment she had spent with Ryder was worth all the years she would spend without him. It was that simple. If she could go back—knowing everything that was to come, including the way it would end—she wouldn't change a thing. Quinn had never loved before. Not like this. She knew—broken heart or not—that the sweet would always outweigh the bitter.

"I need to get my ass hopping. We are supposed to hit the recording studio at the end of next month. If I don't start to write, it will be a mighty thin album."

"What about the others?"

Quinn knew that Ryder wrote the bulk of the band's songs. However, Dalton and Ashe were first-rate wordsmiths and Zoe's ability to write a tune was well documented.

"We'll get together. Right now is solo time. The band spends so many days and nights together that we deliberately block out a few weeks away from each other. I have a cabin in Sierra, Nevada. Rustic is putting it mildly. It has a generator and running water. No cell service. A barely passable road."

"Sounds God-awful."

"I love it—for a week. Two max. After that? Pretty much God-awful."

Quinn laughed. "Is there an indoor toilet?"

"I had one put in when I bought the place."

"Smart man. Nobody needs to run the risk of meeting a bear on the way to do his business. Especially at three in the morning."

"There is hot water, too."

"Did I say God-awful? What was I thinking? It is practically the Hilton."

Ryder nuzzled the top of Quinn's head with his cheek. He hadn't shaved in two days, and the stubble snagged her hair. She found the tug on her scalp oddly appealing. Then again, it was Ryder. There wasn't much he could do that she didn't like.

"You could come for a visit."

"To your cabin?" Quinn's heart rate increased. "What about your songwriting? Besides, I need to get back to work."

"You won't disturb me. Bring your camera. The mountains are a photographer's dream. You'll make a fortune on the pictures." Ryder lowered his voice to a deep, sexy timbre. "At night, we can play Parcheesi and dab Aloe Vera on each other's mosquito bites."

"You make it almost irresistible."

Quinn didn't know how to take Ryder's invitation. He sounded serious. Yet the tone was teasing. He would be happy to have her company—but would he care if she turned him down?

"It is tempting, but I better not."

"How about for a long weekend? I dab a mean Aloe Vera."

The more Ryder pushed, the better it was for Quinn's ego. However, her ego was just fine the way it was. Her heart was another matter. At this moment, leaving him was doable. It wouldn't take much—like a long weekend—for Quinn to forget her common sense—not to mention her pride.

"There are plenty of women who would be thrilled by the invitation. Especially if it involved you dabbing their anything."

"I don't want *any* woman. I want you." Ryder's eyes narrowed. "You pulled away. What is going on, Quinn?"

Quinn didn't pull away. She jumped to her feet and walked across the porch.

"Stop pushing, Ryder. Please?"

"Tell me what happened?" Ryder stood, but to his credit, kept his distance. "Is it the cabin? I know it isn't a bungalow in Aruba, but—"

"I don't care about that. I don't care about the indoor toilet or hot running water. I—" Quinn took a deep breath. How the hell had she backed herself into *this* corner? "That has nothing to do with it."

"If you won't speak to me, how can I know what's wrong? How can I fix it?"

Normally, Quinn would have cheered Ryder and that piece of wisdom. She valued talk over silence. For once, she didn't think the truth would do either of them any good.

"You won't like what I have to say."

Blissfully unaware of the bombshell coming his way, Ryder sent her a cocky smile.

"I'll judge that for myself. Hit me with your best shot."

It felt like Ryder had issued her a challenge. Quinn never backed down from one of those. "I'm in love with you."

Quinn had wanted to knock the smile off Ryder's face. She got her wish—and then some. Ryder's face turned white, and he looked slightly sick to his stomach. She hadn't expected him to jump with joy, but this was borderline insulting.

"No, you aren't."

"I know how I feel, Ryder."

Obviously frustrated, Ryder sighed. "Quinn. I can't—*I don't*—love you."

"I know." Before Ryder could react, Quinn cut him off. "I know it would be easier for both of us if this hadn't happened. And I know the smart thing would have been to keep it to myself."

"Amen to that," Ryder grumbled.

"Hey, fella." Quinn jabbed the air in Ryder's general direction. "You're the one who pushed. But you know what? I'm glad I said it."

As she heard her words, Quinn realized it was true. Perhaps it wasn't wise to put herself out there with no hope of anything but disappointment and heartbreak. But there was something freeing about saying the words. She loved her parents. But she was *in love* for the first time in her life. And damn it, whether he knew it or not, Ryder needed to be loved by someone other than his millions of anonymous, blindly adoring fans. He had let her in—further than anyone else. She had seen his demons. They didn't scare her. She wasn't repelled or shocked. She loved Ryder Hart. Not the rock god. The man. Fears, foibles, and all.

Looking at them, one would have thought Quinn was the one rejecting Ryder. He looked so distressed. So hurt. On the other hand, Quinn felt strangely at peace. Perhaps the truth did set her free.

Ryder turned away, his hands reaching out to grip the porch rail. "I don't want to hurt you."

"Then don't." Quinn wrapped her arms around Ryder's waist. Resting her head on his back, she breathed in his scent. "Be my friend, Ryder. Let me love you."

"I am your friend, Quinn. That will never change."

"Don't be sad, Ryder. I'm not."

Seemingly resigned, Ryder took Quinn's hand. Tugging, he reversed their positions.

"Tell me what to do," Ryder whispered, his breath caressing her ear.

"Hold me." Quinn turned. "Kiss me." She sighed when he followed her request. Her fingers slid through his thick dark hair, drawing him closer. "Now, take me to bed and love me the only way you can."

Without a word, Ryder lifted her and carried her into the bungalow for the last time. Quinn took in everything. The curve of his lips. The touch of his hands. His taste. One last memory to last a lifetime.

CHAPTER EIGHTEEN

LIKE THE OPENING of an old door in a creepy horror movie, the ropes supporting the hammock between the huge pine trees creaked threateningly. Unconcerned, Ryder shifted his weight. The hammock—and the rope—was new, expertly installed by the skilled technician who had delivered it directly to his door. Not only had Burt Pollard assured Ryder that his company's product would withstand gale-force winds, the man turned out to be a fan.

A little conversation and an autograph later, Ryder had Burt's word that the hammock was there to stay. *And* that nobody would discover Ryder's location. Burt swore his lips were sealed.

Ryder had taken both of Burt's promises with a grain of salt. No matter his good intentions, things happened. But so far—three weeks later—the hammock was rock solid and so was Ryder's much-needed solitude.

As he stretched his arms over his head, Ryder watched one lone fluffy cloud float through the sky. The evergreens that surrounded his cabin didn't let in a lot of light. The trees were thick and had been there for hundreds of years. He could walk for miles without finding more than the occasional clearing. Besides the unpaved road, access was minimal.

It was exactly the reason Ryder purchased the one-bedroom cabin. The chances of someone *dropping by* were slim to none. Visitors were strictly invitation only. Since he wasn't there to socialize, those invitations were few and far between.

The last person Ryder asked had turned him down, and though Quinn's reason was a good one, he hadn't been able to get her—or her reason—out of his head. He missed her. It was that simple. He hadn't laughed since they said goodbye. Or smiled. When Quinn had been with him, he had done both with ease and frequency.

Ryder had lost track of the number of times he had reached for Quinn in his sleep. The sex had been unbelievable. However, it was her company he missed the most. It should have passed by now—the need to be with her. To talk and laugh and do nothing at all but hold her hand.

Ryder sighed. Quinn believed she was in love with him. Closing his eyes, he let himself remember how he had felt in the first seconds after she said the words. Before he was reminded why it was impossible.

Pride. Hope. Reality.

The pride that a woman as amazing as Quinn would trust her heart with him. The hope that maybe Ryder Hart wasn't destined to spend his life writing about something he had never experienced—or believed he ever would. The reality that he didn't know how to love Quinn and if he tried, he was bound to disappoint her—killing her love forever. Like his brown eyes and his lean build, Ryder's genetic make-up was set. Love was not a Hart trait. His father had proven that over and over again.

You aren't your father. Ryder groaned. He could hear Quinn's voice as though she were beside him in the hammock, snuggled close. How many times had she told him that he was a good man? He didn't kick puppies. He didn't hurt the weak and defenseless. That was true—thank God. Yet the facts were what they were. Love—whatever that was—was a mystery. Ryder could see it. He could write words that made the heart sigh. But he had no idea how to live it. Quinn deserved someone who did.

Scrubbing a hand over his face, Ryder absently pulled at his beard. He looked the part of the mountain recluse. He hadn't shaved in over a month. When he looked in the mirror, Ryder barely recognized himself. Now that he was past the itchy stage, he thought about keeping the look. It would make a damn fine disguise—for about five minutes. Fans were a surprisingly observant lot. Long, shaggy hair and a wild beard wouldn't fool the faithful for long.

Shaking off his wandering thoughts, Ryder reached for the guitar he had propped against the tree. The point of this trip had been to write songs for the next album. As always, he found the utter peace and quiet inspirational. Ryder believed the stuff he had written was some of his best. All they needed was some input from his band. They knew how to help him smooth the rough edges—or leave the edges exactly as they were.

Ryder strummed the strings, letting his mind find that place where magic happened. Access wasn't always possible, but when it was, there was no feeling like it. Before he realized it, Ryder played the notes of a song he hadn't been able to brush aside. *Quinn's* song.

No matter how Ryder tried, he couldn't let it go. Every time he began to write, this one melody pushed its way past the others. Stubbornly, he pushed back. Ryder had fifteen completed songs. Why wasn't that enough? Why wouldn't this one leave him be?

The solution was simple. Ryder should pack up his things and head to Los Angeles. It was time. *Past* time. The last time he drove to the nearest town for supplies he had called Zoe to check in. One more week, he promised. That was eight days ago.

Something kept him here. Ryder plucked out the opening chords haunting him. He knew what was wrong. Finishing the song he had started in Aruba would feel like the end to something logic told him was already over. Quinn was out of his life, and it had been his choice. He could stay—alone and frustrated—refusing to let it go. Or he could *write the damn song.*

Ryder swung his legs out of the hammock. Purposefully, he clutched the guitar and headed for the cabin. If he were going to do this, he was going to do it right. He closed the door behind him. Ryder needed three things. A beer. A comfortable chair. And his iPhone.

The cabin was rustic. However, Ryder liked to exaggerate its lack of comfort. The furniture was perfect for a long writing session in the wingback chair, followed by an afternoon nap on the soft as down corner sofa. There was little variety in the view—trees and more trees. But nobody would argue that what could be seen from the large plate-glass window was picture pretty.

The appliances in the kitchen were old. Vintage was the term used by the realtor. Since Ryder didn't cook, nor did he plan on starting, the refrigerator and microwave were all the modern conveniences he needed.

The cabin wasn't home. It was where Ryder hibernated. Rested. Worked. It served a purpose. If he wanted luxury, he would check into a four-star hotel.

Ryder took out a cold beer, twisting the top from the bottle. Finding his favorite spot, he picked up his guitar, reached for his phone, and hit record. As his body settled, he closed his eyes, focused, and waited for the magic.

GETTING OVER A man—the man—wasn't as easy as some would have her believe. There were endless articles chronicling the proper path. Do this, then that, and finally the other thing. Boom. Her heart was mended. As far as Quinn could tell, it was mostly common sense, tears, and a boatload of alcohol. She had never been a fan of taking the advice of a stranger—even one of hundreds who purported to be an expert.

Quinn had been home for a month. She hadn't cried, and she wasn't going to take up drinking. The last thing she needed was a pounding head to accompany her heavy heart. Common sense told her to give herself as much time as she needed. Eventually, she would stop thinking of Ryder first thing in the morning, last thing at night, and every other minute in between.

However, Quinn was certain of one thing. If she wanted to move on, the pictures on her computer—and the ones she had plastered on the walls of her workroom—were not helping.

Pushing back from her desk, Quinn used her chair to slowly turn in a circle. There he was in all his glory. Ryder Hart. He had started as a job—a boost to her career. A stepping stone to bigger and better things. According to her editor at *Rolling Stone*, that was exactly what was about to happen. When her photo layout hits the stands next week, the magazine brass expected record sales.

Exclusive access to the notoriously publicity-shy Ryder Hart Band was more than buzz-worthy. For Quinn, it was a potential game changer. She already had three new jobs lined up and her agent fielded offers from all over the globe. Quinn Abernathy was officially in demand. She wouldn't give Ryder all the credit. It took more than aiming a camera to produce a great picture. But he was a big part of it.

Ryder could have nixed her big break before it happened. Now she had everything she had dreamed of. Unfortunately, dreams were not stagnant. They grew—expanded when she wasn't paying attention. Professionally, she was golden. Personally? Quinn wasn't sure how to answer that. She wasn't miserable. Or inconsolable. She was… sad. Not as sad as a month ago. But the difference was negligible.

"What am I going to do about you?" Quinn asked, scanning the printed pictures.

There were hundreds from the tour. However, her favorites were the ones she had taken in Aruba. Ryder wearing the fedora. Handsome didn't begin to describe him. Sexy. Magnetic. Ryder was a natural in front of the camera. Quinn could have made a small fortune off *one* of the shots. Closing her eyes, she sighed. That would never happen. The moment had been too personal to share. Instead, she chose to torture herself with image after image. She couldn't have him. Why not spend hours reminding herself?

Straightening her spine, Quinn slammed her hand down on her desk. "Enough."

When had she become a self-involved wallower? Whether he was here or not, loving Ryder was something to celebrate, not mourn. Determined, Quinn pulled the first picture from the wall. Then the next. And the next. She had each one cataloged and filed on her computer. Making prints had been self-indulgent foolishness. Quinn was booked on a flight to Boston at the end of the week. It was a short trip, but she was determined to make a fresh start when she returned. That meant not having Ryder's face greet her as though he lived here.

"I live alone, Mr. Hart." Quinn sealed the photos in a manila envelope before exiling them to the bottom drawer of her desk. "Someday when I have gained a little perspective, I might let them see the light of day. But for now, I can at least pretend that out of sight means out of mind."

Armed with a new attitude, Quinn took a break. It was afternoon, and she had skipped breakfast. Unless the grocery elves had paid her a visit, her cupboards were bare. She always kept peanut butter on hand. The bread wasn't fresh, but she wouldn't call it stale either. With a glass of milk, it would do just fine. She was just reaching for a plate when there was a knock at the door. It had to be one of her neighbors. The tenants were very good about not letting strangers in. If it were a delivery or a guest, she would have heard the buzzer.

Quinn wasn't exactly dressed for company. She had combed her hair that morning, pulling it back into a messy bun. She wore no makeup—nothing new when she was at home. Her jeans had seen better days, and the baggy t-shirt was a faded yellow from many, many washings. Feet bare, Quinn padded across the hardwood floor. She didn't bother to check the peephole. Her neighbors had seen her after a three-day bout of the flu. If she hadn't scared them off after that, she wasn't worried.

The second Quinn opened the door, she regretted her decision. Zoe Hart didn't wait for an invitation to enter—she barreled into the apartment. There was no point in asking how Ryder's sister had gotten into the secured building. One look at Hurricane Zoe and only a fool would have stood in her way.

It was obvious that something had Zoe wound up. Without preamble, she tore into Quinn. "You unscrupulous, duplicitous, greedy bitch. We trusted you. No, I take that back. Ryder trusted you. The rest of us trusted Ryder. He will never forgive you."

Perhaps it was a lack of food, but Quinn's first thought was that she should have combed her hair. And put on some lipstick. When an avenging angel came to call, it didn't help when she looked like she had just stepped off a fashion magazine, and Quinn looked like she was one step away from homeless. Zoe's jacket alone must have cost a fortune. The gray leather set off her blue eyes to perfection. Then Zoe's words kicked in, and Quinn's appearance became the least of her concerns.

"What did you call me? Unscrupulous? Duplicitous? Greedy?"

"Don't forget bitch," Zoe growled. Her heels clicked as paced across the small living room.

"I'll give you that one." At the moment, the other woman labeling her a bitch was the least of Quinn's worries. "But you'll have to explain the rest."

Blue eyes blazing, Zoe took something from her purse, tossing it on the coffee table.

"How much did they pay you? I hope it was plenty." Zoe looked Quinn up and down. "You certainly didn't spend it on your wardrobe."

"Now who's the bitch?"

Quinn picked up the paper. It was obviously a supermarket tabloid. One of the big ones. The headline was typical—overblown and filled with conjecture and innuendo.

The Secrets of the Ryder Hart Band. The backstabbing. The jealousy. Is the end near? An inside source tells all.

"You've been around long enough to know how these rags work, Zoe."

Quinn winced at the badly photoshopped pictures. Ryder looked like he was ready to murder Dalton. Ashe and Zoe were in some kind of odd, supposedly romantic clinch. It was typically awful.

"I would agree if I hadn't read the story. There are things in there that have never been printed before."

"About Ryder?" Suddenly concerned, Quinn rifled through the pages.

"About all of us."

Quinn skimmed the two pages. There were more bad photographs. The rest was personal but hardly earthshaking. Mostly things about Dalton. Ryder was hardly mentioned.

"It wasn't me, Zoe."

"Right," Zoe sneered. "All the years we've been together without more than the occasional crap speculation popping up, and suddenly the band is featured on the cover of every tabloid in the country. Not to mention the internet gossip sites. Why now?"

"Is this really all over the place?" Quinn sat down, giving the article a closer run through.

"Yes. A friend of mine alerted me to it this morning."

"What did Ryder have to say?" Quinn couldn't imagine that his reaction had been as over-the-top as Zoe's.

"Luckily, he's been someplace where he doesn't have access to this crap."

"Is he still at his cabin in the mountains? I thought he would have been back by now."

"You know about Ryder's cabin?" Zoe's eyes narrowed. "Nice. You have enough information to keep you in ratty t-shirts and ripped jeans for years."

"Damn it, Zoe." Quinn jumped to her feet. "I am not the source. I doubt there is one. Most of the stuff in the article is pretty general."

"And some of it is very specific. Too specific not to come from someone close to one of us." Zoe stared her down. "I came here to tell you that you've been outed. Don't try to contact Ryder. If you do, I will take you down."

With that coldly worded warning, Zoe headed for the door.

"It couldn't have been me, Zoe."

"Why should I believe you?" Zoe asked, halfway out the door.

"I would never do anything to hurt Ryder. Or any of you. I love him, Zoe."

That seemed to make Zoe pause—but not for long. The steel in her gaze hardened. "Join the club. Thousands of women claim to love my brother. It hardly makes you unique." With a swing of her long, blond hair, she slammed the door behind her.

Quinn sank to the sofa. With her index finger, she absently tapped the tabloid. Suddenly, an idea hit her. Pushing aside the front page, her gaze moved down the index page until she found what she was looking for. Quinn smiled, reaching for her phone. Sometimes old contacts came in handy.

Hurricane Zoe. One wouldn't know it to look at the room, but Ryder's sister had left potential disaster in her wake. Hopefully, Quinn could do her part to clean it up.

CHAPTER NINETEEN

RYDER FOUND DALTON and Ashe exactly where he expected them to be. In the recording studio arguing over arrangements. It was always something irreconcilable. The two of them came from different places—geographically and musically. Ryder often wondered how it worked. But it did. Before long, Dalton would give a little. Unless the first move came from Ashe. Either way, when they caught each other's rhythm, nobody in the business could rival their ability to find the perfect mix.

"Have you come to blows yet?"

It was a running joke—funny because, in their hot-headed youth, more than one punch had been thrown. Now, they settled things in a less violent manner. However, Dalton and Ashe had never lost their passion for the music. It gave their recordings an edge that others had tried and failed to duplicate.

"Well, look what we have here, Dalton." When he spotted Ryder, Ashe took off his headphones. "How's it hanging, Jeremiah Johnson?"

It wasn't the most original joke, but it was accurate. Ryder had driven straight from his cabin to downtown Los Angeles without bothering to shave off his beard. He wanted to see his friends—and record a rough cut of his newest song.

"Get it out of your system," Ryder urged. "This afternoon, this look is history."

"It's good to have you back, man." Dalton pulled Ryder close, patting him hard on the back. "A few more days and Zoe would have sent out the National Guard."

"I lost track of time."

Ashe shoved Dalton aside to get in his greeting. Standing back, he gave Ryder the once over. "Other than the Grizzly Adams impression, you look good. Do I detect a spring in your step? You were dragging pretty low before you left."

Ryder thought of Quinn and smiled.

"I had an epiphany."

"No kidding," Dalton winked at Ashe. "Does she have a sister?"

While Dalton laughed at his own joke, Ryder opened his guitar case. After weeks alone, he was anxious to get a second opinion on the songs he had written. One in particular. Quinn's song hadn't turned out the way he expected. The finished product wasn't a mournful lament to what couldn't be.

"No rest for the wicked?" Ashe chuckled when Ryder began to tune his guitar. "You've been back all of five seconds. What's the rush?"

"This song is a little different for me." It was easier to show than tell. "Just listen."

Writing a love song had always been easy for Ryder. There was a tone he set and words he strung together. Those songs had been good. Hell, they had sold more copies than he could remember. But they were by rote. He could have done them in his sleep. When he said *The Road Back,* was different, Ryder wasn't exaggerating. This time, he hadn't written about some nameless, faceless person. This time, the words and music hadn't come from his brain. For the first time, they came from his heart.

Closing his eyes, Ryder strummed the opening chord. He didn't see the look Ashe and Dalton exchanged. Nor did he notice when Ashe began recording. From the opening note to the last, Ryder was lost in another world. When he finished, he hung his head, took a deep breath, and waited.

"What the hell, man?" Dalton shook his head.

"He's crazy," Ashe agreed.

Frowning, Ryder slowly set aside his guitar. Whatever reaction he had expected, this wasn't it.

"No good?"

"You know damn well it's great. Women will weep when they hear it. Shit, I got a little teary myself."

"Me too." Ashe slapped Ryder on the back.

"Then why am I crazy?"

"Because you're here instead of with Quinn. Unless you were communing with some mystery woman for the last month, I assume the song is for her."

"I…" It wasn't that Ryder wanted to deny Ashe's statement. But it was harder than he expected to say the words.

"Give the guy a break." Dalton grabbed three beers from the mini-fridge. He was never comfortable with showing emotions. "We're dudes. We aren't supposed to say that shit to each other." Handing out the bottles, he tapped his against Ryder's. "Save the declarations for your lady."

Ashe joined the toast. Taking a sip, he sent Ryder a speculative look. "Which brings me back to my original question. Why aren't you with Quinn? Play her that song. However you screwed up, that will be an apology she can't resist."

"I didn't screw up."

Ashe snorted. Dalton merely shook his head.

Okay, Ryder conceded, *maybe I had*. But not the way Ashe meant. There had been no blow-up. He and Quinn hadn't exchanged angry words that couldn't be taken back. Ryder's mistake had been not recognizing what had been in front of him the whole time.

"Are you going after her?"

Scratching at his beard, Ryder caught his reflection in the glass tabletop. That was the plan. After he had a shave and a haircut. If he was going to put his heart on the line, he didn't want to show up at Quinn's door looking like Leonardo DeCaprio in the *Revenant*.

"The jet is fueled and ready." Ryder tossed Dalton his phone. "There is a month's worth of songs. You guys can take a listen and we'll start work when I get back."

"Take your time." Dalton connected the phone to his laptop. "Have you seen Zoe?"

"I called her, but it went to voicemail. Is she in the building?"

"I haven't seen her today." The upload from the phone complete, Dalton handed it back to Ryder.

"Ashe?"

"No. I—"

"You're back!" Zoe burst into the studio. Tossing her bag in the general direction of the table, the contents spilling out across the surface. Unconcerned, she threw her arms around Ryder. "I should have known this would be your first stop."

Laughing, Ryder swung his sister in a circle. This was the Zoe he knew as a child. She never hesitated to smile or hug. When they were separated and put into foster care, she drew into herself, becoming shy and reserved. The adult Zoe didn't suffer from those maladies. However, it was rare for her to publicly show her affection. Hugging her back, Ryder savored the moment.

"You know me well." Holding her at arm's length, Ryder whistled. "You always look good, Zoe, but you didn't have to dress up just for me. Nice jacket. Is that new?"

Not quite meeting Ryder's gaze, Zoe tugged on the hem.

"I had an appointment."

Ryder knew his sister. Zoe met everything—and everyone—straight on. The only time she didn't look him in the eyes was when she had done something she didn't want him to know about.

"What's going on, Zoe?"

"And why did you fly to San Francisco?"

"What?" Ryder turned to see Dalton take an airline ticket from where it had fallen from Zoe's bag.

"I went to see Quinn." Zoe lifted her chin defiantly. "And before you ask, I had a good reason."

Ryder's stomach knotted. He could tell by the glint in Zoe's eyes that whatever had happened, it couldn't be good. Still, there was no point in overreacting before he had the facts. He watched as she hit a few buttons on Dalton's computer.

"There," she stepped aside. "See what that *photographer* did."

"I didn't realize *photographer* was a four-letter word," Ashe said.

"Fuck you, Ashe."

"Now, *that* is a four-letter word I recognize."

Ryder ignored Zoe and Ashe. Standing beside Dalton, he looked at the screen.

"*TMZ*, Zoe? Really?"

"Read the headline."

Ryder Hart Band Coming Apart at the Seams. Ryder sighed. It was the same old crap. *TMZ*—and their ilk—had the band breaking up every other month. Mostly, it had to do with his *mysterious* disappearance.

"They used the fact that I was out of town to up their advertising revenue. What does it have to do with Quinn?"

"This time, it's more than speculation, Ryder. They have facts that nobody knows but us. All the tabloids are running with it. This time, that ubiquitous inside source is real."

"You don't mean Quinn?" Ryder laughed. Then he realized Zoe was serious. "You're wrong, Zoe."

"What is it about that woman?" Zoe looked at Ryder, shaking her head. "From the moment you met her, you lost your common sense. She used you to make a quick buck, Ryder."

"Have you read this?" Ashe asked Dalton.

Dalton's reaction was grim. "I did."

"Quinn couldn't have done this," Ryder said emphatically. He wanted his bandmates—his friends to understand.

"What makes you so certain?" Zoe challenged.

"Because most of the shit concerns me," Dalton answered before Ryder could.

"So?" Zoe saw the facts; she couldn't understand why they weren't as incensed as she was.

"What Dalton understands without me having to explain is that I didn't tell Quinn anything about him. Or Ashe." Ryder met his sister's gaze. "Or you. She has a lot of ammunition that she could have used. But it all has to do with me. Nothing I shared with her—nothing, Zoe—is in that article."

To give her credit, Zoe had the grace to look contrite. Tentatively, she reached out her hand.

"I was certain I was right."

Since she was little, Ryder had done everything in his power to protect Zoe. How could he stay angry when she tried to do the same for him? As misguided as it had been, her actions were guided by love. He took Zoe's hand and squeezed. Ryder couldn't be certain, but he thought he saw a trace of moisture in her blue eyes. When was the last time he had seen Zoe close to tears? It was too long ago to remember.

"Quinn will understand." Dalton gave Zoe a restrained kick in the butt. Before she could release her wrath, he pulled her in for a hug. After a brief hesitation, she hugged him back. "It was this knucklehead who screwed up, Ryder."

"Quinn struck me as a forgiving woman." Knowing Zoe had her limits, Ashe refrained from a full-blown hug, opting for one arm and a quick squeeze. "She won't slam the door in your face. But just in case? Bring flowers and talk fast."

It wasn't bad advice. But ordering flowers was easy. He could have two dozen roses waiting for him at the airport. No, Quinn needed his words, not an easy gesture.

"Ryder?" Zoe asked as he grabbed his jacket and headed for the door.

Impatient, Ryder sent her a questioning look.

"May I drive you?"

It wasn't an apology. Zoe would wait until they were alone for that. A car ride to the airport would be a good start. Once Ryder worked things out with Quinn, it would be up to his sister to smooth things over.

Ryder slung an arm over Zoe's shoulder.

"Come on. I have a woman to woo."

THE ADVANTAGES OF living in San Francisco were too numerous to list. Quinn had fallen in love with the city at first sight. The culture. The abundance of fresh produce and seafood. The people. And the fact that no matter where she went, the workout she received walking up and down the many hills was better than anything she would find at an expensive fitness club. The street outside her apartment building was a perfect example. A simple trip to the grocery store and she could almost picture her muscles getting stronger—her legs getting long and lean.

Quinn gripped the handles of her eco-friendly totes. She had gone a little overboard, but she justified the purchases as necessary pantry staples. Her cupboards were bare. The dried pasta and boxed crackers would last for months—years, if push came to shove. Fresh fruit and vegetables were always a must. When she was in the mood for a big green salad or a crunchy apple, nothing else would do.

Admittedly, she could have passed on the freshly baked Caramel Pecan Dreams. But a dozen of the irresistible treats hadn't added that much bulk to her already overflowing bags. Like the salad and the apple, when Quinn needed a sweet treat, there was no substitute for ooey-gooey. The fact that they reminded her of Ryder purely coincidental.

Shopping had been a good distraction. However, as Quinn rounded the corner and began the last of her trek home, she couldn't help but think about Zoe and her accusations. Did Ryder believe his sister? Did he think she had taken his trust and broken it into a million pieces? Money was a huge motivator. Perhaps, like Zoe, Ryder would forget everything he had learned about her and think Quinn cared more about padding her bank account than their friendship—or her love.

The truth wasn't pretty—in cases like this, it seldom was. Quinn had called a contact at the tabloid. The woman owed her a favor—a big one. She had initially balked at revealing the source—it was against the paper's policy, and even gossip rags had ethics. Of course, those ethics were surface-shallow and easily skewed to fit the situation. It didn't take Quinn long to get the information she needed.

A few years ago, she had suppressed some pictures that would have ruined the other woman's marriage. Quinn would never have published the photos. She had deleted them from the camera and destroyed the hard copy. However, a favor had been promised. Until today, Quinn hadn't been able to imagine a reason arising for her to cash it in.

Stopping halfway up the hill, Quinn set the bags on the sidewalk. She took out her phone, checking the texts and missed calls—for the tenth time. No, make that eleven. Nothing had changed. There was nothing from Ryder. Either he was still at his cabin or Zoe had gotten to him and… What? Quinn closed her eyes, her head falling back. It was the not knowing that drove her crazy. If Ryder believed the worst, Quinn wouldn't blame him. Or so she told herself. Zoe was his sister. They were enviably close with a long and emotional history. Quinn was new—a blip on his timeline. But damn it, she wanted him to at least hesitate before condemning her outright. Was that too much to expect?

Call him. It wasn't the first time the thought had crossed Quinn's mind. She ran her thumb over Ryder's number. It was tempting. With a shake of her head, she put her phone away before she gave in. The ball was in his court. He could get in touch or delete her from his life altogether. It was a depressing thought. Ryder wasn't her lover. With the push of a button, she would cease to be his friend. What would that make her? Irrelevant? Forgotten? Quinn sighed. She knew what she was. Pathetic.

Quinn had just bent to retrieve her bag when she heard the music. The faint sound of a lone guitar picking out a melody that was strangely familiar. *Twinkle Twinkle Little Star?* Whoever was playing wasn't an expert, but Quinn admired the effort. It was better than she could do.

As she drew closer to her apartment building, the sound grew louder. Intrigued, she recognized the young girl. Molly Ionesco lived with her mother and older brother on the third floor, one down from Quinn. Della Ionesco was a hard-working single mother who was raising two well-behaved children. They weren't close, but they would stop and chat occasionally.

"You're doing great, Molly. When did you start playing?"

"Last month. Mom bought me the guitar for my birthday. It's hard."

"So I understand. I recognized the song you were playing. That's a big accomplishment."

The ten-year-old grinned, showing Quinn the gap where her front tooth used to be. Molly was a pretty little thing with big brown eyes and straight, shoulder-length hair. She would grow into the guitar, but right now, it was almost as big as she was. Determined, the girl scrunched up her face and haltingly repeated the song.

"That's better, Molly." The voice came from behind Quinn. "Remember. Technique is easy. Play with passion. That's the secret."

Ryder. Slowly, Quinn turned as though afraid she was hearing things. He could have been an illusion, but if he were, Molly must have had the same hallucination.

"My school is having a talent contest next week." Tongue stuck out in extreme concentration, Molly played the last two notes. "All I care about is beating Tami Reinhold. She is *so* stuck up. Thanks for the lesson."

Waving goodbye, Molly raced up the steps and into the building, clutching her guitar to her chest.

Ryder chuckled. "Passion. Petty jealousy. Whatever works." Still smiling, he looked at Quinn. "Cute kid. She kept me company while I waited for you. It seemed only fair to give her a quick tutorial."

"I wonder what Molly will say when she finds out that Ryder Hart gave her a music lesson?"

"I introduced myself. She was not impressed."

Quinn doubted that. If she knew anything about tweener girls, Molly began burning up her social media accounts the second she entered her bedroom. As for Quinn, she tried to figure out why Ryder was here. He didn't look angry. In fact, he looked relaxed, carefree, and sexy as hell. She hadn't thought she was a beard fan. But on Ryder it worked.

"Have you spoken with Zoe?"

"I have." Ryder no longer sounded relaxed. His dark eyes narrowed. Grim. Quinn didn't know if that was directed at Zoe—or her. "Let's not talk about it out here."

Ryder took the bags from Quinn. Without a word, she started up the steps.

"I thought you would call."

"I planned on coming to see you before the crap with Zoe went down. She simply accelerated my timetable." Ryder waited until the elevator door closed behind them. "Sorry about the beard and long hair."

"The look works on you." Every look worked on Ryder.

"You think so?" Looking pleased, Ryder pulled at the curly hair above his lip. "Maybe I should keep it."

"God, no," Quinn exclaimed.

"You said it worked."

"The beard is sexy as hell, Ryder. But the world wants to see your handsome face."

"And you?" Ryder moved closer, backing Quinn against the wall. "What do you want, Quinn?"

Swallowing, Quinn opened her mouth to answer just as they arrived on her floor.

"Saved by the bell?" Ryder laughed as they walked down the hall.

"You know what I want, Ryder. Nothing has changed." Quinn opened her apartment door. Standing aside so Ryder could enter. "Just put the bags on the counter."

"Zoe screwed up."

Ryder leaned against the counter, his arms crossed over his chest. His scuffed hiking boots, faded jeans, and plaid flannel shirt suited his overall look. Mountain man chic.

"I know why she did it. You are always looking out for her. She wanted to do the same for you."

"I'm glad you understand. But that doesn't change what Zoe did. I know you had nothing to do with that story, Quinn."

"Just like that?" Relief flooded through Quinn. She didn't know whether to laugh or cry. A little of both wasn't out of the question. "Not even a moment of doubt?"

"No." Ryder didn't move, but his intense gaze searched Quinn's face. "Only a fool relies on blind trust, Quinn. I knew before I read it. That article isn't your style. If you wanted to make a fast buck, you would have sold the pictures."

"I will never sell them, Ryder."

With deliberate steps, Ryder walked to her. Taking Quinn's face in his hands, he lightly kissed her lips. "I know," he whispered, kissing her again. "If I didn't, I wouldn't be here."

"I meant what I said, Ryder. Nothing has changed."

"And for me, everything has changed. I love you, Quinn. No doubts. No hesitation. I'm yours if you'll take me. Think hard," he said, covering her lips when she would have spoken. "If you say yes, you'll be stuck with me for the rest of your life."

Quinn waited for the tears. It seemed like one of those moments when a woman was supposed to cry with happiness. When her eyes remained dry, she broke out laughing. She had never done things the way they were supposed to be done. Why start now?

"The rest of my life? I was hoping for longer. Forever and beyond."

Grinning, Ryder pulled Quinn close. "That sounds like a good song title. If you promise me first rights, you have a deal."

Needing to touch him, Quinn quickly unbuttoned Ryder's shirt. Tugging, it hit the floor followed quickly by his t-shirt.

"I have questions. Dozens of them."

"Me too." Ryder disposed of Quinn's jacket. "Do you love me?"

"Yes." Quinn sighed as Ryder kissed her neck.

"Then the rest can wait."

Before Quinn could do more than blink, Ryder sent her shirt and bra to the floor. The touch of his hands was enough to make her brain fuzzy. She wanted this—wanted him. Ryder was right. He was here. He wasn't going anywhere. And he loved her. That was all that mattered. They could fill in the details later.

"I've missed you," Ryder whispered the words in her ear, his tongue bathing her lobe before he bit down, eliciting a moan from Quinn.

"Me?" Quinn teased, cupping him between his legs. Through the heated denim, Ryder's erection jumped in her hand. "Or this."

"It's one and the same," Ryder groaned when her grip tightened. "Thank God."

Before she could think of another quip, Ryder made it clear that playtime was over. He lifted Quinn into his arms and strode toward the bedroom. All things considered, it made no sense, but a thought suddenly occurred to her.

"I have ice cream in my shopping bag."

Ryder gave her an incredulous look then burst out laughing. "I'll buy you some more. Later. Much later."

"It's salted caramel," Quinn stated, hiding her grin.

"I don't care."

"Good answer."

Taking Ryder's face between her hands, Quinn kissed him. He lowered them to the bed, never breaking contact. She couldn't get enough. His taste. The feel of his lips against hers. She was a starving woman taking her fill. Ryder was the only man who could satisfy her cravings because *he* was what she craved. Nobody else.

"I'm sorry. I was an idiot to let you go."

"I agree." Rolling to her knees, Quinn unfastened Ryder's jeans. She eased them over his hips and down his legs. "You came to your senses."

"I did," Ryder shuddered when she kissed the inside of his thigh. "Do you forgive me?"

"There's nothing to forgive. You're here, my love." Quinn licked Ryder's stomach, then his chest. "I love you."

"I love you." Ryder rolled Quinn to her back. "It feels good to say it. I love you, Quinn. I love you." When he heard Quinn's chuckle, Ryder smiled. "Too much?"

"Never. It's music—the sweetest you've ever played."

The look in Ryder's dark eyes made Quinn's heart beat faster. He wanted her. He loved her. It was all there. Too much? She would live a lifetime without growing tired of his words or his touch or his gaze.

"Forever?" he asked, lowering his body to hers.

Quinn opened her arms and her heart, breathing a sigh of happiness. "At least."

CHAPTER TWENTY

DINNER CONSISTED OF take-out pizza and cookies for dessert. It wasn't a grown-up choice, but Ryder figured they had plenty of time to eat healthily. *Forever.* He liked the sound of it. The future had always been about his music and his friends. Dalton, Ashe, and especially Zoe. Their band and their careers. That had been the focus of Ryder's life for so long. That single-minded focus had made him a very successful, very rich man. It had also almost cost him the love of his life.

"Are you cold?" Quinn asked when she felt Ryder's shudder. She pulled the blanket higher.

"I'm fine." Ryder brushed his lips over Quinn's bare shoulder. Dinner in bed with Quinn—naked. It made the food taste that much better. "Continue with what you were saying?"

"Right." Quinn reached for the last slice of pizza. The box was at the foot of the bed, and her movement gave Ryder a nice view of her rounded butt. "I understood that Zoe wanted to protect you. I admire her intentions—even though her venom was aimed at me."

"Zoe knows she was wrong."

Quinn nodded. "It's fine, Ryder. My only concern was how you would react."

"You thought I would jump to the same conclusion as my sister?"

"I wouldn't have blamed you."

"Come on. Tell the truth." Ryder searched Quinn's eyes. "You would have been disappointed."

"Disappointed, yes," Quinn nodded. "However, I hoped you would ask for my side of the story before you made your final condemnation."

"Final condemnation?"

Quinn rolled her eyes. "If you tell me that's a great title for a song, I swear…"

"No. Maybe for a head-banger band." Ryder thought about it for a second, deciding his initial instinct had been correct. "I like the way you phrase things."

Quinn hesitated. "What if there had been something damning in the article? Something private that you had shared with me?"

"It would have raised a red flag." Ryder wasn't going to lie. "I had realized that I loved you. I think—I know I would have come to you before I *made my final condemnation*." Ryder said the last bit with a deep, doom-laden tone.

"Funny." Quinn jabbed a finger in his ribs. Knowing his weakness, she hit his ticklish spot with admirable accuracy.

"That's playing dirty." Since Quinn didn't have a similar affliction, Ryder chose a different form of retaliation. His deep kiss turned Quinn into a sighing, pliable woman. "Now I can have my way with you."

"You already did. Twice." Smiling, Quinn pushed Ryder away. She took a sip of water before biting into her pizza. "I found the source of the story. Norris Mayhue."

"Dalton's brother-in-law?"

When Quinn nodded, Ryder reached for his phone, cursing a blue streak. "Way to bury the lead, sweetheart."

"You distracted me," Quinn reminded him. Then she mumbled, "And don't call me sweetheart."

"Get used to it. I'll be calling you all kinds of things in the years to come."

"Years to come?" Quinn beamed. Realizing what he had said and liking the sound of it, Ryder beamed back. "Will all the things you call me be nice?"

"I doubt it." Dialing Dalton, Ryder laughed. "We are bound to rub each other wrong—on occasion. Take it from someone who has spent a lot of time around people I care about. Arguments happen. It can be a good thing."

"I was young when my parents divorced. But I remember that they argued—all the time. That was *not* good."

Understanding her hesitation, Ryder took Quinn's hand, giving it a comforting squeeze. "I didn't have parental role models either. We'll figure out our own way."

"Trust and respect." Quinn brought his hand to her lips. "And love."

"We already have all three. We're way ahead of the game." Ryder met Quinn's gaze. "Sweetheart."

"You're right." She waited two beats. "Baby."

Giving her a quick kiss, Ryder nodded. "There you go."

Ryder frowned when Dalton's phone went to voicemail. He looked at the time. Eight-thirty. Unless Dalton had gotten lucky—which wasn't out of the realm of possibilities—there was no reason he shouldn't answer. After leaving a brief, *call me*, he hung up.

Quinn slipped out of bed. Pulling on her robe, she began cleaning up. "Are you worried?" she asked as she tossed a used napkin into the empty pizza box.

"Concerned." Tapping the keypad, Ryder brought up Ashe's number. "Dalton has always had a short fuse. He's better than he used to be, but I want to make certain he doesn't to do something stupid."

"Ryder." Ashe sounded upbeat. That was a good sign. "Tell me you have good news. Should I break out my tux?"

"You don't own a tux."

"You're right. I burned that sucker when I turned eighteen. I swore I would never wear one again, but for you and Quinn, I'll make an exception."

"It's a little too soon for that." Ryder had to ask Quinn to marry him before they planned the ceremony. "Is Dalton around?"

"Listen."

Ryder waited. It didn't take long for him to hear what Ashe meant. The sound was faint but distinct—like hail hitting a tin roof. Relaxing, Ryder gave Quinn a thumb's up.

"How long has he been at it?"

"Close to an hour. Dalton will wind down soon." Though Ashe tried to hide it, Ryder could hear the concern in his friend's voice. "He called his sister as soon as you left."

"He suspected it was Norris?"

"That's right. Dalton wanted confirmation before he said anything to you. You know that Maggie can't lie worth shit— especially to Dalton. The bastard got a lousy thousand bucks for the story."

"At least Dalton chose to pound his drums instead of Norris."

"It was a near thing," Ashe said, tone taking on a serious note. "It wasn't what was in the article, it was the sense of betrayal. Dalton sends his sister money every month. We all know that she doesn't see very much of it. And this is how Norris pays him back? It hit Dalton pretty hard."

"Is Zoe there?"

"I'm waiting with the bottle of bourbon. Zoe has a sympathetic shoulder. Between us, we'll get Dalton to the other side."

"Thanks, Ashe. I hate not to be there, but…" Ryder reached for Quinn. A second later, she took his hand.

"Is it all good on your end?" Ashe asked.

"Luckily, I have an understanding woman. So, yes. All's good."

"Then take care of each other. We have Dalton's back. See you when we see you, brother."

"Family comes in all kinds of packages."

Ryder should have known that Quinn would understand She had seen them together. Zoe was his sister. Ashe and Dalton were his brothers. Simple as that.

"They have been there for me no matter what."

"We'll leave first thing in the morning," Quinn said with matter-of-fact conviction. "Unless you think we should go now."

"Dalton has Ashe and Zoe." Ryder slid his arms around Quinn's waist, resting his head on her soft breasts. "Thank you."

"Hey, I'm getting the brothers and sister I never had." Quinn smoothed back his mop of hair. "Make that brothers. I don't know if Zoe will ever accept me."

"She will." Quinn looked at him, doubt—and laughter—shining from her eyes. "Eventually. Zoe is a hard nut, but she can be cracked. I have faith that the two of you will end up the best of friends."

"I don't want to push my luck. I'll settle for her not sneering whenever I walk in the room."

Smart woman. Ryder toyed with the belt. One tug and all of Quinn's lovely skin would be his to explore. Reading his mind, Quinn slapped his hand away.

"I have questions."

"Of course, you do." Ryder liked Quinn's inquisitive mind. And since her beautiful body wasn't going any place, he didn't mind settling back and letting her ask away. "What would you like to know?"

"What changed?" Quinn hopped onto the mattress. Sitting cross-legged, she angled her body until she and Ryder faced each other. "I know you love me."

Taking her hand, Ryder nodded.

"What is different now? When we parted, you were emphatic." Keeping his hand in hers, Quinn placed them over Ryder's heart. "This belongs to me—thank you very much."

"I missed you." Ryder knew it was an oversimplification, but it was the best place to start. "Then I *really* missed you. And no, it wasn't about the sex. Or at least not all of it."

"I missed you, too. I wish I had known you felt the same. It would have saved me some sleepless nights."

"I had a few of those." Trying to find the words was so much easier when he set them to music. "I've never liked singing to someone."

Quinn laughed—as he knew she would. "You do a great job of faking it."

"On stage is easy. Or sitting around with my friends. I'm talking about one on one. It feels strange. I wrote you a song." Taking his phone, Ryder pulled up the recording. "Remember the tune I hummed in Aruba?"

"I thought you were joking."

Quinn looked so pleased that Ryder was glad he had taken the time to record it for her.

"I was. But the tune wouldn't leave me alone. For some reason, I resisted, but the pull was too much. After you listen, I hope you'll understand."

It was hard to remember the last time Ryder felt these kinds of nerves. There had been a time when he was just starting out when he questioned whether he was a songwriter. Playing guitar and singing? His confidence knew no bounds. Ryder had the cockiness of youth on his side teamed with a hunger for success. A thousand experts could have told him that he would never make it. Ryder wouldn't have believed them. But putting his thoughts—his feelings—down on paper was something else.

Dalton and Ashe had drawn him out. Finding out that his friends were writers made the idea less foreign. One collaboration and Ryder had never looked back.

This was uncharted territory. Ryder had put his heart on the line. He knew with an unwavering certainty that he could trust Quinn. With his life. With his secrets and with that surprisingly tender, vital organ. He loved and was loved in return. But the fact that she held so much power made Ryder vulnerable for the first time since he was a child.

From the first note to the last, Ryder's eyes never left Quinn's face. He saw the wonder. The smile. The joy. The tears. Most of all, he saw that he got it right. The many countless reasons Ryder loved Quinn were in that song. Simple yet infinitely complicated.

"You wrote me a song."

Feeling a little teary himself, Ryder took a tissue from the bedside and wiped the moisture from Quinn's cheeks.

"I did."

"You love me." The way she hiccupped the last word made Ryder's smile widen.

"Who knew this damaged heart had it in it?"

"I did. At least I hoped." Quinn brushed her lips against his before snuggling close with a happy sigh. "What's it called?"

"*The Road Back.*"

"Thank God," she said emphatically. "I was afraid it was something like *Quinn's Song.*"

"Too obvious?" Ryder hadn't considered naming it after Quinn. He would have changed the title if she had her heart set on it. He should have known. They thought alike in so many ways.

"Too corny."

"And that is reason number three thousand six hundred and five as to why I love you."

"When are you going to record it?"

"Do you want me to? It belongs to you. Your decision." Ryder knew it would be an instant classic. But if Quinn didn't want to share something so personal, he would understand.

"Are you crazy?" Quinn exclaimed. "Ryder Hart loves me. What better way to let all those grasping, fucking groupies know that my man is off the market."

Ryder didn't know what he had done to deserve Quinn. His life had been good before they met. Why he was given more was a mystery he refused to question.

Pulling Quinn close, Ryder kissed her temple before he whispered in her ear, "I don't fuck groupies."

EPILOGUE

RECORDING SESSIONS WERE notoriously long. No matter how prepared or well-rehearsed, musicians were human. Singers forgot words. And then there was the dreaded technical glitch. That moment where the stars aligned for the perfect moment. Music and vocals blending to perfection. Boom. High fives all around. Then *boom*. The producer announces that the take was ruined.

Ryder had seen it all. Lived through the disasters and came out the other side. Which was why on the day they were to lay down the vocals for *The Road Back*, he prepared Quinn for long hours with stretches where nothing happened. It was her first time witnessing this side of the business.

"It isn't anything like you see in the movies."

"I understand."

"I don't want you to be disappointed."

"I won't be." Grinning, Quinn held up her camera. "I have permission to take pictures."

Nobody had objected when Quinn put in her request. Not even Zoe raised a fuss. As Ryder predicted, his little sister had warmed to Quinn. It was slight. The first step was when she issued a genuine invitation to go shopping. When they returned with no visible signs of blood, Ryder considered it a success.

Moving to Los Angeles—at least temporarily—had been Quinn's idea. She loved San Francisco. However, when the band was recording, Ryder needed to stay in a fixed location. Quinn did not. As long as she had her camera and a laptop, she could work anyplace. Since his house had sold the week it went on the market, and Ryder declared his apartment too utilitarian, they were staying at a downtown hotel.

"We should start looking for someplace permanent," Ryder proclaimed one night after room service delivered their dinner.

"Eventually," Quinn agreed, breathing in the aroma of the

perfectly cooked lasagna. She had quickly gotten used to the maid service and the food on demand. "Are we in a hurry?"

Funny how it worked. If Quinn was happy, Ryder was happy. Talk of moving was shelved until a later date.

"FINALLY," ASHE EXCLAIMED as Ryder and Quinn entered the recording studio. Unceremoniously, he pushed Ryder aside. Winking at Quinn, he scooped her into his arms. "When are you going to run away with me?"

"Tomorrow?"

"Perfect."

"Does that work for you, Ryder?" Quinn asked innocently.

"Sure." He shrugged. "Where are we going, Ashe?"

With an exaggerated sigh, Ashe set Quinn on her feet. "If it's a package deal, I'm out."

"Sorry, pal." Quinn gave Ashe a sisterly kiss on the cheek. "I have a friend."

"No." Ashe held up his hands. "Setups are out of the question."

"Hey, Quinn."

Dalton's hug was warm and welcoming. The drama with his family had blown over—for now. As soon as the album was recorded, he planned on flying east. Whatever had prompted his brother-in-law to strike out couldn't be handled over the phone.

"Are we ready to do this?" Zoe asked as she and Alden Christopher walked from the control booth.

Quinn had told Ryder that she was getting used to Zoe's cool manner. There was warmth hiding somewhere under that gorgeous fashion-plate exterior. No matter how long it took, Quinn was determined to find it.

"Ms. Abernathy." Alden Christopher nodded toward Quinn, his tone neutral.

Ryder rolled his eyes. Though Ashe and Dalton thought he was oblivious to Alden's feelings, Ryder knew how their manager

216

felt. Alden's unrequited love wasn't something he took lightly. But he had a choice. Ignore the situation or fire Alden. For ten years, his way had worked.

Now that Quinn was in the picture, the ball was in Alden's court. If the man couldn't find a way to treat Quinn with respect instead of thinly veiled contempt, Alden would have to go.

Ryder wasn't making a choice. There was none. Quinn was the woman he loved. Period. If it weren't for Quinn, Ryder would have already put an end to the situation. She didn't want Alden forced out because of her. Ryder agreed to wait. However, as he told Quinn, she hadn't done anything wrong. Alden had brought this on himself.

"Are the instrumentals ready to roll?" Ryder asked their longtime producer. The band did the arrangements and vocals. But they left the technical side to an expert and Buzz Sinclair was the best.

"Say the word," Buzz called out from the booth.

Ryder nodded to Dalton. Zoe touched his arm as she walked by and Ashe settled on his stool. Taking his headphones, Ryder went through his usual routine. Breathing in and out. Nodding toward Buzz, Ryder waited for the music. That was where it always started. On cue, he began to sing.

It was like nothing Ryder had ever experienced. No glitches. No forgotten words. Nothing but the blending of four voices creating... magic. Ryder didn't need inspiration. Quinn stood not three feet away. As he sang the last word. As the last note faded, she lowered her camera, her dark eyes telling him everything he would ever need to know.

I love you. Ryder mouthed the words.

I love you, Quinn responded silently.

"What the hell just happened?" Ashe laughed.

Zoe shook her head, a bemused smile on her face. "That was amazing."

"Amazing?" Dalton nodded. "I guess it was."

Ryder opened his arms and without hesitation, Quinn walked into his embrace. He breathed deeply. Surrounded by his friends. Holding Quinn. It was the only place he had ever belonged. The only place he wanted to be.

Ryder covered Quinn's mouth with his, and he knew. He was home.

__TURN THE PAGE FOR A LOOK AT__
__FLOWERS and CAGES__
__(Hart of Rock and Roll Book Two)__
__Coming In September__

PROLOGUE

TRIED, CONVICTED, SENTENCED, and on his way to the state penitentiary, Dalton Shaw had learned two things. He wasn't as tough as he thought. And behind bars, there was no such thing as a guilty man.

The black eye and split lip Dalton sported proved that a cocky attitude didn't impress anyone behind bars. Especially a bruiser who had used up his last strike and was going away for life. It could have been worse. The guard could have broken up the fight after Wiley Malone had done permanent damage.

"I wanted to smash that pretty face into a pulp," Wiley growled as he was dragged away. "Next time, Shaw. There will be one. Count on it."

The odds that Dalton would wind up in the same prison as Wiley was better than even money. The judge who sentenced him made it a sure bet. Three years—less than one if he kept his nose clean. But it was a long time to watch his back.

"There are rules," Ryder Hart, told him during their last visit before Dalton was relocated.

"What do you know beyond what you've seen on television?"

"I've done some research. So has Ashe. Zoe was the one who found you a tutor."

Ryder, Ashe, and Zoe. Dalton's bandmates. Friends. Family—a bond stronger than any blood relation. They were his lifeline and the only thing that had kept him sane. None of them had believed Dalton would do any significant amount of time. He didn't have a record as an adult and only minor scuffles as a minor. Beating the shit out of someone—no matter how well-deserved—was serious. But hard time? It didn't make sense. Unless you added in the fact that Dalton's victim lived in a small town where his daddy's influence ruled. Dalton's lawyer had tried to get the trial moved out of the county, but the judge refused.

"I need a tutor to go to prison?"

Ryder nodded. Dalton knew his friend was trying to keep a positive outlook, but his dark eyes were shadowed with worry. "Jock Lowe. It isn't exactly *Miss Manners*, but there is a definite way to do things."

"Fuck that, Ryder. It's prison."

"And like you said, all we know is what we've seen on TV or in the movies. Forearmed is forewarned, Dalton. Listen to what the man has to say."

Dalton knew Ryder was right. But it seemed so final. Like a movie, he hoped for a last minute reprieve. The sentence had been passed. Tomorrow the bus would take him to his new home.

How the hell had this happened? Dalton was twenty-two years old. The future had seemed so bright. *The Ryder Hart Band* had its first album coming out next month. The buzz was good—better than good. After years of barely scraping by, they were about to hit it big, and Dalton wasn't going to be there to share the moment.

"You need to hire a permanent replacement."

"Why? Are you planning on becoming a career criminal?"

"No, but—"

"Nobody can play the drums like you. It won't be the same, but we'll get by until you're out. Eight months—tops."

"What if it's longer?" The thought made Dalton sick, but it had to be said. "Things happen. The gray jumpsuit I'm wearing is proof of that."

"That's why we hired the tutor. He'll tell you how to avoid trouble." Ryder gripped his arm. "I'll never forgive you if you don't come back to us, Dalton."

"Time's up," the guard called out.

"I'm scared, Ryder." It was the first time Dalton had admitted it to anyone—even himself.

"We'll visit every week. Ashe, Zoe and me." Ryder hugged him. "Stay strong, brother. More important, stay smart."

The next morning, the bus to the prison was filled to capacity. Wiley Malone sat near the front, glaring at Dalton as he walked past. The tutor Ryder hired had given Dalton a plan—a course of action—beyond watching his back and cowering in his cell. It wasn't foolproof, but it was something.

Ankles manacled, Dalton shuffled to his seat. The man he was chained to tripped, sending Dalton crashing into the side of the bus. His shoulder took most of the impact.

"Sorry."

Dalton shrugged it off. Thanks to Wiley, his body was already covered in bruises. What was one more?

"Don Fitzgerald." The man held out his cuffed hand.

"Dalton Shaw."

"I shouldn't be here."

Closing his eyes, Dalton sighed. *Here it comes,* he thought. Since his arrest, he hadn't met a single person who took responsibility for their incarceration. If he believed every story, he heard the criminal justice system got it wrong one hundred percent of the time.

Railroaded. Screwed over. Framed. Pick your term. When those doors locked them in their cages each night, the prisoners slept the sleep of the unjustly incarcerated. Some were tormented by the knowledge. Others accepted their fate. But go ahead and ask. Not one of them was there because they had done the crime.

"I'm telling you, man, I blame that bitch I married. Sure, the drugs were mine, but the police never would have found them if I hadn't been provoked into knocking the shit out of her. A man can only take so much lip, right? She made such a racket the neighbors called the police."

Dalton closed his eyes, picturing himself smashing Don's face into the bus window. He wondered if a broken nose would shut the asshole up. Probably not. There was one good thought. At least Don's wife was rid of her abusive husband for the next three to five years.

"What did they jack you up for?"

"They didn't."

Don frowned. "I mean what shit did they trump up on you, man?"

"I put a man in the hospital because he liked to use his wife as a punching bag."

"Huh?" Don looked more confused than before. "You ain't saying you did it?"

Don's exclamation of disbelief got the attention of half the bus. Dalton felt like an exotic animal on display. A rare species that the prisoners had heard whispered about but never observed in person.

"That's exactly what I'm saying. I did it." Dalton looked around. "And given the chance, I wouldn't hesitate to do it again."

AFTER THE RAIN
(One Pass Away Book One)

PROLOGUE

LOGAN. LOGAN. LOGAN.

Logan Price closed his eyes, taking it all in.

"Hear that, kid?" Starting quarterback Gaige Benson slapped him on the back. "Two games under your belt and you're a star. Now let's go out there and add super to the front of it."

The announcer for the team set them in motion down the tunnel with his familiar introduction.

"And now, let's hear it for your division champion *SEATTLE KNIGHTS*."

The roar of the crowd. There was nothing like it. A packed stadium. Fans chanting his name. Few people would ever experience what it was like to take the field in a professional football game.

Logan Price had been working for this his entire life. He could still remember in exact detail the first game he ever saw. Too small to climb onto the stool in his father's bar by himself, his old man had lifted him onto the seat.

Stay and be quiet.

Not an easy order to follow for an active, inquisitive little boy. One look at the game and for once, Logan had no problem following his father's command. The old TV transported him to a foreign world filled with bright lights and shiny helmeted warriors. Logan didn't know what he was watching. He did know he wanted to be one of those men.

A Sunday afternoon in rural Oklahoma. *Lefty's Pub* was filled with after-church drinkers who figured they had done their duty to God and family. The rest of the day was their time. A beer. Or two. Or six. Cronies who understood a man's need to unwind before the start of another workweek.

And football.

If the Friday night high school game was their true religion, the Sunday afternoon games were a close second. As Oklahoma boys, they hated anything Texas. The men of Denville gathered every week to root for whichever team was playing the Dallas Cowboys.

No matter how the games ended. Whether the crowd was happy or disgruntled. It meant more drinking. Hours later, husbands, boyfriends, and sons would stumble out, pile into beat-up trucks, and weave their way home to frustrated wives, girlfriends, and mothers.

As he grew older, Logan's view changed. He moved from the stool to behind the bar. And he promised himself one thing. He would never become one of those men. He wouldn't spend the week at a job he hated. His home wouldn't be a semi-wide trailer filled with hand-me-down furniture and a wife to whom he couldn't face going home.

His Sundays were going to be spent playing football, not watching it.

"Ready to take down this vaunted Arizona defense?" Gaige yelled at him, butting helmets.

Vaunted. Good word, Logan thought. His QB liked to use what his granny called highfalutin talk. Must have been that Ivy League education. He knew that Gaige Benson didn't grow up with a silver spoon in his mouth. He came from the mean streets of Brooklyn. He had the scars to prove it.

Like Logan, Gaige had vowed to get out of the life into which he was born. In the process, he polished himself up like a new penny. He took advantage of his full-ride scholarship to Yale. He didn't spend all his time on the football field. Fancy vocabulary. Fancy clothes. Fancy women. They were all part of the package Gaige purposefully fashioned for himself.

Seventeen years after clawing his way out of the tenement that he grew up in, very little of that borough-rat remained. Until game time. No one was tougher than Gaige Benson. Three-time league MVP. Considered one of the best ever to play the game. No one stood in his way when he was playing the game. He had the scars to prove it.

"Gather round."

Knights head coach Harry Coleman gathered the team close. He had to yell over the crowd, but he had the voice to do it. Booming was putting it mildly. The first time Logan heard it, he stood right beside the man. The ringing in his ears didn't go away for three days.

"Divisional game. If I have to say any more than that, you shouldn't be out here. Go kick some ass."

The defense took the field to start the game. Arizona had a rookie quarterback drafted in the second round from a small college in the Midwest. The only reason he was out there was because the regular starter suffered a concussion in last week's game and the regular backup had food poisoning. Thrown into action at the last minute, Logan swore he could see the guy's hands shaking before he took the first snap. When the ball went sailing between his legs, Logan shook his head.

The moment was too big for some people. For Logan, it wasn't big enough. He aimed for the biggest stage of all. The Super Bowl. It wasn't a matter of *if* he would get there, but when.

"Three and out." Gaige grinned, pulling on his helmet. "Come on, kid. Let's go show them how it's done."

Logan ran onto the field. *Kid.* He shook his head, grinning. From the first day of training camp, Gaige had hung that moniker on him. Ironic since he was almost twenty-five, a good two years older than most of the other rookies. However, he supposed when someone had been in the league as long as Gaige, all the new guys seemed like kids.

"We're starting on the ground," Gaige instructed them in the huddle. "Sweep out left. Basic. Got it?"

Lining up as he had a thousand other times, Logan checked the defense. He knew he was fast. One of the fastest in the game. What set him apart was his anticipation. He had the uncanny ability to read the guy covering him. He knew when to fake left or when to fake right. Stutter step or flat out, in your face, catch me if you can.

His speed got him out of Denville, Oklahoma. His brains and determination got him to the NFL.

The sounds of the game were as familiar to Logan as the back of his own hand. The call from scrimmage. Each quarterback had his own unique cadence. Gaige was a master of mixing his up. Study him all you want. Good luck figuring it out. His teammates knew. A signal just before they broke the huddle.

Pay attention, you were golden. Slack off even once? Gaige could ream a guy out with the best of them. And he had no problem doing it in the middle of the game.

An entire YouTube channel had been devoted to Gaige and his rants. They were as legendary as the man himself. With a ball in his hand, he was cool as ice. The rest of the time, watch out.

No one would ever accuse Logan of lacking focus. Today was no exception. They were driving down the field. First and ten from the Arizona twenty-yard line. He already had three carries of thirty-five yards. It was going to be a good day.

"Ready to take it in?" Gaige asked.

"Always."

"Then show them what you've got."

A quick snap later, Gaige handed the ball to Logan. The offensive line created a seam. Not a big one. Just big enough. Using the push of his powerful legs, Logan surged through. One more step. They wouldn't catch him. No one could.

Like everything connected with the game, Logan heard the snap of the bone with total clarity. The agony that surged through his body was so intense he almost passed out. In the next few minutes, he was going to wish he had.

"Get back." Logan heard Gaige through the haze of pain. "Goddamn it. Move the hell off."

The three-hundred-and-fifty-pound linebacker didn't get off by standing. He rolled. Crushing Logan's broken leg as he went. He would never know if the move had been deliberate. Now, it was the last thing on his mind. He only cared about two things. How bad was the injury and when would he be able to play again.

"Hold on, kid." Gaige took his hand. "They're bringing the stretcher."

The team doctor checked his eyes. Logan knew he was asked some questions. What they were and how he answered, he would never remember. By the time they carted him off the field, Logan knew the break was bad.

"Gaige." Logan reached for him.

"I'm here, kid."

"Is it over?"

"The game?" Gaige walked with him, his head bent toward Logan. "No. But I promise we're going to win the bastard."

They loaded him onto the open cart. They had him secured and the vehicle rolled away before Logan had his answer. He wasn't wondering about the game. It was his career.

To no one in particular, he whispered the question again.

"Is it over?"

AFTER ALL THESE YEARS
(One Pass Away Book Two)

PROLOGUE

SEAN McBRIDE WOKE up with a smile on his face. It happened a lot lately. And he thoroughly approved.

He stretched his long, athletic body. Some mornings every inch of him ached. Such was the life of a professional football player. Everything was about preparing for the game. Focus. Concentration. The goal was to be ready for game day.

He had to hold it together for sixty minutes. Pull out a win any way possible. Sacrifice his body to the football Gods and pray he walked away healthy enough to do it all again next week.

Sean dreaded the day after the game. The adrenaline had long ago worn off and he felt all of his thirty years. There were degrees of bad. Sometimes he shuffled to the shower, the aches and pains palpable, but mercifully bearable.

Then there were the bad days. After a day of three-hundred-pound defensive backs using him as their own personal punching bag, he didn't get out of bed—he crawled.

Bruised from top to bottom, his joints creaked and his muscles protested like screeching banshees. Those were the times he wondered why he did it. He could have been a doctor. Or a lawyer. He could have taken his father's advice and gone into the family business. No seventeen-year-old with dreams of glory in the NFL wanted to think about becoming a butcher. But damn. Cutting meat sounded good on those mornings.

This was a good Monday. His body felt lithe—limber. The bruises were there. That was part of his life. However, yesterday had been one of those rare games when every moment fell into place.

From the kickoff to the final whistle, the outcome of the game was never in question.

Sean caught every ball thrown his way. He evaded the defense. Fast as the wind. Three touchdowns. One hundred and eighty-two total yards. A damn good day for any wide receiver. He would have had more if Coach Coleman hadn't taken him out of the game in the fourth quarter. With a big lead, there was no reason to risk injury when he wasn't needed.

The after-game celebration moved from the locker room to one of the team's favorite hangouts. Naturally the atmosphere was raucous. Cautiously so.

The Knights were having a stellar season. Ten wins, two losses. Sean and his friends had enough games under their belts to understand how quickly that could turn. Injuries tended to come in bunches. So far, they were healthy. However, that was bound to change. The hope was to get to the playoffs with all their major players on the roster.

After the game, they had a few drinks. Three was Sean's limit these days. A few years ago it was a different story. He would have closed the place down after a win. He and his bed partner of the moment would have moved on to someone's apartment, partying until dawn before going back to her place and fucking like demented rabbits. Then he would go home alone and catch a few hours sleep until it was time to grab a quick shower before heading to the Knights' headquarters to review film from the game.

Those days were over. Sean wasn't a kid anymore, high on his own press clippings and more testosterone than brains. Not that he had settled down completely. He could still party with the best of them. However, he chose his moments—ones that never took place during the season.

Women were another matter. Sean liked sex. Always had. If there were a God, he always would. While his bed partners weren't as varied, they were almost as frequent.

Sean knew players who abstained a few days before the game, saving their *juice*. He wasn't one of them. Sean had plenty of juice, thank you very much. Sex was necessary for a happy and healthy mind. For *his* happy and healthy mind.

A big plus to having sex at night was sex the next morning. It was one of his favorite things. A partner, warm and willing.

The perfect way to start the day.

Speaking of which. Smiling, Sean turned over. His hand reached out, expecting to find a soft, sweet woman. Instead, he found cold sheets. Sitting up, he looked around the room. Like the bed, empty. The bathroom door was open and the light off.

Not bothering to cover up, Sean jumped out of bed. Buck naked, he searched the house. She wasn't in the kitchen. Why would she be? She didn't cook, not even coffee. She was on a first-name basis with half the baristas in Seattle.

Was that it? Would she be back soon with two cups of steaming black caffeine and his favorite muffins? Sean was talking himself into that scenario when he saw the note.

He picked up the paper that had been propped against the lamp by the front door.

Sean.

Thank you for the past few weeks. After years of building it up in my mind, I was worried that it couldn't live up to my expectations. I should have known better. It was everything I had hoped for—and more.

We didn't make any promises. No strings were attached that need to be broken. After all these years, you can finally breathe easy. It's over. We are now friends without the expectation of benefits.

When we see each other, it will be as if it, we, never happened.

Sean read the note. Then read it again.

What the fuck? What was in those drinks?

Sean searched his memory for some kind of clue. The bar. His teammates. Then she was there. They laughed. Everything was smooth and easy. They seemed to be developing a rhythm. In his mind, they were together. Not a man and a woman—a couple.

It sounded good to him. He would have sworn she felt the same. He didn't want another woman. He wanted her. In his arms. In his life.

No expectations? Hell. He woke up with plenty of them, only to find out he was alone. Alone in bed. Alone. Period.

Sean scrubbed a hand over his face. He remembered the way she tasted. The way she melted into his arms. The curves of her luscious body pressed against his. Her sighs. His belief he would never get enough of her.

Crumpling the note into a ball, Sean tossed it across the room. Suddenly he felt every ache. His legs felt like lead. Slowly, he shuffled toward the bathroom. He needed a shower. Long and hot. Determined not to look at the bed, Sean's peripheral vision wouldn't let him off the hook that easily. It captured everything. The rumpled sheet. The pillow still holding the imprint of her head. A slash of red on the floor.

Frowning, Sean picked up the scrap of silk. So small he wondered why she had bothered. The image of her standing in nothing but her heels and the panties popped into his head. Unconsciously, his body tightened with desire.

Right, that was why.

Sean ran the smooth material over his cheek, feeling it catch on his morning stubble. He breathed deeply. He smelled vanilla and spice. Her essence. He would never forget it. As long as he lived, he would be able to close his eyes and conjure up her scent. Her taste.

His eyes popped open. *Friends? Nothing more? Bullshit!*

Keeping the panties in his hand, Sean headed for the shower. This wasn't over. Not by a long shot. It was just the beginning.

AFTER THE FIRE
(One Pass Away Book Three)

PROLOGUE

SHE HAD ONCE asked him if he believed in a higher power.

God? Buddha? Fairies dancing around a blazing fire late at night? Something. Anything bigger than us.

Gaige Benson hadn't known what to say. Not then. But as he stood in the empty open-air stadium—the stars lighting the evening sky—he knew the answer.

Football was his religion. The field he played on and the building surrounding it, his cathedral. If a higher power had a hand in it, then his answer was yes.

He believed.

Walking to the center of the field, Gaige took it all in. He found football at the age of thirteen. A boy who saw his future mapped out. Working in a factory. Drinking away his salary. Divorce. Doling out child support without maintaining a relationship with his children. A weekend father, who half the time didn't bother to show up.

The first time Gaige picked up a football, he felt a connection. The first time he threw it, it wobbled with the grace of a drunk leaving his favorite watering hole on a Saturday night. But it didn't matter. He threw the ball again. And again. Until he taught himself to make it spin in a perfect spiral.

At the time, Gaige didn't know his talent could be useful. Where he came from, Brooklyn kids didn't dream of bigger or better. Most of them didn't dream at all. Gaige was no different.

One day he was passing a playground when a football landed at his feet. The boys on the field yelled for him to toss it back. Without thinking, Gaige sent it sailing, a perfect strike. Then kept walking. He was wary of the man who ran after him. Strangers were the enemy—according to his father. They either wanted money or accused you of something you hadn't done.

Gaige took everything his father said with a big grain of salt. Don Benson didn't have a dime to his name. Why would anyone expect to get money from him? And if a man accused his father of something, chances were he was guilty.

But Gaige was a cautious boy. He fought when necessary and ran when he had no choice. The man trying to get his attention was big. His dark complexion didn't worry Gaige. In his experience, a man was either good or bad. The color of his skin had nothing to do with it.

It turned out that this man wasn't simply good. He was the best thing that ever happened to Gaige.

Terrance Aldridge coached the local Pop Warner football team. A boy with an arm like Gaige's shouldn't let his talent go to waste. Gaige listened. Play football? On a field? With other boys? Was such a thing possible? He didn't know if it were a scam—nor did he care. If there were the slightest chance, he would take it.

The only obstacle was getting a parent's permission. Terrance gave him the papers to be signed, telling Gaige to have his folks call him if they had any questions. Gaige didn't laugh aloud, but he wanted to. His mother never asked questions. Unless they were directed at his father. Wynona Benson hadn't made a move in fifteen years unless she received permission first.

His father was another matter. His word was law. Don Benson could do no wrong. If he drank too much and staggered home two days late, it was his right. If he backhanded his wife—just because— whose business was it? He earned the money. He made the rules. End of discussion.

Gaige hadn't asked his father because he knew what the answer would be. No! Not because he thought there was anything wrong with football. He watched it every Sunday—after laying down a bet that he never won. No, he wouldn't let Gaige play because he was a mean bastard who wanted everyone to be as miserable as he was.

Gaige got around it easily enough. He forged his father's signature. It wasn't the first time and it wouldn't be the last. There was no reason to think anyone would find out. His parents didn't care how he spent his days as long as the police didn't come knocking on the door.

He could steal. Lie. Cheat. Hell, his father wouldn't bat an eye at murder. *Do what you want as long as you don't get caught.* The mantra at the Benson house.

Gaige had no intention of his father finding out. He tried out for the team and made it. The money for equipment was another matter. Gaige didn't steal. Or cheat. Lying was a necessary evil. He would have done almost anything to play but it looked like his first and only dream would die before it had a chance.

Luckily, Terrance was able to dip into a discretionary fund to help boys like Gaige. It rankled to take charity. Especially when the other boys on the team had families to pay their way.

"Don't let it stop you, Gaige," Terrance told him. "Remember. And one day, when you have the means, pay it forward, son."

Twenty-five years later, Gaige hadn't forgotten that kindness and generosity. When he saw someone in need, he did something about it. Over the years, the *Gaige Benson Foundation* paid out millions of dollars to charities and individuals. He had filled the board with people he trusted and could count on to distribute the funds judiciously and without prejudice. The first man he had recruited was the man to whom Gaige owed everything—Terrance Aldridge. Friend. Father figure. Teacher.

"Hey, Gaige." Logan Price called out from high in the stands. "You coming? The guys are waiting to go to dinner."

"Five minutes."

Closing his eyes, Gaige breathed in the air. February in Texas. Tomorrow he would play in his first—and last Super Bowl. Win or lose, he was hanging up his cleats. He was thirty-eight years old. He had more money than he would ever need. He had won every award from Rookie of the Year to league MVP—four times.

This season he put everything on the line to get here—including the possibility that he had lost the only woman he had ever loved.

Gaige Benson was known for his razor-sharp focus. Any distractions off the field were left there as soon as the first whistle blew. It wouldn't be any different tomorrow. Nothing would get in the way.

His gaze drifted to the section where she would be sitting. If she showed up. Gaige planned on going out a winner. But what about the day after? Or the day after that? His future stretched out in front of him. He had plans in place. There were hundreds of options for him to consider.

Do you believe in a higher power?

Her voice and that question had haunted Gaige for almost sixteen years. If there were a God, he prayed the woman he loved would find it in her heart to forgive him. He had a lot of years left. He didn't want to spend them alone.

In his lifetime, Gaige Benson had dreamt of only two things. Playing football. And loving Violet Reed.

DREAMING WITH A BROKEN HEART
(Hollywood Legends Book One

PROLOGUE

THE ROOM WAS dark. Too dark for Garrett's liking. A little stuffy, a slight antiseptic smell with an overlay of sex. That's what you got from a cheap motel and furtive lovemaking. Odors and memories you'd just as soon forget.

The sounds from behind the closed bathroom door indicated his partner was trying to remove all traces of their recent activities. It shouldn't hurt. This wasn't the first time, and damn his weak resolve, it wouldn't be the last.

If he smoked, he would have something to do with his hands. Watching his father struggle with lung cancer put the fear of God in him and his brothers at an early age. All four of them had their vices; smoking wasn't one of them.

Get up. Get dressed. For once, be the first to leave. Even if he could find the balls to walk out on her, he couldn't leave her alone at this time of night. In this part of town.

God, it was like a furnace in here. Despite having the AC wall unit on high, Garrett knew it must be hotter in here than outside. The sheet riding low on his hips was too much. Damn modesty. The room was too dark to see anything; if she didn't like seeing his naked body, she could turn away. Garrett whipped off the coarse cotton material at the same moment the bathroom door opened.

"You don't have to go," Garrett said to the shadowed figure.

"Yes, I do."

She always made sure the light was off. Her silhouette showed a tall woman, thin. Too thin. Even by L.A. standards. She was gaining weight — slowly. Garrett could attest to that. He knew it was a struggle. One she fought every day.

Garrett felt the anger drain from his body — his heart melt. Her demands were not capricious whims. They weren't her attempt to gain the upper hand. Her goal was not to manipulate. She had her reasons. They were real. Legitimate.

"It's still early."

Garrett kept his voice low and even. Shouting didn't help. She never fought back. Retreat. That was her coping mechanism. The last time he blew up it was two weeks before she would take his calls.

"I..." she cleared her voice. "His flight gets in at midnight."

"Don't be there."

"You know how he gets."

Garrett knew all right. She was devoted to a man who treated her like crap, forgot her existence ninety percent of the time, yet expected her to be there when he decided to come home. His fists clenched the mattress. It was the only thing preventing him from grabbing her, begging her to stay. *For once, pick me.*

"I don't know when I can see you again."

I don't know if I ever want to see you again. Garrett thought the words. He would never verbalize them. She was his drug of choice. Weeks passed. The need for her grew. Outwardly, his life looked smooth as glass. Inside, the itch grew.

Garrett became an expert at compartmentalizing. His work never suffered. His family never suspected. No one had the slightest clue about what was raging inside of him. *She* knew. Because she shared his unbreakable habit. Enablers. That's what they were. It was sick. Sometimes, like tonight, he hated himself. He wished he could hate her. Then, maybe, he could walk away.

"I'll be out of town for the next month."

Garrett wished he could see her face. Was she sorry he'd be gone? Relieved? Would she miss him half as much as he was going to miss her?

"Take care."

Garrett waited a second, letting the motel room door close behind her. Jumping up, rushing to the window, he pulled back the thin, dingy curtain. He never walked her to the taxi. Even the minutest chance of them being seen was too much.

The ritual of watching until she was safely inside the vehicle, seat belt on, doors locked, was something he never ignored. Nothing bad would happen to her when he was around. It was when he wasn't there that trouble found her. One more frustration. It wasn't his place to protect her. Knowing that drove him crazy.

Garrett grabbed his jeans from a nearby chair, pulling them on. Unlike her, he wouldn't clean up before he left. He would carry the smell of her with him — let it fill the interior of his car. Tomorrow he would pretend it was still there.

Damn it. Enough. He deserved more than this. They both did. One month. When he got back, one way or another, things were going to change.

DREAMING WITH MY EYES WIDE OPEN
(Hollywood Legends Book Two)

PROLOGUE

NATE LANDIS NEVER thought much about the way he looked.

Women seemed to like his face. That was genetics. He was the son of Hollywood royalty. Alone, they turned heads. Together, they dazzled. It made sense that they would pass some of that on.

Nate took it in stride. He was strong. Healthy. His body was trained to do what he wanted it to do, under what could only be called extreme situations. He ate right, worked hard, and played harder.

At some point, his lifestyle would catch up with him. Age would take care of that. Right now, he was in his prime. If he wanted to scale a mountain, that's what he did. Jump from a plane? A piece of cake. Race car driving. Deep sea diving. You name it; Nate was the first one in line.

When he was three years old, his mother called him her little daredevil. Fearless, she swore he gave her wrinkles for worrying what he would get into next. Nate would always laugh, peering closely at Callie Flynn's flawless complexion. What wrinkles? In her fifties, she was, and would always be, one of the movie industry's great beauties. Nothing he or his brothers did could alter that.

As Nate stepped to the edge of the cliff, he didn't think about the two-hundred-foot drop. He'd jumped from higher than this. It was what he did. And he did it better than anyone else. For some reason, today he thought about his mother.

Callie never discouraged him from pursuing danger, even though Nate knew she wished he had chosen a safer way to make a living. She didn't say so, but he knew she worried about his safety. It didn't stop him — he seldom thought about it. Until today. As he waited for the director to signal the camera was rolling, for the first time Nate let himself worry about his mother's reaction if something happened to him.

He shook off the morbid thought. Now wasn't the time. He needed to focus. Ninety-nine percent of the time, if something went wrong, it was due to a loss of focus. Nate took a deep breath. He cleared his mind. Three flashes of light. That was his signal. He squared his shoulders, coiled his body. And jumped.

Nate Landis was a stuntman. Some might say it was his calling. If a director needed it done big and done right, that person called him. Nate loved his job.

He let his body relax as he sailed through the air. The count in his head was precise. If he pulled the ripcord too soon, the shot would be ruined. Too late, he risked ending up a pile of broken bones.

Nate planned every stunt. He worked out the timing, the logistics, and the angles. He never let anyone perform a stunt unless he tested it. Over and over again. He refused to rush. Anxious directors. Bottom-line producers. Some tried to push him into cutting corners.

Few things made Nate lose his temper. His brother Garrett claimed Nate had the longest, slowest burning fuse in history. But he had his hot buttons. Endangering himself and his crew was one of them. Last year, a director, trying to save time, ran a stunt when Nate was away from the set. Poorly conceived and executed, two stuntmen went to the hospital with second-degree burns.

Todd Winesap went to the hospital with a broken jaw and a tarnished reputation.

It took a lot to make Nate mad. But watch out when it happened.

Nate ran the count through his head. Eight, nine, ten. He gave the cord a firm, steady pull. Smooth as glass, the chute opened. Even so, he traveled at a high speed. The parachute was safety measure number one. Number two was the large, air-filled target waiting below.

Having done this stunt hundreds of times, Nate knew what to expect and how it should feel. And he knew when something was wrong.

The air bag, that Nate had personally supervised the placement of, wasn't where it was supposed to be. He didn't have the time to wonder how that had happened. If he didn't act fast, he wouldn't be around to beat the shit out of the asshole responsible.

Grabbing the guide strings, Nate pulled a hard right with all his considerable strength — and prayed.

DREAMING OF YOUR LOVE
(Hollywood Legends Book Three

PROLOGUE

LIGHTS FLASHED FROM every direction. It blinded and dazzled all at once.

Screams drowned out every other sound. This was Los Angeles. Busy streets in every direction. Jet patterns overhead. The excited—in some cases rabid—fans that surrounded the roped-off red carpet made it seem like nothing existed but them and the bright lights.

It shouldn't have been a pleasant experience. Alighting from the over-the-top luxury of a Rolls Royce into chaos and mayhem? No normal human being would willingly seek out such an experience.

However, Colton Landis was not a normal human being. He was an actor.

Colt turned his world-famous megawatt smile on the crowd, eliciting another deafening burst of heartfelt screams.

"We need to get inside, Colt. The movie starts in ten minutes."

"Relax, Deb."

Colt's publicist had been with him for five years. Deb Kline knew how to spin a press release like nobody else. They saw eye to eye on most things. Except how much he should expose himself to his fans. If she had her way, he would zip from point A to point B as quickly as humanly possible.

In this case, point A was the limo, and point B was Grauman's Chinese Theater.

"I'll relax when you are safely inside. Have you forgotten Dallas already?"

"Dallas was an anomaly."

Colt continued to wave and smile. Deb wanted him to curb his accessibility. She had always been cautious, but after a fan somehow breached security during a press conference to announce his next movie, she was particularly leery of events like this one.

"Colt."

"Don't go over there, Colt."

Deb knew the second Colt observed the waving autograph books, her words fell on deaf ears. He believed in giving his fans what they wanted. It was one of the things that made Colton Landis a huge movie star. He genuinely loved his fans. He loved meeting them, speaking with them, having his picture taken with them. Most of her clients searched for any reason to avoid these moments. Not Colt. He didn't have a public persona and a private one. What you saw was what you got—twenty-four hours a day, seven days a week.

Colt made her job as a publicist a dream. Keeping him safe was a nightmare.

He refused to have a bodyguard. Part of it was ego—and he had plenty of that. Many of his parts portrayed him as a big, macho, tough guy. How would it look if he had a bigger, more macho, tough guy constantly shadowing him? Not great for his reputation. He would look weak. And in Hollywood, perception was everything.

It was a valid argument. Not so valid? Colt believed that, for the most part, his fans were harmless. Not that he was a naïve Pollyanna. There was no need for Deb to point out the entertainment world's tragic examples of the heinous acts obsessive fans could commit.

Colt lived the life. He grew up watching his superstar mother traverse that fine line between making herself accessible to fans and maintaining some much-needed privacy.

However, he didn't have a family to consider. No wife. No children. His life was his own. A bodyguard would mean he was giving in. Turning his life over to fear instead of embracing every single moment of his fairytale existence.

"Ten minutes."

Deb didn't know if Colt heard her over the screams. Nor did she care. She was getting him into that theater if it meant grabbing his ear and dragging him along like an errant five-year-old. And wouldn't that make a great picture in *People* magazine? Okay. No ears. *Ugh. This man was going to make her old before her time.*

Colt held a woman's phone at arm's length, including himself in a selfie of her and her three friends.

"I love you, Colton."

Colt couldn't single out the speaker. The cry came from every direction. He waved and called out, "I love you, too."

He signed a few more autographs, moving along the line. Deb was right. He needed to get inside. It wasn't fair to keep everyone waiting. Ten more, he promised himself. It killed him to see the expressions on the faces of the fans who were left out.

"Thanks. See you soon," Colt called out to the crowd.

Handing her signed book to a dreamy-eyed woman, Colt gave the crowd a final wave.

"Ready?" Deb tried to maintain the *stern teacher* expression she had spent twenty years cultivating.

Colt had a way of making her professional mask slip. Thank goodness she was old enough to be his youngish grandmother. While his charm was undeniable, her age and experience allowed her to put the sexual pull that radiated around him into perspective.

Until he turned his smile on her. Full blast.

"Am I that big of a pain in the ass?"

There it was. That naughty twinkle in his deep blue eyes that made the world swoon. On screen, it was irresistible. Paired with dark hair and a tall, muscular frame, was it any wonder the camera loved him?

Reluctantly, Deb returned his smile.

Colt was her client. He was also her friend. She knew he wasn't trying to be difficult. He was being himself. For a man who was adored by millions, catered to on a daily basis, and could buy and sell two or three third-world nations without raising a sweat, Colton

Landis was surprisingly down to Earth. And hard-headed. And opinionated.

On top of that? On occasions such as this one, a major pain in the ass.

Still, if she were honest, there wasn't a single thing about him that she would change. As movie stars went—hell, as human beings went—Colton Landis was a joy to be around. Not that she would ever tell him that. The last thing he needed was another person extolling his endless virtues. Colt hated that kind of treatment. One of the reasons they worked so well together was because Deb didn't kowtow.

Deb was about to hit him with one of the nifty sarcastic one-liners he loved, when a scream came from the crowd. Not a *we love you* cry, but one of terror. Before she could react, Deb saw a man jump over the velvet rope. He carried a knife.

Colt pushed her to the side, effectively putting himself between her and the attacker. *He isn't after me*, Deb wanted to protest. But everything happened so fast, she didn't have time.

In the blink of an eye, the man raised the knife and stabbed Colt.

IF I LOVED YOU
(Harper Falls Book One)

PROLOGUE

IT WAS SOMETHING out of a fairy tale.

Thousands of flickering lights dazzled her senses, almost as much as the tall, wickedly handsome man who so expertly danced her onto the shadowed balcony. The music that filtered from the nearby ballroom only added to the already magical atmosphere.

Women dreamed their whole lives of a moment like this — a prelude to a happily-ever-after ending. Ever so briefly, she let herself drift into that fantasy as if she was one of those women. For a moment, she let herself pretend that her childhood had been filled with the kind of whimsicality that allowed those fantasies to carry over into adulthood.

But no, she wasn't a romantic, hopeless or otherwise. She didn't want a prince to sweep her into his arms and carry her away on his faithful steed. She was more than capable of rescuing herself. She preferred it that way.

The stars were in the sky, not in her eyes.

"I'm glad you asked me to dance," her partner whispered, pulling her closer.

Suddenly, she was nervous. The champagne she downed earlier had completely worn off. No more floating on a cloud of false courage. If she was going to do this, she was going to have to do it on her own.

"Jack," she said. Damn, it was hard to sound seductive when your voice squeaked. "Jack." That was better, lower, and slightly husky. She'd read somewhere that guys liked husky voices.

"Rose."

"Yes?"

"Nothing, I just thought we were saying each other's names." He put his lips next to her ear. "I like the way you say mine."

"Jack." Good Lord, she had to stop repeating his name. "I need a favor, Jack. A big one." Or should she say, she hoped he *had* a big one. Rose groaned to herself. At least she hadn't said that aloud.

"I'll help if I can."

"You're the only one who *can* help." She took another deep breath. "I need you to take me home and screw my brains out."

www.ingramcontent.com/pod-product-compliance
Lightning Source LLC
Chambersburg PA
CBHW071142170626
46809CB00002B/736